"The story's haunting ambience will remain in the reader's thoughts and feelings for a long time after experiencing this exquisitely depicted story of love, betrayal, forgiveness, haunting memories, and so much more!"   —Crystal Book Reviews

"From Poughkeepsie to Paris, from the razzmatazz of the twenties to the turmoil of World War Two and the perfume factories of Grasse, Mackin draws you into the world of expatriate artists and photographers and tells a story of love, betrayal, survival, and friendship. As complex as the fragrances Mackin writes about, *The Beautiful American* is an engaging and unforgettable novel. I couldn't put it down."   —Renée Rosen, author of *Dollface*

"An exquisitely imagined and beautifully rendered story of the talented, tragic, gorgeous Lee Miller."
                    —Becky E. Conekin, author of *Lee Miller in Fashion*

"A gorgeous tale. . . . I envy those who get to read it for the first time."   —Book-alicious Mama

"Jeanne Mackin blends a tale as intoxicating as the finest fragrance. Spanning wars both personal and global, *The Beautiful American* leaves its essence of love, loss, regret, and hope long after the novel concludes."
                    —Erika Robuck, author of *Call Me Zelda* and *Fallen Beauty*

"Jeanne Mackin's luminous novel about Man Ray and his model-mistress, Lee Miller, evokes the iridescence of 1920s Paris, when youth and artistic freedom and sexual excess were all that mattered. *The Beautiful American*, which readers will rank right up there with *The Paris Wife*, takes readers from the giddiness of the flapper era to the grittiness of World War Two. It is a brilliant, beautifully written literary masterpiece. I love this book!"
                    —Sandra Dallas, *New York Times* bestselling author of *Fallen Women*

"Lovers of the film *Midnight in Paris* will definitely enjoy this."
                                                    —Chick Lit+

"The setting is fascinating, the real and fictional characters intriguing."   —*RT Book Reviews*

Other Novels by Jeanne Mackin

The Beautiful American

The Sweet By and By

Dreams of Empire

The Queen's War

The Frenchwoman

A LADY
of GOOD
FAMILY

JEANNE MACKIN

NEW AMERICAN LIBRARY

New American Library
Published by the Penguin Group
Penguin Group (USA) LLC, 375 Hudson Street,
New York, New York 10014

USA | Canada | UK | Ireland | Australia | New Zealand | India | South Africa | China
penguin.com
A Penguin Random House Company

First published by New American Library,
a division of Penguin Group (USA) LLC

First Printing, June 2015

REGISTERED TRADEMARK—MARCA REGISTRADA

LIBRARY OF CONGRESS CATALOGING-IN-PUBLICATION DATA:

Mackin, Jeanne.
    A lady of good family / Jeanne Mackin.
        pages cm.
    ISBN 978-0-451-46583-2 (softcover)
    1. Farrand, Beatrix, 1872–1959—Fiction. 2. Women in landscape architecture—
Fiction. 3. United States—Social life and customs—1865–1918—Fiction. I. Title.
    PS3563.A3169L33 2015
    813'.54—dc23   2015001019

Printed in the United States of America
10 9 8 7 6 5 4 3 2 1

Set in Adobe Garamond
Designed by Spring Hoteling

To all gardeners, everywhere

The place had an air of refinement . . . one felt more and more that some moonlight nights in May . . . the ghosts of the people who once lived there must come back. Again their long dresses trailed rustling over the walks, and the sound of their voices laughing, for no one could cry in such a garden.

—Beatrix Jones Farrand

A LADY
of GOOD
FAMILY

A Garden for First Meetings

*T*his is the most difficult type of garden to design, since who can tell when first meetings will occur? However, if you are inclined to plan for the unforeseen, to hope for limitless possibility, I recommend a garden that includes elements of the romantic, the antique, and the implausible.

The romantic element should include a series of intersecting winding paths, trails from which, at the beginning, one cannot see the ultimate destination but only guess at it. The gravel for these paths should be very fine and make only the slightest whisper of noise when walked upon.

The antique element should include a small folly or casino, a shelter of some sort in which those meeting for the first time can find objects to feed their conversation. First meetings often involve a certain amount of shyness, diffidence, and anxiety. It is therefore helpful if the garden provides distraction.

The implausible should include a plant growing out of place. I *do not normally recommend such a thing. Plants, after all, know where they like to grow and do not like to grow. Roses do not like shade and ferns do not like direct sun. If, however, you can convince creeping speedwell to grow in one twist of the gravel path, this serves as a reminder to those meeting for the first time that life is full of uncertainty and unexpected happenings. Above all else, we must cherish the mystery.*

For plants I recommend pines as a backdrop, especially Roman umbrella pines if your climate will allow them. If not, a very small grove of Black Forest pines or, even better, pines from the Odenwald area of Germany, planted thickly.

Flowers should include angel's tears daffodils of the narcissus species. They are smaller than other varieties and require a more observant eye; Aquilegia vulgaris, *or common columbine, which looks best grown in semishadowed areas;* Chrysogonum virginianum, *goldenstar, which will bloom all summer in case the first meeting should not occur quickly.*

And roses, of course. There should be roses in all gardens, and in a garden for first meetings the rose should be Rosa gallica "Officinalis," *the old apothecary rose, also known as the rose of Lancaster. This rose, with its very dark green foliage, blooms just once in the season, reminding us that first meetings are not to be taken for granted. It will also spread of its own will, sending out shoots in all directions, and is a good plant for sharing.*

ONE

My grandparents had a farm outside of Schenectady, and every Sunday my father, who worked in town, would hitch the swaybacked mare to the buggy and take us out there. I would be left to play in the field as my father and grandfather sat on the porch and drank tea and Grandma cooked. My mother, always dressed a little too extravagantly, shelled the peas.

A yellow barn stood tall and broad against a cornflower blue sky. A row of red hollyhocks in front of the barn stretched to the sky, each flower on the stem as silky and round as the skirt on Thumbelina's ball gown. In the field next to the barn, daisies danced in the breeze. My namesake flower.

I saw it still, the yellows and reds and blues glowing against my closed eyelids. The field was my first garden, and I was absolutely happy in it. We usually are, in the gardens of our childhood. I, who had lost so much, wondered if I could ever be truly happy again.

When I opened my eyes I was on a porch in Lenox, a little tired from weeks of travel, a little restless. My companions were restless, too, weary of trying to make polite conversation, as strangers do.

Mrs. Avery suggested we try the Ouija board. We had, before that, been discussing rose gardens, and the new hybrids, especially the Miriam yellow with its garish, varying hues.

"Roses should be red or pink," Mr. Hardy complained.

"Or white," added Mrs. Ballinger.

"I like the new hybrids," I said. "Those bold colors."

"Oh, dear," said Mrs. Avery.

Guests at the old inn, we perched in a row of rockers, recovering from a too-heavy supper. There was me, just back from campaigning for the women's vote in Tennessee; Mrs. Avery, the youngest of us all yet seeming the oldest, a rabbit of a woman who spoke too quietly; Mrs. Ballinger, as round as a pumpkin, with hair dyed the same color; and Mr. Hardy, a tall, gaunt man who stooped even when sitting.

It was a late-summer evening, too warm, with a disquieting breeze stirring the treetops as if a giant ghostly hand ruffled them. Through the open window a piano player was tinkling his way through Irving Berlin as young people danced and flirted. In the road that silvered past the inn, young men, those who had made it home from the war, drove up and down in their shiny black Model Ts.

It was a night for thinking of love and loss, first gardens, first kisses.

The moon was cloud covered, and the inn's proprietor did not turn on the porch lights, since they drew mosquitoes and moths. We sat in darkness, except for the occasional small flare when someone lit a cigarette.

An uneasiness charged the air, the feeling that something was going to happen. It is an uncommon sensation in summer, when the world seems to have settled into its own idea of Eden. The wind had a premature autumnal feel to it. "You feel the seasons in a garden, the passage of time," my friend Beatrix told me once. "Whether you want to or not."

The hotel had a rose bed in front of the porch. I wondered whether the roses were the same variety as what had grown in the garden at Vevey, Switzerland, where I had first met Gilbert. Pink roses all look alike to me. Perhaps that's what Gilbert thought of me that evening at Vevey when we met. One pretty American girl looks much like all her sisters.

In a way, all hotels look alike, too. Some are grander than others, some have the Alps for scenery, some a little town in Massachusetts. I was staying, as my finances required, in one of the less grand inns of the town, but I was always aware that in those Berkshire hills nestled some of the most famous houses ever built, cottages where Melville and Hawthorne had resided, and later, after Lenox became fashionable with the wealthy, the larger estates where Vanderbilts and Morgans, and the writer Edith Wharton, had passed summer days.

I was content to be in an inn, where strangers come and go and you feel a bustle of life about you, what Mr. Henry James described as the rustling of flounces and late-night dance music, the cries and sighs as young people court and play.

Fashionable young girls did not wear muslin flounces anymore. Those were as out of style as calling cards.

We had, that night, already finished a game of bridge, and I had fleeced the others of their pocket money. I was usually popular with my peers, but not with their children. They found me a very expensive proposition, a bad influence. That from grown children who danced the black bottom and tango, the young women with their skirts almost to their knees.

What had most shocked me, during my years of campaigning, were the young people who had tried to shout us down, who did not want change. You expect complacency in older folks, not in the young. "Aren't you satisfied with your homes, your husbands, your children? Leave politics to the men!" they had shouted.

Thank God my daughter, Jenny, had not felt that way. She had bailed me out of jail when needed, housed me often despite her husband's antipathy toward me, and wined and dined a judge now and then when required. She had also paid in advance for my week at Lenox, so that I could rest after my traveling and marching.

"Penny," said kindly Mr. Hardy, interrupting my thoughts.

I liked his face. It was open and somehow vulnerable. You could see that his life had not been easy, yet he was not bitter.

"I was thinking about gardens, and then about politics, and

power, and men and women," I said, but no one encouraged me to develop this conversation.

Instead, Mrs. Avery suggested we try the Ouija board. Since the war, it had become a national obsession.

"Let's," I agreed eagerly. "Perhaps Mr. James will come through." He had died four years before, and I would have enjoyed a message from the master. Henry James' letters to my dear friend Minnie had been so entertaining, and of course she had shared them, as he had meant her to do.

Mr. Hardy, grumbling a bit, went in to fetch the board as Mrs. Ballinger, Mrs. Avery, and I rearranged our chairs around a wicker table.

After we set up the board, placed the planchette in the middle, and put our fingertips on it, we waited.

And waited.

"Someone is not being open to the spirits," said Mrs. Avery with more than a little whine in her voice. A stronger breeze stirred the treetops. Inside, the piano player tinkled his way through "Oh! How I Hate to Get Up in the Morning."

"Maybe they don't like the music," suggested Mr. Hardy.

We laughed. Then the pointer moved. Just once. When we opened our eyes, it had settled over the *M*.

"You got your wish, Mrs. Winters," Mrs. Ballinger told me, sounding envious. "It was to have been a message from the master."

"Or my sister, Mary," said Mrs. Avery. "It was, after all, my idea. It should have been a message for me."

"For that matter, it could have been from my poodle, Mariah," said Mrs. Ballinger.

"A useful letter, *M*," agreed Mr. Hardy. "Could be anyone, anything. He pushed his chair away from the table and refused to continue. We restored our chairs to the assigned row and ignored the Ouija board.

"Nights like this, when I was a child, we told each other ghost stories to pass the time," said Mrs. Avery. She had grown up on a farm near Rochester, and though I had known her for only a few days, I already understood that her childhood had been harder than mine. She had fled the hardscrabble farm life, and now she looked fondly back upon what she had hated at the time.

"Silly things, ghost stories," said Mrs. Ballinger. We all turned to look at her, trying to convey the message that ghost stories were no sillier than a woman of her age wearing that shade of pink with that color hair, but Mrs. Ballinger was oblivious to such subtlety. "Silly," she repeated with a condescending sniff. "Give me a good romance anytime."

A car backfired just then and jolted Mr. Hardy out of his sulk.

"I saw a ghost once," he said. "A lovely thing, all white and floating. Back when I was a boy in County Cork and almost dying of typhus."

"That was an angel," corrected Mrs. Avery. "I've never heard that ghosts are lovely."

"It was my poor dead mother hovering over, and from what I've heard, she was no angel," Mr. Hardy said.

"I've never heard of anyone who ever really saw a ghost," said Mrs. Ballinger, her voice even more condescending.

"I once saw the ghost of Nero in Rome," I said. "In Piazza del Popolo. It was all the rage that year. Anyone who was anyone saw him."

"Rome." Mrs. Ballinger sniffed, indicating that for some reason Rome was beyond her approval. I suspected she had never been there.

We rocked in our chairs, listening to the crickets and watching eerie, silent sheet lightning flash in the eastern sky. The crickets were very loud with their ratchety, ratchety, and the frogs in the brackish pond sounded like they were auditioning for the Anvil Chorus. Silence, human silence, was difficult that night, and I felt a need to talk. They would be voting on the amendment in Tennessee in two days, and my nerves were taut enough to be strung on a violin.

"I know someone who saw a ghost under very strange circumstances," I said, thinking of that *M* and seeing in my mind's eye a piece of stationery with that single ornate initial on it. "Shall I tell you the story?" I asked.

"Yes!" said Mr. Hardy with enthusiasm.

"Oh, Lord," sighed Mrs. Ballinger.

"It begins in Rome," I said.

"I've never been," said Mrs. Avery. "I bet it's lovely."

"I've been many times," I said. "Rome and Paris. London. We used to live like nomads. Newport in the spring and summer, New York in the autumn, Europe in winter. We all did, though of course such travel was new to my family, since money was new to my family. I met my husband on my first trip to Switzerland, and even after the babies came we went back every year. He insisted. 'My dear,' he would say, 'you don't mean to say you are going to buy this year's gowns in New York rather than Paris?' So we would pack up the children and the nurses and later the governesses and board the steamer, seeing the same faces over and over, because society was all doing it. The *Lusitania*, the German torpedoes when they came in 1915, ended that."

Mr. Hardy's mouth clamped into a straight, sad line. He had lost a son in the war.

"Well," I continued. "The story begins in Rome, in the gardens of the Villa Borghese. Mr. Henry James wrote about them. My friend Beatrix Jones was there, touring Europe, to look at those gardens. She's the famous garden designer. The first American woman in the field, really, and making an excellent job of it. Even her male counterparts agree on that."

"Women just don't know their place anymore," grumbled Mr. Hardy. He gave me a sideways glance of disapproval. I still wore my purple, yellow, and white rosette on my cardigan, the badge of the suffragists. He, like a good many men, was worrying over that upcoming vote in Tennessee, the last state in the union to debate giving women the vote. He was not in favor.

"We will not speak of politics tonight, Mr. Hardy. We are in the Borghese gardens with Beatrix. Rome. Early spring," I insisted.

"Oh, Lord," repeated Mrs. Ballinger.

TWO

1895
Rome, Italy

"Is it possible to have a haunting without a sense of evil attached to it? Last night poor Mrs. Madden kept insisting she felt the presence of someone, some spirit, and instead of feeling afraid, she was comforted." Mrs. Frederic Jones, christened Mary but known to friends and family as Minnie, frowned. Why had she brought this up? She hadn't meant to speak of it. Everyone knew Mrs. Madden was, well, to be kind, a bit unmoored.

"I should think so," said Mrs. Jones' daughter, Beatrix. "It would be like—let's see—like spring in the garden before the first seedlings are up. You can feel their presence even though you can't see them."

"Mr. James would disagree," said a third woman, Edith Wharton. "I think he rather feels that this world and that other world are like Europe and America, with a vast ocean between them. Any spirit still lingering on the wrong side of the ocean must have a grievance, and a grieved spirit must have some sense of anger or wrath. Interesting concept, though, a harmless spirit. I wonder . . ." Her voice trailed off as it sometimes did when her thoughts moved from public discourse to a more private daydream. She looked pale, an indication that she had not slept well.

The little dog curled on her lap grew restive and barked to be set down. Edith held it closer.

"Nightmares again, Edith?" Minnie, her sister-in-law, reached over and patted the dog's head. Edith had been "unwell" for the past year, suffering from depression and nerves.

"A very strange one," Edith said. "A long avenue of trees, ashen olive trees, leading to a house I knew was haunted. The ghost was a woman who had been locked up by her husband . . ." Her voice trailed off again. Her hand fluttered in the air for a moment as if she were waving at someone, and then fell into her lap. Her dog barked once more, a high, demanding sound that echoed through a stand of umbrella pines.

"Hmm," said Edith's husband, Teddy. "This is the result of spending so much time reading and scribbling. More fresh air, perhaps. A good long walk after dinner."

"The house was called Kerfol. Such a strange name." Edith ignored Teddy's comments.

"Blasted city," said Teddy. "We should never have come to Rome."

"But I wanted to see Minnie and Beatrix, and they were in Rome," Edith said.

"It was that nurse who told you ghost stories as a child." Teddy found a new source of blame, landing on one closer to the point than the city of Rome. Edith as a child had been ill in Germany, had almost died of typhoid, and her nurse had passed the long hours telling old village ghost stories to the child. Lord, how we torment our children.

Another wife, at this point, would have said, "Yes, dear," and dropped the subject. Edith instead gave Teddy a scathing glare.

Mr. Wharton was a man who simply ignored what he could not comprehend, the type of person who never read a novel or poetry. This, Edith had discovered, was not a good quality in a husband. When she most needed encouragement to pursue her work—her scribbling, as he called it—he simply smiled and said, "My dear, perhaps we should go for a ride. Get you out of that dark library."

"Well, I don't know houses called Kerfol, but the nervous excitability of ghosts would account for Mrs. Ford's experience," said Minnie, anxious to fill a hostile silence. "She swears she saw Nero's ghost when she visited the Piazza del Popolo. A raging old man in a white robe, making obscene gestures."

"Did he have his fiddle with him?" Beatrix asked. "Some people are so gullible. Ghosts. Really. It is the result of being too much amid all these old places."

"Women, my dear. Men are not so sentimental as to go looking for Nero's phantom in the Piazza del whatever it was," said Teddy. He was very handsome, with a dashing reddish brown mustache and fine blue eyes, but there was something unfinished about him, like a portrait still on the easel waiting for the artist's final touches.

Teddy and Edith, though seated side by side, seemed a world apart, as couples do when both have come to the realization that the marriage is a failure and there they are, stuck with each other.

Edith had been a young woman hungry for approval when she wed. A daughter born twelve years after her mother had already produced the two required sons, she had been a lonely and to a large extent ignored child. When handsome young Teddy Wharton proposed, she accepted with what she thought was love or at least the possibility of it. It turned out to be relief, and relief is a short-lived emotion. Within months she realized that a love of small animals, their only shared passion, was not enough to sufficiently bind man and woman together.

She had tried to ignore her compulsion to write, to create stories and other worlds with more interesting people than those around her; she had tried to become a good society wife—tried, in other words, to become what others expected of her—only to find that such behavior . . . teas, the constant round of leaving calling cards, the interminable dinner parties, consultations with cooks, and other wifely duties . . . left her physically and emotionally ill. And so she had begun writing again. Some of her work had been published, and now Teddy had a literary wife. Not quite the thing, in New York or Newport.

And Edith was stranded on a silent, cold island of marriage with a man she neither loved nor was loved by.

"Piazza del Popolo. That's where Nero's ghost is seen," she said now, her voice metallic with irritation.

Their knowledge of Roman ghosts having been exhausted by that brief conversation, the four of them sat wrapped in the silence of early-spring heat and foreign places, each secretly wishing to be elsewhere. The Borghese gardens were all very well. But there was an unpleasant sense of requirement to the visit. When in Rome, one must visit St. Peter's Square, the Spanish Steps, the Trevi Fountain, the Pantheon, the Baths of Caracalla, the Borghese gardens, and so they had, dutifully, done so.

This tour of European gardens was to further the education of her daughter, Beatrix, but Minnie was more interested in the Common People than in gardens. Her eyes were focused inward, on the suspicious doings of a certain Nurse Henrietta back in New York, who sometimes filched from the infirmary where Minnie performed charity work.

Minnie sat straight-backed in her chair, both feet flat on the ground, the proud posture of a woman who could trace her family back many generations, whose ancestors had tossed tea into Boston Harbor, whose lawyer father had visited President Lincoln in the White House; a woman raised to know good wines, read in several languages, arrange flowers. Minnie knew how to dress for a Patriarch Ball and what to order at Delmonico's, but she also knew that life was serious and short, and a wise woman would use her time well. Minnie, suffering through her own failed marriage, had learned the value of good works and doing one's duty.

Some of this wisdom she had already passed on to Beatrix,

who sat listening and watching. Waiting, she would have said, though she didn't know what for; perhaps simply waiting to become who she was meant to be, free of interference, of the need to please others. And that is one of the hardest things in life to achieve, especially for a woman.

While her friends had been dreaming of marriage, Beatrix, with her mother's approval, had planned for a career in landscape design. She wanted to add beauty to the world. A fresh morning, a wheelbarrow, and a dozen bushes to be planted or trees to be pruned, no one in shouting distance to yell at her that she was grass staining her dress or ruining her hands—that was what she wanted of life. A lady's hands said everything about her, Uncle Teddy had stated once, glancing disapprovingly at hers.

After only a month of the planned six-month tour, Beatrix already missed her home and garden in Bar Harbor. She wanted to be digging in the winter-freshened soil of Maine, planting the first lettuces and peas, working to the music of gulls crying overhead and rollers breaking against the rocky shore. In Bar Harbor, gardens were not far removed from a wilder nature; in Rome the gardens seemed beaten into submission.

Bar Harbor was more home to Beatrix than either New York or Newport, and their cottage there was a house of women; of long, easy days and Sunday afternoons spent discussing books and music without male bluster and tumult. Her father and mother had ceased living together soon after arriving at Mount Desert Island. There had been shame for Minnie in that separation—a failed marriage was a failed marriage, no matter who was to blame—but a measure of peace as well.

Now, sitting in that public garden in Rome, Beatrix was all too aware that her long-absent father was only two days' travel away, in Paris. She was used to having an ocean between them. She thought she preferred it that way.

Perhaps that's why she later sent for me to come visit her in Rome, to provide a little taste of home. We had become very good friends. I was in Paris that spring with Mr. Winters and our three youngest daughters. Our two sons were in New York, studying, and the eldest daughter, Jenny, was at Mrs. Prim's Academy in Geneva, Switzerland. Mrs. Prim wasn't her real name, of course, but that was how I referred to her.

"I don't wish to leave the girls," I told Mr. Winters when Beatrix's letter arrived for me. And I didn't, not even for Beatrix.

"It is unnatural for a woman to spend so much time with her children," said my husband, who had spent very little time indeed with his own mother. "You should go. It will do you good. I'm not certain Paris agrees with you." I suspected that my presence did not agree with Mr. Winters at the moment. It was the racing season and we had had enough quarrels over his gambling and his numerous broken promises that he wished me out of the way. At my husband's behest, I reluctantly packed my travel case and prepared for a trip to Rome, to visit Beatrix.

Probably it was just as I was packing my new walking suit that Beatrix was sitting in the Roman sunshine, her strong fingers yearning for the crumble of soil. It was maddening for her to sit feet away from a weed popping up in a flower bed and not be able to bend over and pluck it.

However, when in a public garden, or a private one owned by

another, one did not squash aphids no matter how thick they were on the petunias, or pull weeds. One merely sat, like the elderly, the infirm, or the merely lazy, and admired what others had done, or had not done, or had not done well.

Beatrix sighed and studied the scenery. All those moldering buildings and old ruins. That weed taunting her from the edge of the gravel path was driving her to distraction.

"One must expand one's horizons," Minnie said for the dozenth time. "Remember there is a purpose to all this. There is always a purpose."

The purpose, of course, was to learn, to study, to experience. To see how other people experienced the wonder that was life, what they made of it, how they shaped it. That was what travel allowed.

That spring of '95, though, there were more English and American people in Rome than there were Italians. They filled the benches, the gravel walks, the little terrace tables, the men all in gray frock coats and tall hats, the ladies in their pastel silks tightly cinched at wasp waists. They talked of the midnight escapades of the Prince of Wales, the tennis matches at Wimbledon, the debutantes of the New York season.

They talked, Beatrix thought, of everything but Rome. She was twenty-three years old that spring. It took determination, in those days, to be twenty-three, of a good solid New York family with sufficient income and attractive appearance, and remain unencumbered of a groom. She had busied herself with work and study at the Arnold Arboretum in Boston, and now she ran her quick, bright eyes over the Borghese grounds, taking in the expanse of lawn, the temple in the distance, the crumbling *casina* in the other direction. She was trying to ignore that single taunting weed with all the effectiveness of a child trying to ignore a plate of cakes.

The flowering plant beds were severe in their geometric rigor and the temple not well placed, fronted as it was by that little fake lake in the middle of what was obviously a dry plateau. Like a tableau vivant waiting for the posers to arrive. No. More like something in a dream from which one is eager to awake. What would Mr. Olmsted think of all this, he who had designed Central Park without a single straight line, who made the plantings follow the lay of the land and the granite outcroppings, rather than the other way around?

"Lovely day, isn't it?" An American matron had stopped in front of their café table and addressed Beatrix's mother. She looked vaguely familiar, though Teddy was completely indifferent to her presence and had already looked away with as much condescension as he would have shown a waiter.

Edith's little dog barked so insistently that she placed it on the ground, where it ran at the stranger and worried the hem of her gown.

The American matron smiled even more broadly. She had light brown hair graying in broad streaks, thick brown eyebrows over impossibly pale blue eyes, and a pointed face, all giving her a wolfish look. Gathered around her was her pack of three daughters of marriageable age, decked in pale colors and trailing skirts. They swayed, twirled their parasols, and kept looking coyly about, like girls in a ballroom waiting to be asked to dance.

"Lovely day," Minnie agreed, nodding but still not remembering. "The sun is quite pleasant."

"It is a bit warm, though." The woman eyed the glasses of lemonade, the shade of the umbrella, the free chair.

Mrs. . . . Mrs. . . . Beatrix couldn't for the life of her remember the woman's name, only that they had met at another woman's home, probably in New York, although it could well have been there, in Rome. Traveling was an excellent occupation, except it required so much memory, and the only details in which Beatrix was truly interested were plants and landscape. Her memory for Latin taxonomy names was inexhaustible; for matrons, brief.

"A bit too warm, perhaps," agreed Edith, squinting a bit from the sun.

Mrs. Of-the-Forgotten-Name eyed Edith with a distinct lack of approval. It was rumored that the Wharton woman had written poetry as a young girl. She had even published in journals. Unsuitable. And that niece, Beatrix. Yes, she had heard about Beatrix Jones. Imagine, a lady digging in the dirt, standing in the sun for hours, working for a living. In truly good families, even husbands didn't work for a living.

"Well," said Mrs. What's-Her-Name, angry that she hadn't been asked to sit with them. The Jones family was strange, but they were of old blood and old money. The Joneses and Whartons were just the kind of society she needed to get those three daughters married off, to get them, finally, onto Mrs. Astor's list of those to be invited to future balls and New York charity events. What luck to run into them in Rome!

But now the Joneses and Whartons had as good as snubbed

her in a public place. Bad enough that they couldn't remember her name, but not to offer her a chair and a place in the shade under their sun umbrella—that was too much.

The woman flushed. "Will we be seeing you this evening?" she asked. "So many dear friends have sent their acceptances, I can't quite keep them straight. The princess Constanza will be there." She had already resolved that if the Joneses and Whartons did not attend her musical evening, she would find a way to make them sorry for the slight.

Minnie remembered now, with a visible sigh of relief, who this inconvenient woman was. "Thank you so much for thinking to invite us, Mrs. Haskett." They had met in New York a few years before, and Newport before that, at various charity balls and public events. Her husband had speculated and accumulated a fortune in one of the industries, but Minnie couldn't remember which. He had died recently, heart trouble. She recalled now that Mrs. Haskett always had her three daughters in tow. They seemed especially difficult to marry off, still being paraded about after so many seasons. And then Minnie repented of that thought, for wasn't the same being said of her Beatrix?

"I do worry, though, that my headache may keep me in this evening," Edith said.

"It must not," Mrs. Haskett insisted. The three daughters smirked.

"Beg pardon?"

"I said, Mrs. Wharton, that your headache will probably disappear between now and nine thirty and I would so hate to have you miss the music. Signor Lucente is on violin, and Madame Granados will be singing. Perhaps Miss Jones will also sing for us. I hear she has a lovely voice."

Beatrix pretended to find a loose thread in her crocheted bag and did not respond. Mrs. Haskett's eyes narrowed.

Mrs. Haskett was a social climber of consummate skills. In a few short years she had risen from her beginnings as a shopkeeper's daughter in Montana to a society wife, sans accent, sans homemade clothing, sans a Western taste for bread dipped in bacon grease.

But when she first arrived in New York as a young bride, she had hit the brick wall of Mrs. Astor's dislike of the nouveau riche and stalled there, smashed on the sidelines of old families and old money. Her widowhood had not advanced her cause—single women could be so hard to seat at a dinner party—and though she was invited to parties and balls, they were not the right parties and balls, not the exclusive ones in the Fifth Avenue mansions. Bitterness and envy smoldered in her like an autumn bonfire that will never die completely out but only smoke away, threatening the houses in the near vicinity.

And now, having made it as far as Rome, as far as a private tea with the princess Constanza, who, though of questionable character, was a bona fide princess of an old Savoy family, she was being snubbed yet again by the New York brigade. She would not have it.

"Till this evening, then," she said. "Come, girls. We will be late for our appointment with the hairdresser." She turned and stalked away, head high as though sniffing the air for her next attack.

A group of young men, mustachioed and with swinging canes, appeared on the walk and set the three Haskett daughters into a fit of simpers and giggles.

The Whartons and Joneses watched the blushing girls and their mother disappear down the gravel path.

"I thank whatever fortune guides me that my Beatrix is not silly," said Minnie. "Imagine making it your life's work to marry off those creatures."

"We must go to her party, I suppose," Edith said.

"She knows I had forgotten her name. I saw it in her eyes. How unpleasant." Minnie sighed.

"I would have remembered her if there was any distinction to be remarked," Beatrix said defensively. "They do all look alike, don't they? Some simply wear larger jewels and more padding in their hair. I do wonder if there are any New Yorkers left in New York."

"You need more exercise," said her mother. "You are sounding bored. Perhaps you should walk a bit. We'll stay here."

In fact, it was Minnie who was most bored. Beatrix was still being taunted by that weed, and those in the midst of temptation are not bored. But one of the advantages of being a mother was that one's faults could so easily be assigned to one's daughter. Not that Minnie was unpleasant about it. She and Beatrix were close and loving, certainly closer than Beatrix and Minnie had ever been with the third part of the family trinity, the husband and father.

Mr. Frederic Jones, Edith's brother, was currently, and had been for some time, in Paris with his mistress. If, in some rare minutes, Beatrix, with her soft gray eyes, regal height, and long, straight nose, reminded Minnie of that straying husband, she never said so. She had once loved Freddie, well enough to defy dear Henry James' fearsome edict that they should not wed.

Early during Freddie's brazen adulteries, Minnie had tried to forgive him because of that supreme favor he had once done her: bringing her in contact with Mr. James. Henry had been a college friend of Freddie's and, knowing the man well, had gone to New York to plead with him not to wed the serious bluestocking Mary Cadwalader Rawle, not because of any imperfection in Mary but simply because of oil and water. That was what he had said. They would never mix well, never be happy together. He had been correct, as always. Henry knew human nature.

Freddie hadn't been at home to receive the warning, that afternoon of many years before, so Henry had called on Minnie, instead to voice his doubts about the coming nuptials. It was impudent on his part, even a little rude, but Minnie hadn't taken it amiss. She had already read his stories and reviews in *The Atlantic Monthly* and was flattered by the attention of a man of his reputation. In fact, she quizzed him closely on his opinions of Sir Walter Scott, and they spent a pleasant hour together discussing not marriage or Freddie Jones but the novels of Scott, which Mr. James admired and Minnie did not. However, Minnie was in love with Freddie, and Henry James hadn't been able to talk her out of the marriage. Despite that, they had been friends ever since.

"You do look bored, Edith. So am I." Teddy tugged at his collar and then, understanding his words could be considered boorish, gave his wife a false smile of reassurance. "My immediate company is charming," he quickly added. "As always. But all these gardens and ruins. What good are they?"

"You ask what the point of a garden is. Really, Teddy." Edith tapped her foot with impatience.

Beatrix shifted in her chair, feeling the perspiration that made her clothes stick to her back and arms, and longing, absolutely yearning, to lean over and pluck that weed.

THREE

"Your story is very gossipy," protested Mrs. Ballinger, the creak of her chair pausing for a moment as she leaned across Mr. Hardy to complain. "I'm not certain I approve."

"It is important to reveal character as well as situation," I explained. "That would have been Mr. James' defense for detail. Beatrix would have said that the soil must be thoroughly prepared before the planting. Gardeners pay attention to detail. I do not invent, and if you are to understand what follows, you must understand what Beatrix was thinking at the time. I will continue now, Mrs. Ballinger."

"Do," said Mrs. Avery.

Lightning split the Lenox sky in two like a theater curtain. Girlish shrieks and laughter sounded from the parlor where the young people were dancing.

"Storm's coming," said Mr. Hardy, smiling. He was remembering, I thought, a storm of his youth, when a bolt of lightning sent a pretty young girl, shrieking and laughing, into his arms. "I like a good storm. Cleans the air," he said.

My husband, Mr. Winters, had enjoyed a good storm as well. He used to bet on how long it would take for the rain to arrive, once the first lightning struck. He'd bet on which raindrop would trickle down the window first. It was his flaw, his fatal weakness. But he had carried excitement with him the way another man might bundle the daily paper under their arm. I think it was because he had spent so much of his youth and childhood abroad in Switzerland, where because so much is forbidden he had grown up with a sense of outlawry.

That is the problem, you see, with the overly strict rearing of children. If even little things, such as putting one's elbows on the table and saying "damnation" when a toy breaks, are condemned as criminality, then the child feels himself to already be a criminal. In for a dime, in for a dollar.

This was partly Edith's problem, as well, I believe. Her mother had been strict and undemonstrative, making it quite clear she preferred Edith's brothers. Edith learned, eventually, to please only those who pleased her, Mr. James among them.

"Didn't Mrs. Wharton have a home in Lenox?" Mrs. Ballinger asked.

"Not far from here," I said. "But now we are in Rome, not Lenox."

"So sorry you are bored." Edith didn't look at Teddy but stared into the green distance. "The gardens are lovely, though, aren't they?" Her voice was clipped and cold, in contrast to the Roman heat.

Teddy tugged at his collar again and looked at his pocket watch.

I will never marry, Beatrix thought. Never.

She had passed through the first heady years of womanhood, the first balls, first waltzes, first dancing card and house party invitations, quickly discouraging any serious suitor. "My mother," she had simply explained when any young man tried to call on her a little too frequently, implying that her duty to her solitary, hardworking mother made it impossible to accept other affections. Now that most of those young men had already wed, she felt she could easily avoid the issue permanently.

She jumped up, eager to be away from the table. "I will walk." She stepped closer to the taunting weed. She bent. She pulled and plucked. It had fibrous roots rather than tap, just as she had suspected. She put the weed in the pocket of her jacket for later sketching and identification and looked around to see if anyone had caught her in this furtive maneuver. Only Edith, who smiled conspiratorially.

Still, they might never have met, the Italian and the American.

Beatrix could have walked in the opposite direction, away from the temple. She could have strolled through the rose garden or gone into the *casina*. But she chose the temple, that eerie replica of pagan passion.

"Don't be too long, Trix. We have invitations for this evening," Minnie reminded her.

"Fifteen minutes," Beatrix called over her shoulder, already moving quickly away. "That's all." She walked with determination, strides a little longer, a little faster, than was acceptable for a lady during a leisurely afternoon.

An air of decrepitude, a smell of unwholesome rot and stagnation, circled the part of the garden surrounding the temple. It was like moving from one reality to another, and not entirely pleasant.

The temple made Beatrix think of Bluebeard and his wives, knights locked in dungeons. To dispel the gloom, she tried to imagine Uncle Teddy as Bluebeard, trying to lock Aunt Edith into her room. Impossible. Edith would climb out the window and be away, never to return.

They will divorce, too, Beatrix thought. It is just a question of time. What was the point of it, then, courtship and love and marriage? In a garden, things began and ended according to season. In relations between a man and a woman all was disorganization, discord. I will never marry, she repeated to herself.

I dread marriage, thought a young man walking a good distance away. He had been taking the air before going home, enjoying a walk between the lawyer's office and the dilapidated palazzo he inhabited with his father. The lawyer had been unpleasant, his voice bordering on a continual sneer, his statements full of ultimatums and warnings. Shoulds and musts. Or else. Your father insists.

The gardens were full of Americans; the young man who had just been soundly berated by the family lawyer disliked the sounds of their voices, so full of German consonants, not at all soft like his own Italian. The sounds of conquerors, he thought, laden with wealth and greed and taking much of his homeland back with them when they returned to New York and Boston and Chicago. That's what the visit to his lawyer had been about: the possible sale of several artworks. That, and the other business.

Empires rise and fall. He lived in a land of fallen empire, part of a family that was falling even faster than the rest of the empire.

There was no cure for history except to sell: collections, paintings, sons.

Perhaps Mrs. Haskett would be in the gardens again today. He could accidentally encounter her, remind her that she had promised to come look again at the painting.

Ahead of him was an example of the fall of empire: a group of boys, dirty, sly eyed, begging, and worse, their grimy hands snaking into the folds and cuffs of passing men and women, searching for coins, watches. They had surrounded a young woman and were practicing their street skills on her. He saw her face, the terror behind the forced calmness of a tight smile. He changed direction and headed toward the crime in action.

Still, they might never have met. He could have waved from a distance, yelled something the boys would have understood, driven them off with words. But he kept walking toward her.

Beatrix, suddenly surrounded, trapped by the clamoring children, was forced to a complete halt.

Where had they come from, this cluster of noisy urchins, each one beautiful enough after a necessary washing to pose as an angel? As she stood, speechless, they grew bolder, tugged at her sleeves, jumped up at her. "Me, me," they shouted. "Choose me for your guide. A penny. Only a penny, miss."

She felt one little hand snaking into the folds of her skirt, searching for a pocket, a purse. The scene changed from charming to fearsome as the children swarmed ever closer, forcing her in one direction, then another. She couldn't breathe, couldn't escape. She put her hands over her ears, trying to shut out their cries.

They pressed closer, suffocating her. She became dizzy and was afraid of stumbling, of falling beneath the frenzy of screaming children, being trampled by them.

"Alt! Attenzione!" A man's deep voice scattered the boys. One by one, the hands and shoulders and knees that had been closing on her flitted away.

She opened her eyes to see the last of the children scurrying off, sticking his tongue out at her over his shoulder.

"Are you all right, miss? May I help you to a bench?" The man's voice was melodious, with soft middle vowels, slightly rolled *r*'s. His hand was on her elbow, guiding her, and still flustered, she pushed him, her long arms windmilling in panic. He backed away.

"Pardon," he said more stiffly.

"No, please pardon me." She offered him her hand apologetically and looked straight at him. This was Beatrix's way. Direct, open, no coyness.

Their eyes met in a shock of recognition though they had never met before. Did all birdsong, all conversation, cease for a heartbeat when their eyes met, or did they merely imagine it? You know the moment, don't you? This one, and no other. If you have never experienced this moment, you have my condolences for your loss. Whatever comes after, the moment is worth it.

Beatrix, though, was already thinking, There is still time to stop this. She could simply turn away and hurry back to her table, her family. But she stood her ground.

He had a kind face, a good face. Olive complexion, black hair and eyes, but with none of the leer or suggestion that traveling women often faced in strangers' eyes in public places.

Her face was flushed pink, the color of distress that comes over women with hair that particular shade of auburn. Her nose was long and sharp, her mouth and eyebrows straight, no hint of a curve. A handsome rather than pretty woman, with pale gray eyes full of sweetness, though when she was crossed they became the color of a cold rain.

"Sorry," she said. "Thank you. I will sit for a moment. Catch my breath." Her voice, he thought. It sounded of arias and violins, danced up and down scales within those few phrases.

He extended his arm, palm up, in the direction of the bench. He did not attempt to touch her again.

"They can be troublesome, these little boys," he said, sitting as far away from her as the bench allowed. "It is better not to walk on your own in these gardens."

"I see that now," she said, her breath once again slow, steady, her golden voice even lighter, lovelier.

"May I introduce myself? Amerigo Massimo, at your service."

"Miss Beatrix Jones."

"Ah. American!" He seemed surprised. She did not have the air of the conqueror.

"Surely you enjoy a steady supply of them in Rome."

He laughed. "Even so."

"Amerigo," she said. "The name of my country."

"Yes. In fact, he was simply a mapmaker. In my family, the first son is always named Amerigo. In your language, it translates as Henry, does it not? It means ruler of the home. And Beatrix means blessed, the bringer of joy." He stopped short, embarrassed. Surely that comment had been too personal, not the sort of thing you say to an unknown woman in a public garden.

They fell silent then, both uncertain of what would come next. They had not been formally introduced, and indeed their meeting had been under unfortunate circumstances. He will go back to his friends and laugh at the silly American, she thought. She will go back to her family and sneer at the shopworn Italian, he thought.

He was shopworn, an Americanism he had grown fond of, though he had learned the word in even more embarrassing circumstances—at Mrs. Haskett's musical evening last week, whispered as he passed by. His suit, though of good quality, then as today, had been mended; his boots, polished till they reflected like a black mirror, had once been worn by his father and were older than many of the young women in the gardens that afternoon.

But she, the American, dazzled in her newness. They usually did. New frock, new hat, new boots, everything so new she sparkled with it. She wore her wealth more lightly than most of them, though, and by that he recognized breeding. Her earrings were small, though the dark amethysts were of excellent quality and well chosen to go with those pale eyes. The silk of her frock had a subtle sheen rather than a glare. Her hat had a single silk flower on it and no ribbons. He liked the openness of her gaze.

His expression pleased her equally. There was no nuance, no flirtatiousness, no double meaning. It was as honest as the sun. Yet she was very aware that he was a man, she a woman. Eden, she thought. That first look between Adam and Eve must surely have been a look of wonder and appreciation, of curiosity, of Eve thinking, He is for me, and I am for him.

The thought alarmed Beatrix. She had come to Italy to study gardens and art, not fall in love. This was not part of her plan and never had been. A volunteer, she thought. A plant that pops up where it has not been planted, a poppy in a cornfield, an oak sapling in a bed of speedwell. She knew how to deal with volunteers. They were dug up and discarded or rerooted in a more appropriate place.

Don't be a schoolgirl. I shall never marry, she thought, yet she understood that inevitability a seed feels when the first drops of spring rain seep down to its resting place, awakening it.

"Well," he said, clearing his throat, a touch of shyness suddenly appearing. "I seem to have frightened off your potential guides. They were really pickpockets, you know. They are uneducated, these boys who accost visitors in the public places. If you wish, though, to view the Caravaggios, I will be most pleased to escort you. You must not go alone into the *casina*. Most unfortunate, but one must tell the truth about one's city."

"Yes," she said. A single word. That, too, pleased him. They walked in silence, an arm's length between them.

As they approached the *casina*, the shadows grew thicker and closer together; the open vista of the gardens changed to something quite different. Trees hovered over; shrubs close to the ground grabbed passing ankles. The air grew warmer, even more stagnant.

The *casina* smelled of damp and cat piss, but the white columns were lovely, the arched windows placed to frame scenes as beautiful as those hanging on the gallery walls. I must remember this, Beatrix told herself, burying the strange excitement she felt under a student's obligation to observe. What is viewed outside a window is as important as what is viewed from the center of any garden. Pleasure and beauty. That was what gardens brought to the world, her world. It was what she wanted to give back to the world. Eden, she thought again. The garden before the fall.

Several clusters of visitors, mostly women escorted by the occasional male, father or brother or fiancé of one of them, paced the gallery where the Caravaggios were hung. They looked in her direction when Beatrix entered with Amerigo. One or two whispered. Rome was a large city, but not so large that people of a certain class were not continually encountering one another. Beatrix thought she recognized one or two faces from afternoon teas, musical evenings, concerts. She nodded and pretended to be deep in conversation with Amerigo to avoid the inevitable confrontation when pleasantries must be exchanged. She was hopeless with names.

Beatrix stood closer to Amerigo to deepen the impression that they were not in the gallery to share small talk with others. This was the mistake, of course. By that evening a certain circle of expatriate Americans in their rented foreign drawing rooms and parlors would be talking about that step closer. My dear. She put her arm through his. Such intimacy. Does the child know nothing?

Amerigo understood the purpose of Beatrix's gesture and leaned slightly closer. Yes. A deep conversation, one that should not be interrupted with niceties. "See the brushstrokes in this corner. It is said an apprentice, in a fit of temper, painted over the master's work in this area, for spite," he said loudly as one of the matrons passed them.

Beatrix peered studiously at the painting.

That squint that would surely produce lines at the corners of her eyes in a few years made his heart skip a beat.

They stood in front of the *Madonna of the Palafrenieri*, and the glow of the Madonna's rusty apricot dress cast a blush over Amerigo Massimo's face.

"She looks a little like you," he said.

"Not at all," Beatrix protested, despite the auburn hair and white skin of the Madonna.

"Of course, you are right." His voice changed. He became what he had promised, a tour guide. "This painting once hung in St. Peter's, but it was removed. It was considered to have insufficient decorum for the subject matter."

Beatrix nodded. The Madonna was sensual, her lips parted, her dress revealing more than should be revealed in a church, and the Christ child was no longer an infant but a young boy, standing fully naked and bathed in light. The figures spoke of physical beauty as well as the spiritual.

They moved on to the next painting. Here, she thought, is a

source of dread. The boy, that dreadful boy, so serene, almost indifferent, as he holds up the gory head.

They were standing in front of one of the larger works, *David with the Head of Goliath*, and there was so much Amerigo Massimo wished her to see in the painting. Could she appreciate its glory, the beauty of the shepherd boy, David, dangling the grizzled head of his enemy in his left hand, the decapitating sword still in his right hand? The slingshot of legend was nowhere to be seen, as if Caravaggio were saying, See how victory elevates one from the humble to the grand. Engraved on the sword were the letters *H-AS OS. Humilitas occidit superbiam.* Humility kills pride. Beatrix remembered the phrase from one of her Latin primers.

"To fully understand this painting is to understand that every victory carries the germ of its own defeat," Amerigo said.

"The boy is so beautiful. Like an angel," Beatrix said. "A killing angel."

"The head of Goliath is Caravaggio. It is a self-portrait." The boy model painted as the shepherd, David, had been Caravaggio's lover. Could she see that?

Her quick blush said yes, she saw, she understood the intense sexuality of the painting, the older lover totally defeated, destroyed by the young beloved. This painting was not about victory in battle, but about the cruelty of desire. She felt the hot blood suffusing her cheeks, and more, she understood the aging painter's lust for that beautiful boy, that destroying angel.

I should not have brought her here, he thought. She wore no wedding ring; she was an innocent, even though Italian girls of her age were mothers two or three times over.

"Why did the artist not paint in a background?" Beatrix asked, ignoring the assaulting sexuality of the painting. "That deep blackness covering everything behind them. Why?"

"You must dream what is there," Amerigo said. "You must paint it in your own imagination. Caravaggio did not like to put pretty gardens in his paintings."

"A specimen," she said.

"Pardon?"

"In a garden, if the tree or shrub is of exceptional quality, one plants it alone rather than in a grouping, and in front of a different planting that does not call attention to itself."

"Ah. Like an only child, adored and protected."

Beatrix flinched slightly. She was an only child. "Yes," she said, not yet knowing that he, too, had grown up in solitude, an only child.

"You must have for your home an exceptional gardener, a man with such wisdom and craft." He and his family hadn't had a gardener for many years, only old Magda, who threw buckets of water over the potted trees in the courtyard when she remembered, and raked up leaves, stuck seeds into pots with peasant abandon, indifferent to color and texture and arrangement.

"Yes," Beatrix admitted. "The plans are mine, though. I designed our gardens myself. I do much of the maintenance as well."

She said it with pride and more than a touch of defensiveness. He, like most, had already assumed it was man's work.

"American women! Such viragos of cleverness and ambition!"

Was he mocking her? She stole a quick look at him. His face

had closed like a book. They were being watched, she saw now. Mrs. Haskett had come into the *casina* with her three daughters.

Hadn't the woman said she had an appointment?

Amerigo strode forward and made a little bow. He said something under his breath. Mrs. Haskett answered in an equally quiet voice. Beatrix understood immediately that they already knew each other.

"I must get back to my family," Beatrix said. "I have been gone too long."

"Miss . . . Jones, isn't it?" Mrs. Haskett said, knowing full well it was Beatrix but wanting to return the insult she had suffered an hour before. "We meet again." There was an unpleasant note in her voice. Her eyes went back and forth, from Beatrix to Amerigo, and there were questions and judgments in her gaze.

"I will take you back to your family," Amerigo said, turning away from Mrs. Haskett. "It is not wise to walk alone here."

Beatrix felt Mrs. Haskett's gaze burning into her back as they walked away.

They returned by a different path, shorter, he promised, since she was in a hurry. It curved behind the *casina*, as natural in its flowing lines as a stream. This path suited her better than the formal allées, with their too-strict geometry, their insistence on order above all else.

"Look," she said, just as the path began to turn into a formal allée and the vast expanse of the Borghese gardens came again into view. A lone flower grew between the flagstones, a pale and fragile stem of veronica. "It is blooming in a very dangerous place. See, it has already been trodden. And it is blooming very early."

He bent and she held her breath, thinking he intended to pluck it for her. Such a silly gesture, even though it was only a volunteer, something growing out of its proper time and place.

Instead, he straightened its stem, turned it up toward the sun. "It will not last the season, or even the week. But one must give it its chance."

Beatrix closed her eyes, feeling the sun on her face, thinking of herself as that plant growing where it should not, yet being given its chance. She could almost imagine he had touched her face rather than the veronica.

He kept a formal distance between them, but when they approached uneven steps he took her elbow. By unspoken agreement, the second time this happened he kept his hand on her elbow. They moved a little closer, their steps matching, and it seemed to Beatrix as if a new center of gravity had been created, that Rome and Europe and the planet earth and all the stars of the universe now revolved around them. They had begun with a miracle, that little flower blooming out of season, out of place. She was certain there were other miracles to follow.

I shall never marry, a little voice echoed back in her thoughts, and she felt the private earthquake of dissonance that occurs when one's purpose no longer suits one's emotions.

He pulled her hand through the crook of his arm, and they walked like that, not speaking, both totally transported by that casual contact with the other. When they came in view of the table where Edith and Teddy and Minnie sat, Beatrix slid her arm out of that tender angle between his forearm and breast. When they made their farewells it was with a great deal of formality. She felt the change in herself, though.

Mrs. Haskett, watching from the *casina*, also felt a slight shift of the earth beneath her feet when she saw Amerigo Massimo making that formal little bow to the American girl, Beatrix Jones. The forced and constant smile on her face disappeared.

FOUR

That evening, in their suite at the Hotel d'Italie, Minnie
Jones sat retucking strands of dark hair into the chignon
low on her neck as Beatrix read to her. The spine of the Baedeker
was as broken from use as that of the ancient family Bible; on the
round, cloth-covered table towered a pile of books on the history
of Italy. Tomorrow they would visit the Casa Respiglia and the
Roman Forum; the next day they would travel to Frascati to see
Villa Aldobrandini and the ruins of Tusculum. Their custom had
become to read in the evening before, as preparation for the next
day's visits.

Despite their efficient preparations, this trip felt unusual,
fraught somehow. Like others of her class and set, Minnie had
traveled often to Europe. One of her recurring dreams was that
of waking up on a ship, in the middle of the ocean, and not remembering if she was being carried to or from Europe. But once
the divorce was finalized, her life would be altered. Europe would

be where he lived, with his mistress. Every drawing room she walked into would buzz with the scandal and more than a touch of judgment for her failures. Or worse, pity.

The thought of pity from others made Minnie slam her brush onto the table. Beatrix paused in her reading.

Mother and daughter sat still and silent. "Do you want to discuss it?" Beatrix asked after a long while.

"No. There seems nothing to say. Read again that part about the facade of the Villa Medici," Minnie said. "I like to know what I am looking at." Her voice suggested that once, when she had been young and vulnerable, she had not known what she was looking at when she first beheld Freddie Jones. Mr. James had warned her, and she hadn't listened.

A large vase of dahlias stood on the book-strewn table, sent not by her husband but by her husband's lawyer, who was preparing the papers in advance of her visit. It was deemed wasteful to discard them, yet mother and daughter pointedly avoided looking at those awful orange dahlias from the even more awful lawyer who represented Mr. Jones in his divorce proceedings against Mrs. Jones.

It had been sadly appropriate, Beatrix thought, that the lawyer had sent dahlias. Had he known that the plant was famous among gardeners for its morphological variations? Plant a dahlia from seed and you'll never be certain of what it will grow into, not the color or shape or height. A seed-grown dahlia was the epitome of unpredictability; a seed-grown dahlia is as dangerous as a marriage based solely on youthful passion.

"Who was that young man you were walking with?" Minnie

asked now, putting down the brush and turning from her mirror to her daughter. "Today. At the gardens."

"Signor Amerigo Massimo," said Beatrix, who had never told a lie to her mother, nor kept a secret. "He rescued me from a group of boys who were pestering me."

"A good face. Even seen from a distance," Minnie said. "He seemed to be a gentleman."

"He was. And I won't see him again, I'm certain."

"Beatrix, you are already becoming a little set in your ways. You have decided against marriage, I know, and therefore have closed yourself off from the possibility of passion. Don't turn away. I am your mother, and I will speak of this. Not all marriages become disasters. I worry that I have set you a bad example. Edith as well. She and Teddy. Well, I won't say more."

"You have been the best of examples." Beatrix sat next to her mother and put her arm around her shoulders. "You have allowed me to become independent."

"People will soon whisper that you are becoming an old maid."

"Let them. I have my work, my gardens. I will make a profession of it."

"A woman landscape designer." Minnie raised one arched eyebrow. "They will more than whisper about that."

"Let them. We can't live in a manner meant to merely suit casual conversation. Signor Massimo was startled when I spoke of my work, but he quickly ascribed it to American eccentricity."

"Your conversation with him seems to have progressed to private matters." Minnie stood and rearranged the books on the table. Her impulse had been to hug Beatrix, but her daughter was several inches taller and such a style of embrace had been difficult for years. That was the Jones' blood showing up. Her own family had been smaller in stature.

"We had been discussing a Caravaggio, and the painting had made me think of gardens. Did you know that Caravaggio did not like to paint landscapes?"

"He probably found them too pretty, too common. Though how one can find Caravaggio's work to be pretty is beyond me." Minnie turned back to the mirror and tied a black choker around her neck. She stared thoughtfully, comparing Beatrix's auburn coloring and smooth skin to her own darker hair, the beginning of lines at eyes and throat.

"I worry," she said to her reflection in the mirror, "that I have been too modern of a mother. In my day, the only decision a girl made was what color her wedding travel dress should be." That wasn't exactly true. She, not her mother or father, had chosen Freddie. They, like dear Henry, had had doubts. And they had been correct.

"What ideas you have." Beatrix laughed. "Do you think you should have locked me in my room when I insisted on moving to Boston to work with Mr. Sargent at the arboretum?"

"No. You would have left anyway. You would have climbed out the window and might have injured yourself. Couldn't have that. Are you ready for dinner, Beatrix? Let's see if the carriage has arrived. Annie, bring my wrap!" The maid came with her arms full of light woolen shawls, blue for Beatrix, yellow for Minnie.

. . . . .

O r so this is the story Beatrix told me. She does not embellish; gardeners know better than to force excessive color or outrageous shapes into a flower bed. The result is garish. Moreover, the event as she described it rings with authenticity, especially that bit about the weed she wouldn't allow herself to pull. I have seen Beatrix in gardens not her own, witnessed the impatient sighing and tapping of toes at a flower bed not well arranged, a fruit tree in need of pruning. She knew better than to interfere with another's work and garden, even when badly done, even when accidents like weeds make it difficult to admire a rose bed. And as for the volunteer that Amerigo tried to save, later, what could better corroborate the scene, the meeting? Only a passionate gardener or two people in love for the first time would even notice such a thing.

It is important to establish what Mr. James would call credibility. You'll understand why later, when I must write of things that are not as easily authenticated as the Latin tag of a plant.

But Beatrix does have imagination. "Daisy," she whispered after that afternoon in the Borghese gardens, when I had arrived in Rome and we met in the hotel tearoom, "I have seen a face I will never forget. There is nothing remarkable about it, I assure you. Yet . . . it is unforgettable. Am I clear? Remember the white alba?"

The summer before, when I had been visiting Beatrix in Bar Harbor, she had pointed this particular rose out to me during a tour of her garden. My visits to Bar Harbor had become regular by then, since I, Mr. Winters, and many other New York residents escaped the city for the cooler rooms and lawns of summertime Maine. In fact, Beatrix's rustic escape was becoming crowded with visitors, and the private homes on Eden Street were, one by one, being replaced by hotels.

The busier Bar Harbor grew with sailing, hiking, lawn tennis, and dance parties, the more Beatrix cherished her garden, started when she was still a very young child. Eden, she liked to remind me, was one of the earlier names for the island.

The white alba rose she grew there was one of the oldest varieties, having been around since before the Crusades and perhaps even before that. The color, to my eye, was pale and nameless, the scent whispery, the petals soft but nothing like silk. Yet gardeners, ones who knew their materials, always planted some bushes of this rose, and it was this rose that visitors remembered.

"It has a quality of constancy," Beatrix had explained. "It is a trustworthy rose. And it reminds one of so much of the simple goodness of life."

"Like my Mr. Winters," I had said, bending down in Beatrix's garden to sniff the rose. "I know that at this very moment he is still in his dressing room, studying the papers, getting ready to place a bet. When he loses—and he will lose because he always does—he will explain his shortage of ready cash by claiming to have left his money clip in some public place. Then he will buy me a box of chocolates and . . ." Beyond that, one dared not tread, not even with one's dearest friend, for fear of describing an excess of intimacy. "Dear Mr. Winters," I finished. "How constant he is."

"Does he lose much?" Beatrix asked, frowning.

"No more than we can afford, my dear—don't make that face. Every man must have a hobby."

"Of all the people I know, only you have succeeded in finding happiness within marriage," Beatrix said, laughing.

"True. And for that, Mr. James will never forgive me."

Nor would I forgive Mr. James for killing me off in that novella he wrote. True, he renamed his poor victim Miller, Daisy Miller, but everyone in New York and Newport knew he meant Daisy Cooper, who married Gilbert Winters. Yes, that family. Old streets named after them in New England, an ancestral home inhabited by distant cousins in Sussex. Roman fever, indeed. Mr. James killed me off because he believed that I, only one generation removed from the harsh, up-before-dawn farm life, had married unwisely into a family of taken-for-granted privilege. Like his friend Minnie Cadwalader Jones, I had chosen with my heart, not my head, and despite all the advice of love poems and songs, such marriages often wither on the vine.

"You have used me badly," I wrote to Mr. James after receiving the copy of *Daisy Miller* he had signed and sent me. "I accept the label of flirt. I admit my naïveté. But to destroy me with malaria? This is a simple case of sour grapes, dear fox. You cannot accept my happiness, that Mr. Winters and I were designed especially for each other, and grow happier every day." That was true, at the time.

"My dearest Daisy," he wrote back the same day, "perhaps I did purloin some of your circumstances and your charming nickname. But you have made your life. I have made my novel. Let us continue to be friends, and continue on these parallel paths. After all, how many New York matrons can claim the honor of being a Henry James heroine?"

He was right about that. My calendar grew twice as busy after the novel began to circulate. The expense was frightful, because supper invitations must be returned and of course new gowns had to be worn to those dinners.

Mr. Winters was none too pleased. He is, after all, a bit of a cad in the story. Prim, self-righteous, easily defeated. "It is unbearable," he had grumbled. "Henry could at least have written how well I sat a horse, and my infallible rhythm on the dance floor. And he got that night at the Colosseum all wrong. I offered to escort you back to your hotel, and you, little minx, refused."

"It's called creative license, dearest," I said. As for the refusal: I knew exactly what I was doing. Didn't his proposal a few months later prove it?

But this is Beatrix's story. Let us return to it.

FIVE

That evening, after Beatrix's encounter in the Borghese gardens with Amerigo, the meeting that almost did not happen, Beatrix and Minnie, accompanied by Edith and Teddy, attended Mrs. Haskett's musical evening. They felt they must, but what they didn't know was that the damage had already been done. Mrs. Haskett took slight easily and was slow, very slow, to forgive. Mix passion and jealousy with insult and there is guaranteed trouble ahead. It was going to be a difficult evening.

There are two ways to acquire an ancient and noble Roman house. The first is to marry the son of the house. This was beyond Mrs. Haskett's abilities. She had a sharp-faced attractiveness, an animal quality of health, but she lacked youth. First sons, heirs, tended to marry young women, and she was middle-aged. The second way to acquire an ancient palazzo, of course, is to simply purchase it. This was not beyond Mrs. Haskett's talents, since the late Mr. Haskett had left her a tidy fortune. My

Mr. Winters had been a friend of that family and we had spent long evenings gossiping about—and, true, also being jealous of—that fortune.

The old house, as the merrily widowed Mrs. Haskett called her Roman palazzo, was close to the fashionable Spanish Steps, not far from where the poet John Keats had died seventy-five years before. He was one of Minnie's favorites, and she often recited from memory his "Ode to a Nightingale." "Singest of summer in full-throated ease," she whispered to Beatrix that night as they climbed the steps to the palazzo. There were forty or so rooms, two separate courtyards, and enough American modifications to make the old Roman families sneer with distaste. They did, however, accept her invitations: her personal chef, we had been told, had been lured away from the Ritz, and she hired the best musicians available.

Beatrix's party arrived promptly, followed by their two maids and one manservant, only to discover that most of the other guests had decided to follow the European custom and arrive half an hour late. The huge halls and reception rooms were almost empty, except for the predictable down-at-heel bachelors and poorly paid *professori*, who arrived as soon as possible so that they could dine for free at the buffet. Rows of servants in red satin and white stockings and white wigs lined the rooms, waiting, and a trio of violinists tuned their instruments with a series of squeaks and twangs.

Mrs. Haskett herself was still upstairs in her dressing room, so Edith and Beatrix, Minnie and Teddy, sent the maids and footservant to the back of the house, found a door into a pleasant courtyard garden, and sat there, feeling strange and a little miserable.

At ten, the music began and their hostess came to find them, apologizing profusely and insincerely for having kept them waiting.

"What a day it has been!" she exclaimed, pretending to have forgotten she had met them in the Borghese gardens. Insult for insult. By then the other guests had arrived and the palazzo buzzed with activity.

An unfamiliar soprano of great beauty but questionable vocal range sang Mozart and Goldoni in the yellow parlor. Beatrix tried to close her ears to the faltering notes, but ears are not like eyes: they will not abandon the world as easily as eyes do. The music seeped into her consciousness, reminding her of things better forgotten.

A late supper with ices and greenhouse strawberries was provided in the conservatory, amid a great quantity of orchids and ferns. It was, Minnie kept complaining in Beatrix's ear, a great crush of people.

"But look at the orchids!" Beatrix whispered back. "Do you think I will be permitted to tour the new greenhouse?" The violin trio in the conservatory was playing a waltz, and Beatrix couldn't help swaying a little to the music.

"They will be certain to ask you to sing," Minnie warned her. "Will you?"

Before being accepted as an apprentice at Arnold's Arboretum in Boston, Beatrix had studied to be a concert singer. As

Amerigo had already discovered, she had one of those voices that made people hold their breath when they listened, not wanting to break the magic even with the noise of their own breathing. When she sang, her voice made people remember first love and cradling their first newborn in their arms, or a certain moonlit evening with an irresistible lover.

"No," Beatrix said to Minnie that night in Rome. "I will not sing for Mrs. Haskett. Not even as payment for a visit to the private greenhouse, not even if she is once again offended."

She and Minnie moved deeper into the throng.

On this particular evening, the five salons of the house were opened to the party. Guests in formal and very expensive evening attire wandered back and forth, admiring the crystal chandeliers, Aubusson tapestries, and large collection of recently acquired pictures, mostly old masters, all hung from walls and ceilings newly reinforced with American dollars and ingenuity. It was rumored Mrs. Haskett had a staff of no fewer than three curators, hired away from the Louvre, scouring Europe for her purchases.

Beatrix found it compellingly repulsive, this combination of new wealth, greed, and impersonal tastes. She found her repulsion to be just as repulsive, as if somehow her disapproval was part of this scheme, accommodating Mrs. Haskett's rampage. The mix of so many brilliantly colored satin gowns, randomly placed Fra Lippis and Berninis, huge urns of ferns, roses, and orchids, made her fingers ache for soil, her neck for the feel of sun browning the nape . . . for the honesty of labor. The salons of the palazzo made her miss the simple single drawing room of her mother's New York brownstone, the cozy comfort of the Bar Harbor cottage.

"How soon can we leave?" she asked Minnie, extending her hand to a count who had clicked his heels and bowed over it.

"An hour more. Anything less would be rude. Do smile, Beatrix. You look as if you are about to have a tooth pulled."

Minnie had known in advance that the evening would be distasteful. Mrs. Haskett, like other nouveau riche, had a reputation for overdoing things. But Minnie was determined that her daughter should have a taste of Roman society whether she wished it or not. It was dangerous to turn one's back on the untried and untested. Life was, after all, an experiment. What is the planting of a single desiccated seed if not an experiment in hope?

It was inevitable that some of the experiments would be failures, but some would not be. Marriages, for example. Hers had failed, but without the marriage there would have been no Beatrix, and that single child was worth all the possible failures of the world. There was the single seed blossomed into a lovely woman, a future, a life to outlast her own.

"I think I would rather be at the surgeon's," Beatrix whispered back.

The rooms were too crowded for her. Tall as she was, she still felt herded like a wayward sheep, pushed this way and that. She had become ensnared in a group of young girls in silken pastels who were carrying her away from her mother, toward the table of ices.

The violinists were beginning another waltz, and couples swirled into the middle of the room. Across the way, a young man waved enthusiastically and began pushing through the crowd toward her. She knew Timothy Whipple from the Newport tennis club and understood that he wished an association with her. She found him boring, one of the indiscriminate mass of young men who study lethargically at Harvard and then settle into society and family life with equal lethargy, rousing only for games of tennis or bridge—young men who do their duty with little enthusiasm, who seem permanently asleep by the age of thirty. She had no desire to waltz with him in this overcrowded room.

"Miss Jones!" Another hand reached out to her.

"Signor Massimo." She could think of nothing to say, once the name had been said. But she grasped his hand and let herself be pulled out of the current of humanity.

"It seems my fate to rescue you from swarms. Come, this way." He guided her to an alcove festooned with red and gold velvet curtains. They sat on cold white marble. "Are you enjoying your stay in Rome, Miss Jones? How strange to have—how do you Americans say?—bumped into you, twice in one day."

"Yes." She winced at her lack of inventiveness. In New York ballrooms she was not this naive, tongue-tied maiden. Rome seemed to be rendering her speechless. They did not look at each other. They did not look at each other so hard that the other's face was all they could see in their mind's eye.

"Shall I bring you some punch?"

"No, thank you. Don't leave. I mean, if you leave . . ." She stopped.

"I see. That young man still waving at you from across the room will claim my place. Then, I will guard it with all my strength."

That seemed to be the end of their conversation. They sat there, side by side, neither looking at nor touching each other, yet conscious only of the other, as if the soiree was a mere stage setting for what was to occur between them, except they had forgotten their lines.

Had she really met him only that afternoon? Why the sense that he had always been there, at her side? When he brushed at a bit of lint on his coat sleeve, she felt it was a gesture she already knew. She had already known his evening cologne would be vetiver, and that the handkerchief in his pocket would be simple linen with neither lace nor monogram.

The waltz ended. From the next room she could hear subdued applause, a woman's voice announcing a set of songs she would perform accompanied by the violinists. The musicians played the opening notes of Zerlina's aria from *Don Giovanni*, the song that promises a remedy for pain and ends with Zerlina placing Don Giovanni's hand over her heart. There was a problem, a false start. The soprano cleared her throat and the violinists began again. This time she joined them, her coloratura voice sending the sensation of honey through Beatrix's veins.

"A fine love song," Signor Massimo said when she had finished.

"Her final notes seemed to quaver."

"It is true her voice no longer has the clarity for which she was so famous in her youth. But still, it is a fine love song."

From across the room, she could see Timothy Whipple staring at her and whispering to another young man at his side. Their faces were stormy with disapproval until two young women stopped before them, laughing, saying something that made the two boys bend closer to their whispers, forgetting Beatrix and the Roman who seemed to have claimed her for the entire evening.

"How long are you staying in Rome?" Amerigo asked, still not looking at her.

"Just days. I am here to see the gardens and monuments, and then there are other cities I must visit."

"Ah! You wish to return home and style your gardens in the European manner."

"Not just my gardens. Others as well. I am to work in the profession. And no, not exclusively in the European style. We need a new style for our New World."

"But that is the work of laborers, of men," he protested.

"There are some who believe it can also be women's work," she answered quietly.

"Americans." He smiled and shook his head. "So industrious, so new in their thinking in that New World."

"Not all of them." Her father, the man she hadn't seen for years, had sent a letter of complaint when he heard his daughter was pruning trees and turning compost at the Boston arboretum. "She will ruin her hands. Who will marry her?" Beatrix had read the letter after her mother had crumpled it into a ball and left it for the maid to take away.

"Your father doesn't approve," Amerigo guessed. "They are a difficult breed to please, fathers. Mine as well."

They sat in silence as the music changed from Mozart arias to Brahms' *Liebeslieder*. Beatrix understood enough German to appreciate the lyrics: "The underbrush is trembling, struck by a bird in flight. My soul trembles in the same way." Gardens for joy; dark woods for danger. Brahms knew how to place love, she thought.

No, she told herself. This is not love. She sat up straighter, lifted her chin higher, and purposely looked in the opposite direction, where Amerigo's face could not fill her peripheral vision. She carried a fan Minnie had given her, and she opened it now, revealing the antique garden painted on the silk mount. It caught his eye and he reached over to touch it with admiration.

"It is beautifully painted," he said. "May I see it?"

"Certainly." She gave him the fan, still avoiding his gaze, pretending to be entranced by the dancers. They were so careful to avoid touching each other's hands in this exchange that the effect was stronger on them than actually holding hands would have been. That moment was, I believe, the closest Beatrix ever came to coy flirtation.

"I do not recognize the flowers they have painted," he admitted, handing back the fan after a moment.

"That is because they don't exist. They are, as far as I can tell, a strange hybrid of peony and calendula. They were the painter's fantasy."

"I see. Poetic license." The music changed yet again, to a quick-paced polka, and the room filled with the laughter and shrieks of the dancers, the rustle of silk and clink of glasses, young girls dressed in garden colors, their partners in black and white, whirling and changing formation like shards in a kaleidoscope.

This is wrong, Beatrix thought, feeling overwhelmed. We should be in a quiet garden; we should hear birds, people speaking in the distance. She shifted restlessly, and he misunderstood, thinking she was tired of his company.

"Sadly, I see someone I must speak with," he said after a few more moments. "You will excuse me?"

Beatrix should have spoken that line; the woman should be the person to end the encounter and the conversation. But there had been little conversation, only that magnetism of their two bodies leaning slightly toward each other.

"Yes," she agreed. "I must find Mother. I have left her too long."

"Perhaps we will meet again." He took her hand and kissed it, formally. "I hope so."

Had her silence offended him? Beatrix worried. She was, then, too inexperienced to know that his confusion was even greater than her own, that he could no longer sit close to her without putting his arm about her waist, and that, of course, was impossible.

She watched him go, his back stiff and straight in the black evening jacket. His clothes were not of the most recent fashion, and that added to a timelessness about him, a sense of age beyond his own youth, as if he walked surrounded by an invisible crowd of ancestors. They are never alone, these Europeans, Beatrix thought, even when they seem alone. A sudden urge made her want to call him back to her. She did not.

She looked to the side and saw young Mr. Whipple watching, disapproval on his face.

"That was your rescuing knight from the Borghese, wasn't it?" Minnie, gliding effortlessly through the throng, came and sat on the marble bench next to Beatrix.

"Yes."

"He has gone into the yellow salon. I just saw him with a young person who seems to be on warm and familiar terms with him."

"It is none of my affair," Beatrix said.

Is this how it begins? thought Minnie. With a Roman? Rome was so far from New York. Would she become one of those lonely mothers who received cards and foreign shawls and leather purses in the mail, but almost never saw her daughter? I want my daughter's happiness, she told herself. And I want her close to me. Is it impossible to have both?

Minnie, herself an only child who had lost her own mother at a young age and had been for years separated from her husband, realized how dependent she had become on her daughter's companionship. They began and ended each day together, could finish each other's sentences, knew each other's preferences and dislikes. To lose that closeness at a time of life when she was unlikely to find an intimate relationship—not that she wished to remarry—would be a difficult thing. Beatrix was so woven into the fabric of Minnie's daily life that she thought she could hear that fabric tear when she saw Beatrix sitting with her Roman acquaintance.

Minnie considered the situation. A careful, calculating mother would, at this point, accept or at least plan for the inevitable and make gentle and subtle inquires about the young man. He seemed well-bred, perfectly acceptable. But who was his family? What were his prospects? Minnie was alert only to the fact that her twenty-three-year-old daughter had never, as far as she could tell, been in love, and she was terribly vulnerable.

She held herself responsible for this, for her daughter's childhood filled with the cold, bitter silences of an estranged husband and wife, that singular witnessing of the death of love rather than its inception. It is a shame, she thought, that children are born after the fact, after the passion.

No. She would make no inquiries about the Italian. He had a good face and good manners. That would have to be enough. Even if the coincidental meetings turned into a love affair and the affair went wrong and became heartbreak, her daughter would have experienced those days, even just minutes, that can make an entire lifetime worthwhile. She would have had what Edith called "heart history."

As for marriage, for a daughter living in Italy, she could not force herself to think about it.

The next day began with a cloudburst. Rain glittered in the air, catching brief reflections of light like jewels shining in a woman's dark hair. In the hotel's dining room, voices were hushed and the waiters moved silently through the thick, humid atmosphere of white cloths, chandeliers, and silver services.

"Shall we cancel our sightseeing?" Edith asked, pouring cream into her coffee. She broke off a corner of buttered toast and fed it to her little dog, who sat next to her chair, dark eyes large with longing.

"Fine with me," Teddy grumbled. "Beastly weather. These eggs are cold. Waiter!"

The three women waited patiently as Teddy complained loudly to the waiter and demanded a fresh plate. The other diners in the hotel restaurant seemed evenly divided into two groups on this matter of service: the Americans and English nodded agreement, while the French and Germans smirked into their napkins. Since the hotel catered mostly to Americans, Teddy had a largely sympathetic cohort. Still, Beatrix was embarrassed. Why couldn't her uncle eat as the Romans ate, a simple breakfast of bread and cheese or cold meat? Why insist on eating as New Yorkers did even when they were not in New York?

"As I was saying," Edith continued, once the new plate of hot eggs arrived. "What shall we do today?"

"I think we should alter our plan to suit the day," Minnie said, "and visit the catacombs instead of the forum. Stay out of the weather."

"Another old pile of stones," Teddy grumbled, forking eggs into his mouth.

"No, dear," Edith said. "The catacombs are underground, so it should be called another old hole in the ground, by your standards."

Teddy glared and pulled at his waistcoat. He always put on weight when he accompanied Edith abroad, sacrificing, he complained, his sturdy sportsman's figure to Edith's peripatetic whims. He missed his horses and his hounds.

"What do you think, Beatrix?" Minnie asked.

Since there were gardens in neither the forum nor the catacombs, Beatrix didn't really care which they visited. She'd had a sudden vision of leaves dancing overhead, boughs of oak reaching toward one another. There was a nest of robins in one of the branches, chirps rising in the breeze as the mother robin, worm in beak, landed on the edge of the nesting twigs to feed her brood. A memory. Bar Harbor in the spring. Such simplicity: strange to remember it amid the Michelangelos and Corinthian columns of Rome.

"It is decided, then," Edith said, though it hadn't been decided at all. "I'll arrange for a guide. We leave in one hour."

Exactly one hour later they walked out of their hotel and down the congested Corso to the church of San Sebastiano. The rain had turned to a fine drizzle, dulling the already dull colors of the ancient ochre city and muffling their steps.

Even on the widest streets of Rome, Beatrix felt hemmed in, confined. True, streets were congested in New York and some of the new buildings jutted up past a comfortable horizon. Even so, New York had more sky, more green, more sense of the presence of soil beneath the bricks. Rome, the eternal city, felt of artifice, contrivance, a kind of architectural stubbornness. We have always been here. We will always be here, the stones seemed to say.

The gray, rubble-strewn church of San Sebastiano on the Via Appia Antica was one of the smaller and older churches in the city. The facade had three arches supported by slender columns on the ground level and three large windows on the second level. It was in particularly bad repair in a city full of monuments in bad repair, large cracks zigzagging over it like frozen lightning bolts.

"Not auspicious," said Teddy. "However did you choose this place, Minnie?"

"The crypt has a Bernini I thought we might find interesting."

The robin of spring simplicity sang in Beatrix's imagination, a song of rising and falling chirps, so distinct it seemed strange to know they were sounding only in her memory. They seemed so real.

"And you will, I assure you." Their guide stepped out of the shadows to greet them, a brown-robed, tonsured monk of indeterminate age. Cistercian. The order that brought the Inquisition to Rome. Beatrix felt both intrigued and slightly repulsed.

The monk greeted them in heavily accented English. "I am Brother Tommaso. I speak your language well. There is nothing worse than seeing a wonder and not being able to comprehend it because the words are a barrier. Is this not correct?" the monk asked.

"Absolutely correct," Minnie agreed. "Are we to see wonders?"

The monk was tall and lean, with deep furrows in his face running from nose to chin. He had been handsome once in the way of Latin men, dark and intense with a springy walk suggestive of power. Beatrix wondered why he took vows, what he gave up, if he had regrets. Had there been a girl in his village, one who still mourned him? Perhaps another man's wife who thought of him at night as her husband snored heavily at her side?

Beatrix had a thought, as fast as birdsong, an image of Amerigo in his home, a woman at his side, pressing her hands on his shoulders, and a thrust of jealousy made her gasp in surprise.

Foolishness, she told herself. Stop it.

"The wonder of the ages, of the earth itself," the monk promised. "We will walk in single file. I will lead. Signor"—he nodded at Teddy Wharton—"will be last in file. Yes?" He addressed the question to Beatrix, not Mr. Wharton, as if he sensed her curiosity about him, her wandering thoughts.

"Agreed. Let's get on with it." Beatrix braced herself with a deep breath, dreading the closed, small places she was certain they would encounter.

Brother Tommaso pulled open the heavy wooden door and signaled them through. Inside, he gave each of them a candle and lit it.

"By the third level, we will be in darkness," he said. "But there will be drafts, so guard your candle."

Again, that odor of cat piss permeating everything. Rome was a city of cats; they slunk through the ruins in furry hordes, more sure of themselves than even the monk guide. We are outsiders, Beatrix thought for the hundredth time. They don't like us, but they need us. We are yet one more invasion in their eternal city.

"These catacombs are the easiest to access, so there is much damage to them," Brother Tommaso apologized. "Graffiti, stones carried away, sarcophagi smashed. As you see." He held his candle higher, the better to illuminate the ravages of centuries of vandalism. The first level of the catacomb looked like a rubbish pile. They kicked loosened stones out of their way as they walked, following the beacon of the monk's candle.

Down stone steps, slippery with damp, hollowed in their centers from millennia of footsteps. Beatrix already longed for the light, for openness. The passage was so narrow she would have touched both walls had she spread her arms.

"The catacombs are carved from tufa," Brother Tommaso said in a practiced voice. "Volcanic rock is soft, easy to shape. You may pick up one of the stones and scratch it with your fingernail. Test it."

Beatrix did. It flaked, leaving grit under her nail. No nourishment in it, she thought. Nothing could take root there, even if there were light, perhaps not even moss or lichen. It was good only for the already dead.

"Come," said the monk. They stepped into deeper shadow, and then into darkness, their candles lighting the way.

The second level was a little wider than the stair passage had been, and lined on either side with what seemed like shelves carved into the rock itself. "These cubicula were carved in the fourth century. This is where the bodies were laid to rest," Tommaso said. "At one time there would have been hundreds in these catacombs, but alas, there has always been a market for relics, for crushed bone and mummy powder." He sighed at the general gullibility of a frail humanity.

Beatrix, adjusting to the darkness and feeling slightly freed by it, felt an impulse to find a bone, to bring it back to Bar Harbor and crush it into powder, to feed that powder to the rambling rose that splayed against the south wall of the house. Would the rose know that it was now part Roman?

Minnie had more practical concerns. "How did they die, the people laid to rest in this catacomb?"

"Lions in the Colosseum, probably," Teddy said with relish.

"Some martyrs, yes," the monk said. "Others, perhaps the Roman fever. Perhaps a plague. Who knows? Death comes to us all, no matter what the path."

Minnie held her candle close enough to her face that Beatrix could see her expression. She's thinking of Father, Beatrix thought. The divorce. A different kind of death.

They moved deeper into the darkness. "The mausoleum of Marcus Clodius Hermes," said Brother Tommaso, holding his candle high to illuminate the cubicula. "See the paintings here, on the entrance wall. A funeral banquet."

Beatrix stepped closer to the wall, moved her candle in a circle as she studied the ancient faded wall painting of wealthy Romans dressed in flowing tunics and heavy earrings, reclining before tables spread with clusters of grapes, haunches of meat.

"And the miracle of the calling out of Cerasa's demons." The monk paused before another section of the painted wall.

"Cerasa's demons?" Edith asked, interested. She had been quiet until now, breathing slightly heavily behind Beatrix. "Ah, yes, the man in the cave. Christ cast out his demons and they went into a herd of pigs and then over a cliff, squealing."

"You are not a believer," Tommaso said quietly.

"I am not a disbeliever. We must both be content with that."

"I thought there would be . . . remains. Skeletons. That kind of thing," Teddy said, plainly disappointed.

"In many of the catacombs, yes, there are. But not in San Sebastiano. They have all been removed. Reburied or looted." The monk, slightly taller than Teddy, peered down at him, his gaze a reprimand for desiring the grotesque over the merely antique.

By now Beatrix's eyes had adjusted to the thick darkness. She could see in the way she thought seeds underground saw, with their whole being, not just a single sense. She could see the cold emanating from the underground stone walls, the warmth in the center of the passageway where they stood clustered together. Time itself seemed visible, the long marches of centuries floating in the motes illuminated by their candles. The candles themselves seemed like a constellation of distant suns. Invisible planets circling them in the swirling darkness.

She thought she saw a movement in a corner shadow, movement where none of them stood, and had a sensation of being observed. They who had come to see wonders were in fact being watched by some invisible presence—she could feel it. She thought she heard the patter of feet, felt some rough furred animal of shin height rush past her. A cat, she told herself. Only a cat.

Edith's little dog whimpered, and Beatrix heard, rather than saw, Edith bend down to pick it up and stroke it for comfort.

"Now we will see the painting of the Gorgon's head, the Triglia, or funeral banquet room, and the Platonica, where Peter and Paul were buried," said Brother Tommaso. He held his candle at an angle that illuminated his sharp cheekbones and made black caverns of his eyes. His face had become skeletal through a trick of light.

Again, something in the shadows moved. There was a blur, a soundless shift that no one else seemed to notice.

This place is unwholesome, Beatrix thought. She had visited cemeteries, stood before towering chiseled monuments of loss, and peered down at flush markers half buried in the grass, but this city of the dead was different. There was a complete absence of light, of life, aside from the feral cat that had brushed against her. Even in cemeteries there is life, she thought, but only when they are above ground, in open air. There are flowers and trees and birds and breezes to remind you that time stopped only for the person for whom you grieve. Here, everything had stopped.

"Death awaits you at the end of the dim vista." It was something Nathaniel Hawthorne had once written to her mother in a letter she had saved. Beatrix the child hadn't understood the phrase when he read it so softly, so casually, teacup in hand. But now, in that closed, suffocating underworld, she thought she understood. She shivered and longed for the light, the open sky.

Years later she would remember that moment, how wrong it felt to dishonor the dead with dank darkness, and when, after the Great War, she was asked to design memorials for those fallen in battle, she placed the memorials in patches of sunshine, where flowers could grow around them.

"No," said Beatrix. "I don't want to see the Gorgon's head. I don't want to go deeper into the catacomb."

"Ah." Brother Tommaso sighed. "A shame."

"Indeed, I am ready for some fresh air." Her mother took her by the arm. They turned around and began to retrace their steps.

"Hope the rain stopped," said Teddy, following behind.

When they emerged into the light, Beatrix felt like Persephone running away from Hades, hating the sterile darkness where nothing could grow except regret. She lost her footing on the last step, and when she reached into thin air, trying to regain her balance, her mother's hand grasped hers. For a blind, confusing second she had expected the hand of a man who wasn't even there with them. She had reached out for Amerigo.

SIX

"I had a painted fan once," said Mrs. Avery. "It had such strange flowers on it, like Beatrix's fan. My mother gave it to me when I was sixteen."

"I bet you looked charming, holding that fan," said Mr. Hardy, in a pleasant rather than flirtatious manner. Mrs. Avery had the surprising ability to bring out the nature of those around her: Mrs. Ballinger became even haughtier, while Mr. Hardy became kindly. In the days that I'd been in Lenox, I noticed that people tended to gravitate to Mrs. Avery, thinking at first, as I had, that they would be nice to her, and then discovering that they enjoyed her company. In a garden she would have been the smallest and palest of flowers, yet one with a very sweet scent, I imagined. Alyssum, perhaps. You barely know it is there, but a garden would not be complete without its fragrance.

"Useless things, painted fans," said Mrs. Ballinger. "I'm glad they've gone out of favor. Worse than kidskin gloves for getting lost or stepped on and ruined."

"But how beautiful they were," I said. "Fans and gloves. There was a time when you felt naked if you didn't have both."

I had been holding a painted fan on the evening in Vevey when I met Gilbert Winters.

There was so much Mr. James didn't write about that night. The garden, for instance. I had to go down stone steps to reach it. It was halfway between the wrought-iron-balconied front of the hotel, with the beautiful mountains behind it, and the lake itself, so that when I stood in the garden I was tempted to keep swiveling my head about to take in the scenery. I knew better, though. My grandparents blew on their soup and ate peas off their knives, but I had been instructed by a careful governess and kept my head and eyes looking straight ahead. Most uncomfortable.

Thankfully, I had already taken in the scenery for two nights before Mr. Winters appeared in the garden, so the temptation to swivel my head and gawk had been thoroughly tamped down.

I saw him sitting on the bench in the twilight, my little brother plaguing him with demands for candy, and I thought, I must rescue that gentleman from Raymond.

He stood, of course, as soon as I approached. Our eyes met. Music floated down to us from the hotel, a waltz, and for a dizzy moment I thought he intended to ask me to dance with him. I would have, despite how slippery some of the stones were. Instead, he gave me a polite little bow and looked immediately away. Undoubtedly, his tutors had studied the same etiquette book as my governess. I looked away as well, not to be outdone in this business of proper manners.

We stood, both pretending to be completely absorbed by the scenery. There was I, seventeen, fresh from Schenectady; there was he, handsome and seemingly indifferent, though I was wearing a particularly pretty dress that evening, with enough bows on it, as Raymond had commented, to make a pink streamer to the moon and back.

I didn't know yet that Gilbert was in Vevey for two purposes: to visit an aunt, upon whom he was somewhat financially dependent, and to begin the process of recovering from an affair, for his mistress, an older widow, had sent him packing the week before. A young girl was not told of such matters; I had to discover them later, in Rome, through careful eavesdropping at several salon doors.

Gilbert would never explain to me what had gone wrong between them, but wrong it had gone, which pleased me greatly. By the end of that evening in the garden in Vevey, I had already decided I would marry him.

His aunt refused to allow me to be presented to her, of course. She hadn't heard of my family—very few had—and she decided instantly I was common because I had allowed a strange man to talk with me in the hotel garden. Her disapproval helped my cause, I believe. Every man, even one raised by aunts in Switzerland, has a bit of the rebel in him.

"Did you just sigh, Mrs. Winter?" Mr. Hardy asked, concern planting a furrow between his brows.

"I was just remembering something," I said. Another flash of lightning split the sky, and a gust of hot air blew on our faces. Mr. Hardy wore a white linen suit and he had opened the collar and loosened his tie, as my grandfather used to do after Sunday dinners in the hot summer. When I looked at him, my inner eye saw a yellow barn against a blue sky, a row of red hollyhocks.

"A happy memory, I hope," he said.

"Very."

"What disturbed you this morning, in the catacomb?" Minnie and Beatrix were in their Roman hotel suite again, reading the morning's mail and drying their shoes before the small coal brazier that the concierge had brought up to drive the chill damp out of their rooms.

"I didn't like the atmosphere," Beatrix said. "The air was heavy with mold and rot. It felt like being buried alive."

"Like a vestal virgin. That's how they were punished if they broke their vow of chastity."

"You do acquire the strangest facts, Mother."

"That's from Murray." Minnie waved a guidebook at her. "He seemed quite pleased at the idea. When women have outlasted their appointed function, what more can be expected from them except to die?"

From the acrimony in her voice, Beatrix could tell that Minnie was thinking of her husband. Or perhaps her husband's mistress, those rooms in Paris where the couple had cohabited for so many years. There had been another letter from his lawyer awaiting them when they returned to the hotel, another discussion of terms and conditions. "Ending a marriage seems to require more legal maneuvers than ending a war," Minnie had commented. "I guess they do have much in common, the two situations."

"It was more than the air in the crypts," Minnie said now, returning to their conversation about the morning expedition. "Something upset you."

"I began to imagine things. Movements in the shadows, someone, something, watching us."

"Rome is giving you fancies. You seem to be changing before my very eyes." Minnie sat in the chair opposite her daughter and watched as Annie poured them coffee from the service tray a bellhop had brought. Their rooms were still being straightened, and a couple of maids peeked in at them from the separate bedrooms.

Their own maid, the very protective Annie, watched them closely. She had decided that all hotel maids were little better than thieves and that nothing would go astray under her careful gaze.

"I hope this trip was a good idea," Minnie said.

"It was a necessary idea," Beatrix countered. "For both of us."

"Yes," Minnie agreed. "We will both go home changed— that is certain. Is that the point of travel? Unfortunately, the travel does not seem to agree with Edith and Teddy. They have decided to leave Rome." The maids finished and left.

Annie gave the bedding a proprietorial straightening, punching pillows and pulling coverlets tighter.

"Thank you," Minnie called to her. "You have been on your feet all day. Why not have a rest?"

"Thank you, ma'am." Annie bobbed a little curtsy.

"The trip does not seem to have improved relations between Aunt Edith and Uncle Teddy," Beatrix agreed.

"You see that, too. No. I would say it has worsened the situation. Teddy used to enjoy traveling, but this trip seems to be causing him distress. That may be the secret to achieving serenity in an intimate relationship," Minnie mused, more to herself than to her daughter. "Two people who simply want to be in the same place at the same time. After a few years of marriage your father and I never even wanted to be in the same room together."

Beatrix leaned over and took her mother's hand, giving it a gentle shake, the way mothers do to distract unhappy children away from the barking dog or grumbling nanny.

"Oh, Beatrix, I shouldn't speak like this in front of you. You will lose heart before you've even tried to live. It wasn't all Freddie's fault, you know, the separation. He needed a wife who would be more devoted, who would spend all her time with him, not in charity wards and committee meetings."

"But shouldn't a woman's world be larger than what he expected?" Beatrix asked.

When Minnie took her afternoon nap, Beatrix sat in their shared sitting room, thinking. Between her mother and her aunt, marriage did, indeed, seem a dismal prospect. But without it, how could a woman experience life fully? Was it better to remain a virgin, safe and unsullied, or to test those vestal vows and eventually be buried alive in the debris of lost love? Passion, it seemed, could not survive the tests of the simple day-to-day routine that marriage required.

She should have been born a man. They did not have to choose between home and profession, tame marital bed and wild, secret passion. She stood and paced, back and forth.

The hotel room seemed too small to contain her restlessness. She would go for a walk and leave her mother to her rest and then her writing table and that letter from the lawyer in Paris that must be answered. Annie was snoring gently in the little dressing area where her bed was set up. Beatrix decided not to disturb her. She could go out alone.

She put on her wrap, the dark-colored one that covered most of her figure, and a plain hat that did not invite glances. She strode quickly down the stairs, through the lobby, and out the door, aware of eyes following her with curiosity and disapproval. A young woman going out alone? There would be talk that evening in the dining room.

Beatrix paused as soon as she had reached the street. Which way? She'd had enough of the places One Must Visit in Rome, enough of formal gardens.

She turned left instead of right, away from the Corso and the popular tourist sections. At the next corner, she walked in the direction of the more open sky, where the buildings were lower; at the next corner she chose the narrowest street and followed it. She walked uphill, turned again, and up another hill.

After half an hour, she was in a neighborhood of rutted streets where housewives had hung their linen out the windows and over balcony railings to air. Some of the houses had enclosures where donkeys brayed; this was the section of Rome where the carters and laborers lived. She could smell cooking cabbage playing in and out of the wonderful honey scent of mimosa. Children paused in their rough play to stare at her, but none swarmed at her as they had in the Borghese gardens.

"Look for beauty in rustic places," Olmsted had told her. This place, this neighborhood, was beautiful. It was full of life and small dreams, the everyday hopes not of those who moved through the rarified atmosphere of the wealthy and the foreign, but of those who knew this place, this soil, the plants and birds and the names of all the local children, the color of the sky in January, in June. The simplicity of it was the same as honesty, in the way that the waves at Bar Harbor were honest, and the barrels in the shops where people bought their pickles and flour were honest.

There, in that rough wooden doorway, a vine climbed up and over the lintel, cooling the ochre walls with white flowers. An urn of geranium and ivy shone red and green against a brick wall. A crawling weed sprawled over a dusty gravel path. It was the same plant she had plucked from the formal gravel walk of the Borghese gardens, but here it looked at home, even pretty. She would have to discover its name.

The homely beauty of this neighborhood took her breath. Why had she wasted her time in all those villas and plazas, with their mathematical precision and coy, artificial plantings?

If Aunt Edith and Teddy could walk down this street, they might enjoy each other's company here, she thought. They might smile together at that birdcage hanging in the window, the pretty pattern of the quilt draped over that railing. They might be friends again.

Beatrix turned in circles in the narrow street, trying to take it all in at once, delighted even by the children who had begun to watch her, to giggle. She closed her eyes and lifted her head, letting the heat of the sun warm her face. The gray morning drizzle, the dark catacombs, seemed a long time ago.

"Are you lost?" An old man stood before her, frowning.

"No. I simply wished to go for a walk. Away from the others. What is this street?"

"Via dei Serpenti." He nodded, frowning with concern.

Now, she thought, he will warn me about thieves and men who are too bold and threatening. He will tell me to go back to the safety of my hotel. But he did not.

"You were looking at that vine," he said, "over my door. Do you wish to see it closer? Come. I will bring you a glass of water. Sit here. Rest." He used his dingy handkerchief to wipe clean a stone bench placed where the hot sun could not reach, then disappeared through his dark doorway.

When he came back out carrying a stoneware pitcher and two glasses, she gratefully accepted one of them. "What is the name of this vine?" She reached up to touch one of the white flowers and rub its waxy petals. It was cool and smooth, like the sweet water he had brought her.

"If it has a name, I do not know it. My mother planted it. She stole a piece from the garden at the villa one day and put it here, by the door. She could make anything grow, even dead sticks."

He spoke slowly so that she could understand. "Would you

like some of the seed?" he offered. "Take it to your home and plant it. They say it lives forever. The vine at the Palazzo dei Serpenti, where my mother stole her cutting, has been growing for many, many years, much longer than this. Perhaps it saw the Caesars. Who knows?" He laughed, showing strong white teeth.

"Where is this palazzo?" Beatrix asked. She had never heard the name before; it was not a part of the usual itinerary of those visiting Rome. Perhaps this would be a chance to see a smaller garden, one for housewives to cool themselves in and children to play in.

"Just there." He pointed to the end of the street. "The housekeeper is Magda. Call for her, and she will show you the garden."

Beatrix thanked him and walked with some hesitation in the direction in which he had pointed. She had grown up in a world where everybody was familiar, whether she was in Maine, New York, or Newport. Strangers were still a bit of a difficulty for her, one she would have to overcome in her chosen profession.

At the end of the uneven cobbled street, she arrived at a large iron gate, rusted and with some bars missing. A jasmine vine sprawled over the top, its ambitious tendrils twisting and twining over the gate and one another and finally even reaching into the thin air, as if it could cling to that. There was a bell with a pull rope, but no one answered to it except a dog who barked from some unseen place. A gray striped cat appeared and stared up at her with large yellow eyes.

"Magda?" Beatrix called, softly at first and then with some insistence. At the third call, an old woman hobbled to the gate.

"*Sì! Sì!*" she called with impatience, only to pull up short when she found a lady standing there and not the vegetable cart she had been expecting.

"Signor . . ." Beatrix didn't know his name. "A friendly man down the street said I might see the garden."

"*Sì.* The garden." The old woman, all in black, with a wizened pale face, looked her up and down and found her acceptable. She opened the gate and the unseen dog stopped barking. The cat disappeared into the undergrowth of the wisteria.

The housekeeper, lurching from side to side in an arthritic stride, chattered quickly and in an accent Beatrix couldn't follow as she guided Beatrix through the high archway of the palazzo's facade and into the interior courtyard. This concept had delighted Beatrix when she first began to observe it: Americans placed their gardens in the front yard, where all passersby could admire them. Romans placed their private gardens in hidden courts where they could be admired only by those living in or admitted to the household.

Such a profusion of flowers in this garden! They were planted everywhere—in urns placed in the four corners marking the cardinal directions; in pots of every size; between flagstones and under benches. Roses climbed thirty feet up the facade of the house, and untrimmed yews exploded between light and shadows. The colors were fabulous, hot yellows next to warm pinks, true reds next to purplish fuchsia. It was the kind of wild, overgrown garden one encountered in dreams, without logic or plan or control.

"*Bello!*" she said to the housekeeper.

"Bellissimo," the housekeeper corrected.

The palazzo was in bad repair, with slipped roof slates broken over weedy graveled paths, mortar crumbling from the walls, windows with cracked and even missing panes. It was, Beatrix realized, the kind of Roman home that a wealthy American would seize upon and redo, boring guests with stories of the palazzo's foundation back to the first century AD and then boasting about the modern wiring and plumbing being installed.

A fire-sale home. The term Mrs. Haskett had used for her own palazzo. How sad, Beatrix thought, that history could be purchased as easily as a painting.

There was the vine, opposite her, its pale green leaves as tender as a baby's fingertips, its white flowers shining starlike against the grimy stone walls of the palazzo. What was it? Beatrix approached slowly, reverentially.

Amerigo, who was in the library having the same argument with his father as he had had the week before, and the week before that, strode impatiently to the window. How could he make the old man see his point? The world was changing. They must change with it. They must look reality in the face and not creep back into ancient tradition, hiding under it like children hiding from a ghost.

"Just one painting. The Sassetta. That's all we need to sell," he said again to his father. It was Amerigo's favorite, and that was why he had chosen that one as a possible salvation for them: to show that if he could bear the pain, so must his father. The small, jewel-lovely painting was a study for the San Sepolcro altarpiece showing the life of St. Francis. It had hung on the wall of the Palazzo dei Serpenti since Sassetta had painted it four hundred years before.

Mrs. Haskett had offered fifteen hundred dollars for it. Enough to pay the taxes, fix the roof, and make some wise investments. She knew it was old and valuable. It would be another trophy for her salon.

Amerigo had danced to Mrs. Haskett's hired musicians, eaten at her extravagant buffet, provided "atmosphere," as she called it, by attending her soirees. He detested the woman. Seeing the changes she had made to the ancient palazzo was like rubbing salt into the wounds. He had played in that home as a child, with the sons and daughters of the family.

"No," his father said, pounding his desk. "We will sell no paintings. And you will obey me."

Amerigo, tired of the endless argument, sat on the wide ledge and looked out. He felt trapped by the crowded house, by the rooms full of books unread for two hundred years, by cabinets of Chinese figurines collected three generations ago, by his own destiny.

Magda was in the courtyard, hobbling amid her pots of geraniums. Amerigo watched as she emptied a pot of water over this plant, pulled dead weeds off that one. He did not realize at first that she was not alone; then he saw that second figure. Who was there with her?

Impossible. The American girl from the Borghese gardens, bending forward to sniff a stem of thyme growing in a terra-cotta urn. Miss Beatrix Jones, who had a fan painted with fantasy flowers. How had she found her way there?

He watched, enjoying the luxury of seeing her when she did not know she was being observed. He noted the openness of the smile she gave old Magda, the way her eyes closed when she bent to inhale the aroma of a flower. Her movements were extraordinarily graceful, smooth and unself-conscious in the way of children at play.

That ease of movement affected him as her voice had when he had first heard it, but that emotion moved from simple admiration to something else. He wondered what she would feel like, this tall, slender American, in his arms. The thought startled him.

"Are you listening, Amerigo?"

"Yes, Father. Of course." But he was not.

He should go into the garden and greet her, offer his hospitality. But to do so would require going onto the mezzanine that housed the family art collection, because the other stairwell was no longer safe. He would, as he always did, pause before the little Sassetta painting, so perfect in its subdued pastels, the delicate filigree halo around the saint's face as he takes the paw of the wolf of Gubbio. That was the legend: the wolf had been terrorizing the people of Tuscany, and St. Francis had asked the wolf to stop murdering and let the townspeople feed him instead. Tamed by the meek holiness of St. Francis, the wolf offers his paw, as tame as any household hound.

That day, Amerigo would pause before that painting and reflect that his father loved the painting more than he loved his son; would in fact sell the son before he would sell the painting.

Perhaps, Amerigo thought, trying to awaken slumbering hope, perhaps I can convince Mrs. Haskett to increase her offer. Mrs. Haskett and her awful soirees, her conquering American wealth.

The wolf, in Renaissance art, was a symbol of avarice, and there was something in Sassetta's wolf's lean, alert face that reminded him of the American art collector.

Thinking of Mrs. Haskett, the way she sometimes addressed him as if he were one of her staff, he made up his mind. He would not go into the garden, to the American girl who had wandered into it. He was weary of Americans.

SEVEN

When Beatrix returned to the hotel, Edith and Teddy had already departed for the train station, preceded by maids and a courier, who traveled in advance to make sure the next hotel suite was prepared according to instruction. Edith had not been happy, Minnie said. She disliked train travel, the stern and inflexible schedules that must be met, the waiting in crowded public rooms.

"Edith left you this. She thought you might enjoy it. You haven't read it yet, have you?" Minnie handed her the spine-broken copy of *The Turn of the Screw*. "It is a ghost story. I don't know how Edith could tolerate having it in her hotel room with her. You know how she is about ghost stories. Perhaps because it is one of Henry's . . ."

"How did they seem?" Beatrix took off her hat and placed it on the table.

"Like a cat and dog forced to share the same cushion," Minnie admitted.

"Poor Edith. Poor Teddy as well, I suppose."

"Before she left, she sent someone to a stationery store to fetch her a dozen journals and four more pens. I think Edith sees a way out of the situation. Work. Work. The writing is becoming more and more important to her. It was a great mistake, stopping when she married. But you. You look radiant, my darling daughter. What have you been up to?"

"I went for a walk and visited a garden. A private garden. All overgrown and wild and the prettiest thing I have seen in Rome, I think."

"Where was this garden? And were you quite safe, alone?"

"Quite safe. Down a little street and off an even smaller street, up into the Monti section. The hills. Via dei Serpenti, it was called. Somewhere near the basilica of Maria Maggiore."

"You overexerted yourself. You're flushed. You should have a rest before dinner."

"I'm not at all tired. In fact, I feel quite exhilarated. This, I think, is what Mr. Sargent wanted me to see when he told me I must travel before I begin my work. The small private gardens, little cracked orange pots against a gray stone wall, red geraniums next to purple stocks. The very still lifes and backgrounds Caravaggio would not paint because they were too pretty, too sweetly domestic. I must try to sketch it, quickly, before I forget."

Beatrix sank into a chair, suddenly feeling a little dizzy. "Maybe I will rest. After I finish my journal for the day." She fell asleep sitting up in the chair and dreamed of dank catacombs leading to an underground moon-shaped garden of all white flowers, *Nicotiana alata, Gypsophila, Deutzia gracilis*: flowers that sang to her, shrubs that danced and held her hand, a fountain from which flowed Latin names instead of water.

M innie and Beatrix spent the next week visiting the Casa Respiglia, Palazzo Colonna, the forum, and the Villa Medici, Beatrix eagerly taking measurements, listing the plantings, making notes of what worked, what might be repeated in a smaller garden, what most definitely to avoid. When she had begun her preparations for the trip, her study of the gardens to be visited, she had imagined the yew hedges would be a foot or so high, more a border of suggestion than anything else. Instead, many of them were sometimes five feet high, turning garden walks into a labyrinthine experience where one often lost sight of the beginning or end of the garden.

The experience thrilled her but also disquieted her. A garden must have a suggestion of mystery, true. But wasn't it possible to have mystery without enclosure? Wouldn't that be preferable? Again, the inner vision of the shore at Bar Harbor, the huge sense of horizon. Gardens were man-made and artificial, yet they must respect what was natural as well.

"I think the gardens at Casa Respiglia were the finest," Minnie admitted when they were back at their hotel late one afternoon, swollen, shoeless feet tucked up underneath them and cool damp cloths pressed to overheated foreheads.

"I think because we were still fresh and energetic when we looked at it," Beatrix said. "Did we receive any mail today?"

"More invitations. Nothing from Paris." The relief in Minnie's voice was apparent. No news from Paris meant no more papers, no more regrets, no more worries about the divorce . . . at least for the day.

"Can't we just stay in this evening? I'm exhausted. And tomorrow we need to visit the Vatican gardens. Perhaps we should rest," Beatrix said.

"My girl, you will have plenty of time for rest when you are old, like me. We received another invitation from Mrs. Haskett, and I think you should accept. Show yourself in society." Become accustomed to the whispering that will occur, once I am a divorced woman, Minnie meant. People will talk and whisper and we must learn to face it.

"If I wanted to show myself in society, I could have gone to Newport for the season. Or stayed in New York," Beatrix said. "Perhaps we should stay in tonight. I have reading I need to do, letters to answer."

"Mr. Sargent and Mr. Olmsted would not have been pleased if you had passed up this tour of gardens. You know they both believed you need to see them with your own eyes rather than just read descriptions. But if you really wish to stay in tonight, I will go to the concert and tell Mrs. Haskett you have a headache from the heat."

"I'll make it up to you. I promise."

Three hours later, after the sun had set and lamps cast flickering shadows in the dark sitting room, Minnie had gone and Beatrix sat by herself, thinking. She should have been writing in her notebooks, recording the visits of the day or writing one of the long, detailed letters Mr. Sargent expected of her garden visits. But the exertion of the day had enervated her. Gardens should refresh, not tire. She was tired, and there was another week of Rome, then the gardens of Berlin, England, even some of France, to be visited.

A warm wind was blowing, bringing a sense of restlessness that, coupled with her physical fatigue, made Beatrix feel off-balance. She was not used to feeling uncertain, not about herself or her life or her expectations. She was used to prompt and efficient decisions and a forward movement void of regret. This evening was a night of uncertainty, though.

A professional female landscape designer. Even Mr. Sargent had had his doubts. He knew she could do it, and do it successfully. But was the world ready for such a thing? She sipped the tea that had cooled in its thin porcelain cup. She unpinned her heavy hair so she could massage her aching temples. This was before women began cropping their hair, and Beatrix's, shook free of its bindings, fell in a dark golden-red curtain almost to her knees.

Released from the agony of pins and rolls and the heavy chignon on the back of her neck, she rose from her chair and stretched, yawning like a child. She wondered if the music at Mrs. Haskett's that evening was any good and realized she didn't care if it was; the cost of listening—the silly chatter and stiff manners—was too high.

She stood and adopted the familiar pose: chin high, arms at sides, elbows slightly bent to allow the lungs full expansion. She tried a few notes of the song she had heard on the Spanish Steps, a *stornello* full of yearning, the notes rising and falling like breath, like the beat of surf on a shore, a tune in a minor key, as old as night, full of shadow.

Standing in the hall outside the door, Amerigo paused, hand already lifted to knock. Was this the American girl singing? What else could it be, unless she had hired someone for her own solitary enjoyment? No. It was she. He could tell the voice, the American accent stumbling slightly around the Italian vowels of the folk song.

What a voice she had! He stood listening, barely breathing, till she reached the last line of the verse and stumbled over the wording, guessing what it might be, trying to fill in missing words with tra-las and da-dums. Then, silence. He lifted his cane to knock on the door with it.

When a knock sounded at the door of their suite, Beatrix assumed it was Annie, who had been sent out to purchase talcum. She swung the door open.

"Oh," she said. Her hand was on the doorknob still; she pulled it away as if the metal burned her.

This is what Amerigo saw when the door opened: the American girl, barefoot, her red-gold hair loose over her back and shoulders. Her thick brows over those pale gray eyes drew together in surprise. Fool, he thought. You should have sent a card up first, had yourself announced. But he had been afraid she wouldn't receive him, or worse, wouldn't remember the name on the card. And he had very much wanted to see her again.

"Forgive the intrusion. I . . . You forgot to take these. Magda sends them." He opened his hand and revealed a tissue paper full of seeds.

"Would you give me a moment?" She shut the door again, leaving him confused in the hallway, and when the door reopened she was properly shod and her hair was bundled up again.

"You are alone? They should have told me downstairs. I would not have come up." The sly clerk at the desk. No wonder he had smiled at him in that overly familiar manner. He would have words with him later.

"My mother has gone to Mrs. Haskett's for the evening. Come in."

She took his hand and pulled him gently into the sitting room. "I am old enough to receive visitors," she reassured him. "It is one of the privileges of being an old maid."

"Surely not," he protested before he realized she was laughing at him, at herself.

"How did you find me?" She removed the evening paper from the most comfortable chair in the small room and indicated he was to sit in it.

Amerigo paused. In fact, Hotel d'Italie was the third hotel in which he had inquired for the two American women, Mrs. and Miss Jones, the mother short and dark, the daughter tall with red hair. Titian-colored hair, he had explained to the men at the various reception desks.

His conscience had bothered him. He had been rude, even if she hadn't known of it. A gentleman did not behave in that manner, spying out of windows rather than properly receiving a guest . . . even an uninvited guest.

Beatrix unwrapped the tissue he had given her and saw the

seeds inside. Magda, he had said. The little woman who had opened the gate for her?

"It was your house?" she asked. She fingered the seeds, testing the pointed ends, looking closely at the tiny stripes on the brown pods. A sense of unreality crept over her as she realized that her unplanned afternoon expedition had led to his home. Plants turn, as they grow, in the direction of the sun. Did he exert some strange influence that drew her to him? Such a thing wasn't possible. Yet, "How strange," she murmured.

"Then you were not looking for me?"

"No. I had wandered off the tourist path and was told I should look at the garden at the Palazzo dei Serpenti. I did not know it was yours. A kind old man down the street directed me there."

"The man must have been Giorgio. He was our stableman for many years." When they still kept horses and carriages instead of hiring them, he did not say. "Very strange," he agreed. "It seems destiny wishes us to be acquainted."

They sat in silence for a long moment, both shy and tongue-tied, wondering what should come next. He was sorry she had put her hair up, though of course it was the correct thing to do.

She worried that he was right—perhaps she should not have received him while her mother was out. He sensed her discomfort and stood again, refusing the ease of the little chair.

A pink slipper, slightly frayed at the toes, stuck out from under a settee. He thought he had never seen anything so intimate, so suggestive, as that abandoned slipper. There were shawls thrown on chair backs, a vase of too brightly colored and half-wilted dahlias, guidebooks spread open over tables and armrests, a smell of pomade and perfume. The complete femaleness of the room overwhelmed him.

"What is the name of the vine?" she asked, trying to kick the slipper back under the sofa. This, she thought, is worse than receiving a man in your boudoir. A hotel room! And not even her maid was there.

"We call it the paradise vine. Because of the fragrance, and because the flowers are the color of dawn. I don't know it by any other name. Magda assures me the seed will grow for you." He paused, smiling an apology for what he was about to say. "She says she saw it in your face, that you make things grow. It will take some years for the vine to climb a wall or arbor." He had been watching her foot trying to maneuver the slipper out of sight. Sensing he was being indiscreet, he looked back up just as she did, also. Their eyes met. They both blushed. They looked away.

"Would you like to go for a walk?" he suggested. That was also risky, on the border of appropriate good manners, but he knew he could not stay alone with her in that room.

"Yes," she said, knowing instantly where she wished to go. "Let's go to the Colosseum. I've never seen it by moonlight, and it is an experience highly recommended to me by a friend. Or is it not safe?"

"If we go for just a little while, it will be safe enough. The fever is not as common as it once was. We will stay for just a few moments."

She put on her hat and coat and they descended the grand staircase of the hotel together. There were murmurs from several white-haired ladies sitting in the lobby drinking their chamomile tisanes. Beatrix smiled at them as they passed. Her mother would get an earful when she returned from Mrs. Haskett's. And then mother and daughter would laugh together.

He hummed as he walked. Was he nervous? Or simply enjoying the mild evening?

"I have heard that tune before," she said.

"It is a *stornello*. A street song. A later verse of . . ." He almost said "the song you were singing earlier," but did not want her to know he had stood outside her door, listening. "Many of the *stornelli* are as old as Rome itself, part Italian, part Greek, part Arabic. Who knows where they came from? That particular song is about a young girl going to a fountain, hoping to meet her lover."

"Can you sing the words?"

Even in the dark she could see the renewed blush that stormed over his face. "No," he lied.

Their steps echoed together, her long-legged stride matching his. He tried not to notice how the muslin flounces of her skirt swung back and forth.

"I think we should take a cab," he said. "It is already late for such a long walk." He stepped into the street, waited till one of the small, open Roman carriages approached, and stopped it. "The Colosseum," he told the driver, a stout man dressed in a dusty frock coat and top hat. "And you will wait for us, once we are there. We will not be long."

The driver replied softly, in words Beatrix did not understand, but she could tell from Amerigo's face that she had been insulted. Amerigo answered him, rapidly and with anger.

"He disapproves. He thinks this is an elopement of sorts, doesn't he?" she asked Amerigo.

As soon as she said it, Amerigo knew that was exactly what he wanted. An elopement. With her. Away from Rome, from his father, from the Via dei Serpenti and the old palazzo for which he was to be the sacrifice. She was no longer a new acquaintance, a foreigner. She was the woman who walked by his side, her skirts swaying.

"It does not matter what the driver thinks," he said, letting the joy of being out in the spring evening with this lovely girl fill his senses the way a good wine does.

The moon was a thick silver crescent in a star-filled sky. When they arrived, half the Colosseum was illuminated by the celestial light; the other half was in darkness. They were the only visitors, they and the stealthy cats and the ghosts of centuries.

"It is beautiful. And terrifying," Beatrix said, standing close to him, their moon-cast shadows merging together into one shape behind them. The many arches of the Colosseum were full of blackness and secrets, dark holes that seemed like doorways to a different world. They walked through the nearest one, their feet crunching gravel, rending the silent darkness.

"You can imagine the lions roaring, before they begin their feasting," Amerigo said. "Or the gladiators, saluting Caesar."

"We who are about to die. Oh, what an awful way to die, so violent and so public, the crowd shouting at you, indifferent to anything but blood." A chill crept down her spine and she shivered. They walked to the huge cross in the middle and sat on its stone steps, the moon casting a second cross before them.

"Why is it the Americans always want to come here?" Amerigo leaned back on an elbow and stretched out his legs, crossing them at the ankles. If this were a picnic, he would put a blade of grass between his lips, Beatrix thought. He would reach up and shield his eyes from the sun. She wondered if he preferred chicken or ham sandwiches.

"I suppose because the guidebooks recommend it. My friend Daisy did as well." Beatrix moved, putting space between herself and Amerigo.

He understood the gesture. He had been feeling it, too, that intense intimacy that had nothing to do with the conversation, as if words and feelings lived different lives.

"I will take you back to your hotel now," he told her. "Come. You have seen the Colosseum by moonlight. If we stay longer, there may be unpleasantness for you."

"You mean Mrs. Haskett will hear about it and spread gossip."

"Exactly."

"I don't care for the Mrs. Hasketts of the world."

"You should. They can harm you in ways you can't imagine."

He was right, of course. If she was to be a professional landscape designer, she must preserve her character. No one would hire a woman of questionable reputation, especially if that woman was the daughter of a divorced mother. A bad or even questionable reputation spread as easily as contagion.

The driver was smoking a pipe when they returned to the carriage. He emptied it on the ground and stamped out the sparks as Amerigo handed Beatrix up onto the creaking leather seat.

"We leave Rome in two days," she told Amerigo when they were again in front of the Hotel d'Italie.

He wondered what she meant by that. It was more than mere information. A request? A challenge? A dismissal?

She was frowning. A line etched itself between her brows and he felt an urge to reach up and smooth that line. "That is unfortunate," he said softly. He didn't have the right, or the courage, to say anything more, or to smooth that line between her brows.

They stood, neither knowing what to say or do next. He cleared his throat. She brushed imagined lint off her sleeve.

"Maybe," he began.

"Or," she suggested.

He thought, She's just a girl. An American girl. He took her hand, gently, and kissed it, not on the knuckles or fingertips, but on the palm, turning her hand over and breathing gently on it before the kiss.

It was the most intimate, most sensual touch Beatrix had ever experienced, and it electrified her. She stood, mouth open in shock, as he breathed gently into her palm and his lips grazed it.

"I hope we meet again," Amerigo said when he released her hand.

"Yes," said Beatrix. "Me, too."

"You could not delay your travels for a day or two more?"

Tickets had been purchased, rooms reserved, invitations accepted. Beatrix and Minnie had made a stringent schedule. "No," she said, hiding her own regret.

Two days later, Beatrix and Minnie left Rome.

Amerigo was in his father's study, arguing with him once again, when their train, with a great lurch and hiss of steam, pulled out of the station. He knew the train schedule, knew when Beatrix was leaving to go north. It was just about the time that his father shouted, "You will do as I say!"

He had thought of going to the station to see Beatrix off with flowers and a basket of fruit. But that would have been too like a suitor's behavior, and he was not her suitor, not her lover. He thought of her low, soft voice and the long whiteness of her hand and wondered if he would have become her lover if they had had more time together. No, he thought. Impossible.

The next day he went back to look at the Caravaggio, David holding the severed head of Goliath, and it seemed he understood better than before the surrendering despair in the giant's face. "Old fool," he said to the painting.

EIGHT

I met Beatrix only a couple of years before these events in Rome, yet our friendship had developed quickly and deeply. We had, she said, a natural affinity, my lightheartedness complementing her more serious outlook.

Mr. Winters and I had purchased a brownstone in New York and a summer home in Newport after we married. He had decided we should settle in America. New York deemed us an appropriate match: my family, thanks to my father's talent for speculating in mines and railroads, had wealth, and his family had lineage. It was how things were done, and if Mrs. Astor's Four Hundred sometimes gossiped about me, at least they accepted me.

They all knew, of course, that Gilbert's aunt had refused to meet me and then refused to attend the wedding, but that only aided my cause. She was much too enamored of Swiss mountains and had cold-shouldered too many people to be herself thought of warmly.

With the brownstone and the summer home came children, and busy years followed so quickly I could barely catch my breath. They were happy years for the most part, except for the occasional quarrels with Gilbert, who insisted I knew nothing about finances and didn't need to worry myself about them; and for those heart-stopping frantic days when the children came down with mumps or chicken pox or some other childhood illness. My children were strong, except for Robbie, with his weak lungs.

In 1893, for our wedding anniversary, Mr. Winters decided I should have my portrait painted, and he asked the great John Singer Sargent to paint it. Mr. Sargent cabled back from Paris a firm no. He was too busy. Mr. Winters did not take no easily and persisted, enduring several curt telegrams from the artist. One day, though, I had been thumbing through a magazine and read that Mr. Henry James was a friend of the artist. Thanks to the "Talk of the Town" column, I knew that a neighbor around the corner on East Eleventh Street was a friend of Mr. James. I sent Mary Cadwalader Jones a basket of fruit and a note, asking her to intercede on our behalf with Mr. Sargent, through Mr. James.

Minnie invited me for tea and a conversation. Her daughter was not at home, so it was just the two of us, chatting in her book-lined, velvet-curtained parlor. Minnie was delighted by my story of meeting Mr. Winters in a garden in Switzerland and I was enchanted by her warmth, her kindly intelligence. She wrote to Mr. James, and to her friend Mary Robeson Sargent, cousin by marriage to the artist, who both wrote to Mr. Sargent. It was arranged that my portrait would be painted when next he was in New York.

This was how matters were arranged, then. One had to know the right people. Letters were sent, cards exchanged. Eventually the wife of the artist's cousin, Mrs. Charles Sprague Sargent, who had heard amusing things about me, invited me to visit when I was in Boston. There was a lung specialist there who promised he could help my son Robbie, so I accepted her invitation.

When I visited the Sargents in Holm Lea, in October of that year, they had another guest with them, Minnie's daughter, Beatrix, who had begun studying botany with Charles Sprague Sargent. She was one of the first students to work with him at the arboretum. That the demanding Mr. Sargent had accepted a female student says much of Beatrix's intelligence and determination.

I suspect Mr. Sargent thought it was his idea to invite the young Miss Jones to study with him. Most likely, Beatrix planted the seed of that idea, and it fell on fertile soil.

She was just twenty-one then, a tall, pretty, solemn girl from one of New York's oldest families. She seemed older than other young girls of that age, as if she had already passed through a stage in which they lingered. She had been working in the Holm Lea greenhouse that autumn afternoon, sorting and sketching seeds and seedpods, and had napped earlier in the afternoon in her room. There was no formal academic program then; when Beatrix studied at the arboretum, she was a guest at the Sargent home.

That day, when she came to join us on the terrace, there were burrs still stuck in her skirts. She wiped at them absentmindedly and shot a questioning glance in my direction.

"Mrs. Gilbert Winters," introduced Mrs. Sargent. "My cousin is to paint her portrait. She is, I believe, an acquaintance of your mother."

"How do you do," said Beatrix, extending her hand. "Yes, I remember her mentioning that she had written to Mr. James on your behalf."

"Beatrix is studying botany and garden design with my husband," said Mary Sargent to me.

I had never before met a lady who studied much of anything, once she was out of the nursery schoolroom, much less a science such as botany.

"You're studying what?" I asked, so startled that the teacup in my hand shook. She might as well have announced that Miss Jones planned to study banking or medicine, things unheard of in those days. Nor had Minnie thought to mention it when I had visited her. Probably she would have thought it too boastful, and ladies did not boast.

"Botany," Beatrix insisted, sensing my disapproval. She gave me a direct, unblinking gaze.

"Won't all that digging ruin your hands?"

"I wear gloves," Beatrix said.

"And a hat, I hope," I said. "Otherwise the sun will turn your hair orange." She had hair that in childhood gets one teased for being a carrot head, and I hoped she was sensitive about it, because by that time I had taken an initial dislike to Miss Beatrix

Jones. So industrious and more than a touch self-righteous. She sat upright in her wicker chair, alert in a way that seemed unnatural to me on a mild, sunny October day.

She seemed so certain of herself, so certain of her place in the world that she could afford to challenge it. I was envious of that confidence, of that straight back.

"I suppose you know the names of all the trees in the Arnold," I said. "By Latin as well as common name."

"All of them," Miss Jones agreed. "The ferns and mosses as well. And tell me, Mrs. Winters, does your hairdresser come on a daily basis? How many pairs of dancing slippers do you possess?"

"Oh, dozens. I don't count," I teased back.

By that time, Mrs. Sargent had leaned slightly back in her lawn chair and was merely observing us, as one does a tennis match, her large and slightly amused face turning left and right, left and right, as we lobbed challenges at each other.

This went on for several moments because I have a stubborn streak. Beatrix, having spent too much of her young life considering goals and ambition, was the same. Each of us wished the last word. Neither was to get it.

"I suggest a truce," said Mrs. Sargent, rising to hand the teapot to a maid, so that it might be refilled for the men, who would soon be returning to the domestic pleasures of a summer afternoon on the lawn.

The "men" of that afternoon were Mr. Olmsted, of Central Park fame, and Beatrix's mentor, Mr. Sargent, of Arnold Arboretum fame. Mr. Sargent had led Mr. Olmsted off an hour earlier to inspect an ill sapling, some sort of fir, I think I recall, to see if their two heads together could identify the source of complaint of the poor wee tree.

Beatrix, I learned later, was out of sorts because she had been left behind with the womenfolk when what she really wanted was to see the fungus plaguing the little fir. The adoration and sentiment that other women gave to curly-haired children, kittens, new hats, and flocked wallpaper Beatrix reserved for trees.

"Truce?" Mrs. Sargent repeated.

Beatrix looked hard at me. I pretended to study something over her left shoulder. But when she smiled, a large, open smile, I returned it. We had both completely misjudged each other, you see, and friendship could not ask for a better starting moment than one in which a misunderstanding must, for the next forty or so years of affectionate banter, be corrected.

I had only one pair of dancing shoes and they were badly in need of new soles, but I couldn't afford another bill at the cobbler's. I had six children and a husband who, I had discovered over the years, liked to gamble.

That was Beatrix's misunderstanding of me: that I was a spoiled society wife with nothing to do but be fitted for her next gown for her next ball. In fact, I was sorely besieged by the duties of motherhood.

Her misjudgment delighted me. I had grown quite afraid of mirrors by then, terrified that any day I would look into one and see a fat middle-aged mother, her face lined and haggard, all humor and girlish lightheartedness long since fled. Beatrix's perception of me reassured me. She saw me as I had been a decade before. What woman would not have been overjoyed by that?

As for Beatrix, I saw a handsome girl who seemed alone, even when surrounded by people; a thoughtful, even somber young woman who knew her path in life. This impression was fostered by her height and her long, straight nose over a very determined chin. Beatrix knew better than to try to compensate for her serious gaze with pink bows and excessive lace; her innate taste and good sense led her to dress in a subdued manner. The plain fabrics and simple lines of her costumes suited her well, though they made her seem older than she actually was.

"For a young woman who enjoys afternoon visits, you have been strangely absent from this household," Beatrix concluded our initial confrontation, and by that I understood that she was prepared to tolerate me, and that toleration, if successful, might blossom into friendship.

"I have been rather busy this year. All those balls," I said.

Just then Mr. Sargent and Mr. Olmsted appeared over the rise of the little hill near his row of white birch, their yellow straw hats glowing in the sun. They were arguing back and forth in a lively manner, not yet having arrived at a shared conclusion about the illness of the petite fir, I assumed. At the same time, a swarm of children appeared from the side garden, a devastated governess trying unsuccessfully to herd them into a semblance of order.

Gil, my firstborn, was seventeen that summer. Home from school, he had agreed to come with us only because he wished to meet Mr. Sargent. His father insisted he study finance, but Gil wished to be an artist. Robert, my second son, was fifteen, too tall for his age, slightly stooped because of his lung problems, and shy. Jenny, thirteen, with huge eyes and such an abundance of curly hair it was difficult to fit hats to her head, and Clara, eleven, were both in short skirts and pinafores. My babies, India, four, and Athena, two, wore little sailor dresses and caps.

"Whoa!" shouted Mrs. Sargent, whooping with laughter at India, who had strewn plucked grass all over her cheeks and hair.

Beatrix watched, slightly overwhelmed. Athena marched up to her, demanding a lollipop. My heart throbbed with love for them. There had been miscarriages as well, so that when India and Athena appeared years after the others, I knew those children would be the last.

"Mrs. Sargent?" Beatrix said, confused. "Do you have other visitors?"

"India, stop crying and make a curtsy to Miss Jones," I said. "Jenny, Robert, Gil, Athena, Clara, meet Miss Beatrix Jones."

"All of them are yours?" Beatrix asked, eyebrows raised. "Dancing slippers indeed." She templed her fingers before her face and peered at me over them. "I shall have to reconsider my initial impression," she said.

Beatrix and I smiled at each other.

That was our first meeting. Others quickly followed, in New York and in Bar Harbor as well, because Minnie and Beatrix invited me to their summer home the following year. In Bar Harbor I realized how serious, how determined, Beatrix was in her goal to become a female landscape gardener.

She had been creating and perfecting her gardens at Reef

Point for years already, though she was still so very young, and the gardens were not merely beautiful; they were emblematic, somehow, of what landscapes should be.

Reef Point, after all, had been purchased by her parents at the beginning of the separation that would eventually lead to the scandal of divorce. I think Beatrix, as well as Minnie, had understood that this was to be a home without a husband, without a father. An incomplete home. And so Beatrix had set about to complete it in the best way she could, to help in the best way she could to bring contentment and peace to the place.

She hadn't forced turf lawns over the peaty soil or created imitations of what other gardeners had done. As much as possible, Beatrix had cultivated plants suited to the conditions of the island: iris and lilies, ferns, roses, asters, wild plum.

When I visited her at Reef Point, it was a paradise of bloom and scent. That, at least, was what the visitor admired. Beatrix had a more critical eye, and even when walking among the roses, she would bend and sift her fingers through the soil, checking for texture, sniff it to see if it was too acidic, then take a handful back to her workroom for testing.

"It isn't enough to be beautiful," she said to me, picking a beetle off a rose and squashing it with her bare hands. "A garden must meet the needs of the soul as well as the senses. You feel at home and somehow enlarged, more yourself, in a good garden. Most of all, the garden must suit the land, not vice versa. The garden should be as much at home in the landscape as the house and the people of the house."

It was a philosophy of life as well as of gardening: pleasure combined with work, beauty with practicality. The garden would both calm and awaken senses and memory. "Daisy," she said, "I know I am meant for other things. Work, for one. I want a created life, not a preordained one. Dancing in ballrooms with New York's eligible bachelors only gets one so far."

In fact, she was so busy with her garden that she all but gave up dancing.

The next year we both went to the Chicago World's Fair. For me, the fair's White City meant gondolas on Venetian waterways, Bedouin tribesmen and their camels wandering the Midway Plaisance, the strange turrets and towers of the Swedish Building, drinking Darjeeling tea at the Japanese Tea House.

After Gilbert and I married, we made several transatlantic voyages to Europe and back. But Gilbert and I never pushed beyond Paris or Rome. "Why would you want to?" Gilbert asked. He had no desire to venture into lands where the hotel concierges did not speak English and where roast beef could not be had for dinner.

I, on the other hand, had wanted to boat on the Orinoco, to taste the honey pastries of Istanbul and visit frozen Lapland. Switzerland, for me, was meant to be the beginning of my journeys, not the end. But I had met Gilbert there, and in Rome he had kissed me in the moonlight in the Colosseum, and that ended my wanderings.

So the Chicago fair was my substitute, that vast expanse of huge domes and gardens seen from the dizzying top of the Ferris wheel—all the lovely foreignness of the world brought to the scrubby shores of Lake Michigan.

For Beatrix, the world's fair meant plants, some familiar and many exotic. There were the strange spindly cactuses dotting the Wild West Show on the Midway, the Spanish cork trees of the Agricultural Building, the rows of tulips outside the Dutch windmill, the date palms of the Sahara. The Horticultural Building contained acres of plants and flowers: Japanese gardens, a tropical garden, an entire field—indoors, under glass!—of snapdragons, and another field of begonias, along with Australian ferns as tall as two-story buildings. There were, a placard announced, sixteen thousand varieties of orchids on display.

Mostly, though, Beatrix loved the Wooded Island, sixteen acres of pansies and roses, all strung with fairy lights so that people could sit there in the evening and be dazzled by the loveliness of the place. It was there, one evening, that Beatrix made what was the largest decision of her young life. She had studied music and still considered the possibility of a career as a concert singer, but her year of work and study with Mr. Sargent was leading her onto a different path. It wasn't a straight line that brought her to her decision; she abhorred ruler-straight lines in gardens and in thinking. Life and landscapes required flexibility and a touch of serendipity. A little rain shower made up her mind.

Beatrix always dressed according to her internal weather. And she always dressed beautifully, like her mother and her aunt Edith. Beautiful costuming on a woman's part is a show of bravery and optimism.

On the second-to-last day of her visit, Beatrix dressed according to her internal weather, which was full of summer and the kind of sensuality that encourages you, as the younger set says, to show off a little. She wore a light summer dress with half sleeves and no collar. I think that glimpse of the belly-bared dancer who'd performed at the fair, Little Egypt, and the strange Eastern music with its eerie pipes and wailing notes, had awoken something exotic in Beatrix's own nature. She was very young, and still making all those choices we take for granted, still shaping herself for an undefined future.

And she was a gardener. She had watched butterflies mating in midair, witnessed the spring courting of rabbits and the yearly litters of barn cats, seen how sprouts shoot out of desiccated husks once they are warmed and watered. There is no more sensual activity than gardening.

Half sleeves and no collar. That's what Beatrix wore that afternoon at the fair. And of course it rained, just for an hour and not heavily, but Beatrix was caught in it and was soaked. She had just left the Manufactures and Liberal Arts Building, where she had been admiring the Remington exhibit. Forty different typewriting machines, all equipped to typewrite in different languages. She was going to the Mines and Mining Building to see the South African diamonds when the rain began.

A gentleman offered her his umbrella, but it was too late to stop the damage. It was one of those rains that begins quickly and heavily, like a faucet being turned on, and ends just a minute later. The gentleman, seeing she was already soaked, folded his umbrella and let the rain soak him as well. He was a young university professor, a historian with a special fondness for Benjamin

Franklin. He told her this quickly and easily, as if it mattered even more than names, which they had not exchanged.

His cuffs were frayed and there was a small hole in his straw hat. Beatrix would remember that, years later. How young he was, how indifferent to his wardrobe, as were many professors.

"Why Franklin in particular?" Beatrix asked, allowing the young man to escort her to the little tram that would take her to her hotel, so she could change into dry clothing.

"I suppose for his wit. And because he loved France. He did not want to cut the New World completely off from the Old."

"And do you love France?" she asked.

"Who wouldn't?"

He accompanied her all the way to the door of her hotel, even though, as she guessed, the return tram fare would abbreviate his supper that evening.

"Bon voyage," he said, tipping the hat with the little hole in it. "I hope we meet again." They didn't, at least not until many years later.

Beatrix, starting to shiver from the drenching, changed into a dress suitable for walking in after dark. She had agreed to meet Mr. and Mrs. Sargent for supper at the Vienna Café, to be followed by a moonlight ride on the Ferris wheel and a tour of the Wooded Island.

Most visitors to the fair preferred to spend the evening on the Court of Honor, a spectacular turreted and domed white city lining a large lagoon, where spotlights constantly swept the sky, the crowds, the fountains, and the statues. But the crowd there, often in the thousands, was shoulder to shoulder. The Sargents preferred a quieter atmosphere.

The Wooded Island was one of the many nature areas Olmsted had included in his design for the fair. There were wooden benches, walkways, Japanese teahouses. Quiet places meant to restore the soul to a calm state after the excitement of the day. It was all illuminated by little lamps that gave the isle a fairy-tale quality.

"You look a bit like Little Red Riding Hood," said Mr. Sargent as they found a quiet bench to share in front of a bed of roses. Beatrix was wearing a white lawn dress with a crimson-hooded linen cloak over it, in case the evening should turn chilly.

"I hope there are no wolves around," she joked back.

"That has always been my favorite fairy tale," said Mrs. Sargent, sighing with fatigue. "The young girl just beginning her life, the kind grandmother, the wolf always lurking about, reminding us of the constant danger of the world."

"In the Grimm version, the wolf gobbles up the girl," said Mr. Sargent, taking off his hat and fanning himself with it.

"I read that version as well. My aunt Edith gave it to me in a collection of German stories." Beatrix unbuttoned her cloak and let it fall from her shoulders onto the bench.

They could hear the roar of the crowds in the distance and saw the spotlights from the court piercing the sky as they, on the Wooded Island, felt very distant from the bustle, in their own little world.

"It is so lovely here, in this very spot," Beatrix said. "As exciting as the fair is, I think I would prefer a quiet garden to it, any day."

"You can hear yourself think," agreed Mrs. Sargent. "My ears will never recover from this visit."

"Would you sing for us, Beatrix?" Mr. Sargent asked.

They had dined at the Vienna Café, where a concert next door had serenaded them with Schubert's *Lieder*. "Sing something that will suit the fragrance of those roses behind us, and the beams of the fairy lights," he suggested.

On an ordinary day, this request would not have distressed Beatrix. She had a classically trained voice, a lovely voice, and the possibility of a career as a concert singer was still available to her in that undefined labyrinth we call the future.

She was greatly moved by that Wooded Island, that large garden, and by Olmsted's vision of a place so perfect for calming the spirit and restoring peace to an overexcited mind. It was gardening at its finest, a realm both natural and artificial, arising from what already existed, the soil, the grasses and trees, the water from Lake Michigan trained into canals and shores, and enhanced by what man had brought to it, the hundreds of roses, willow trees; beds of campion and larkspur flashing color long into the summer twilight; the fragrances of mint and lavender and rose.

It was not by accident that God first put man into a garden. What place is better suited for showing us our own promise and goodness? Certainly not a deep forest, where pagan nature overcomes all, where sharp-toothed wolves and long-knifed robbers roam, and certainly not the seashore, where an almost infinite horizon reminds us of our absolute insignificance. A forest and seashore do not need people. They have always existed and always will. But a garden. A garden does not exist without us. Nor we, without it.

Beatrix thought for a long moment. Of course she would sing for Mr. and Mrs. Sargent, if they wished it. A song was small repayment for their friendship and hospitality, but a song they would have. She decided on another Schubert *Lieder*, one the Viennese singers hadn't performed that evening, "With the Green Lute Ribbon." It was a love song, but a happy one between a young man and maid, and its words had always thrilled Beatrix so much they gave her goose bumps when she sang them. After the boy gives the ribbon to the maid and tells her to tie it into her locks, he says, "Because hope's far reaches bloom green / We are both fond of green. / . . . Then I will know where hope dwells."

It was a beautiful song, a perfect song, in a perfect setting, with the perfect audience. But at the last note of the verse, Beatrix's voice gave way and could not reach the final note. The chill from the rain had gone into her throat. Beatrix froze on the bench, unable to move, to breathe, wishing only that that last quavering note upon which her voice had broken, now seemingly hanging in the air like something tangible—she wished that note would disappear, to never have happened.

That night, at the fair, on the Wooded Island, Beatrix's musical career ended. How could she base her ambition—and she was ambitious—on something as imperfect as a throat that grew chilled in a summer rain shower?

Mr. and Mrs. Sargent did the polite thing and applauded her

as if each note had been true and perfect, but they knew, and Beatrix knew, that the song had changed something. One door had slammed shut, but another was opened to her.

She had been happiest in gardens: her childhood gardens in Newport and Maine, the Sargent garden in Brookline, the arboretum where she had studied.

A gardener, then, she would be. Not an amateur, a professional. She would work for her living, and she would create pleasurable landscapes for her work.

Beatrix sat on the lovely Wooded Isle of the Chicago World's Fair and promised herself that one day she would make something even more splendid.

NINE

"I would like to hear more about Edith Wharton," said Mrs. Ballinger, who was president of her local public library board of directors and a great reader.

"I thought this was supposed to be a ghost story," said Mrs. Avery, tentatively touching the Ouija board still on the table in front of us.

The rain hadn't come, though lightning and thunder had moved steadily closer, disturbing the dark night.

"My wife kept a vegetable patch," said Mr. Hardy. "Grew wonderful tomatoes."

It was almost midnight, but I had no desire to go up to my room and try to sleep. That was one of the most difficult parts of the day for me, entering a bedroom where no other voice would answer mine, no breathing match my own. "You'll get used to it," Jenny often told me. "In time." Perhaps. But I still wasn't. No, I wasn't ready yet for bed.

Mrs. Ballinger shifted in her chair, the telltale motion of a woman about to rise and leave, and I thought if she left, so might Mrs. Avery and Mr. Hardy, and I did not want to be alone. That was one reason why Jenny had recommended I spend a week in Lenox, at an inn. There would be the familiar bustle of the breakfast room, the clatter and conversation of the evening dining room, parlors where I could sit and talk or just watch and listen, and of course the shared front porch.

"Edith and Beatrix were both greatly moved by a good ghost story," I said, and Mrs. Ballinger sat back down. "Minnie found them silly, but aunt and niece shared a predilection for tales of the supernatural, just as they shared a preference for yellow roses and climbing honeysuckle on the front porch rather than wisteria." That, and independence. How I envied them that, sometimes, when Gilbert was cross or sad and the children demanding. "I'll tell you a story Edith told me one night. Do you know the story of the specter bridegroom? It's one of those cautionary tales meant to steer young girls away from questionable choices in matters of the heart.

"It is a story that the German maid told the little girl, Edith, who told it to her niece Beatrix many years later, who then told it to her mother as they rested in yet another hotel in yet another European city, stocking feet warming before the hearth and cups of tea on the table beside them.

"Long ago, Baron Von Landshort lived in a decrepit castle at the top of a mountain in the Odenwald," I told my porch listeners. "The castle was rough and uncomfortable, an eagle's nest surrounded by dark firs that tapped at the windows at night. But

the baron's pride would not let him remove himself to more convenient quarters in town. He liked to look down on his neighbors
from his eagle's aerie.

"His daughter was a blooming rose, but she grew up in solitude, an only child, and with her mother and father living in
separate countries. Her mother had run away from the cold castle
in the Odenwald and the daughter learned early that love was not
to be squandered."

"Oh, no," agreed Mrs. Avery. "Love should not be squandered."

"She sang like an angel, this daughter of solitude. Even the
wild mountain wind stopped blowing when she sang, the better
to hear her. Mostly, though, she liked to work in her garden. She
could make plants bloom just by looking at them. If weeds dared
sprout, they saw the magnificence of their surroundings and
wilted in self-sacrifice.

"On the day her father announced he had found her a groom,
the girl was both cheered and frightened. It is natural for a young
girl to yearn for a husband."

"Absolutely. And she should be obedient to her father's
wishes," said Mrs. Ballinger.

"But she had never met the intended. What if he was cruel?
Or worse, aged and toothless?

"'He comes from a very important old family,' the baron
said. 'Almost as illustrious as our own. I have made the arrangements, and your groom is already on his way.'

"The daughter began embroidering her trousseau. Her morn-
ings were still taken over with care for her garden, but this mag-

ical piece of ground reflected her own state of mind. The garden began to fret, and the weeds, formerly so agreeable in their habit of wilting away, started to grow. Rabbits chewed the little hedges and the knot garden unraveled itself. The daughter knew that her marriage was doomed.

"Her bridegroom, meanwhile, lingered many leagues away in a city full of distraction, gambling dens, and opera dancers. He, too, had his doubts about this marriage, but his father insisted, and his father held the purse, so husband he would be if his father ordered, though he feared the chosen bride would be old or ugly."

"My father disapproved of my marriage," said Mr. Hardy. "That young man should have stood his ground."

"I don't see that gambling and taking up with opera dancers is standing your ground, morally speaking," argued Mrs. Ballinger. I ignored them.

"The time came when the groom must leave his amusements and claim his bride. With a distinct lack of mirth, he packed a travel bag and had his best horse saddled.

"He rode quickly and with few stops to rest and water the horse. He took a forbidden shortcut through a thick, black forest filled with thieves and outlaws. At night, in this forest, you could hear the wolves calling to one another.

" 'I promised my father I would be there, and I will be there, on time, dead or alive!' the bridegroom shouted to the wolves.

"The day for the young girl's nuptials dawned fair. One has to wonder why it never rains on such days in such stories, but it doesn't. She was dressed by her maid in her wedding gown of ivory satin; the last roses from her bedraggled garden were twined into her hair. Thus attired, she was leaning on her chamber casement and looking out when the groom arrived.

"He was filthy with the mud and dust of travel, his face white and haggard, his horse sharp ribbed and lathered.

" 'I was set upon by thieves,' the young man gasped when the baron came down to greet him.

" 'Think no more of it, and prepare yourself for the church,' said the baron, though he was discouraged by the young man's ragged appearance. The daughter, still leaning out her window, sighed. Even under the paleness of fatigue and the dirt of travel, his was a face to make the sun shine. All her worry for nothing!

"The wedding was held, even though the groom limped and his beautiful face was gray. There were deep shadows around his burning eyes.

"When the baron's daughter lifted her veil for the kiss, she felt love stir even more strongly in her. His lips on hers were as damp and cold as stone. He needs a rest, she thought. Still, she was suddenly looking forward to the wedding night. He could rest afterward.

"The musicians played merrily, but the groom did not dance. She loved the feel of his hand over hers, though his fingers were icy. She loved the gleam of his eye, though it was feverish. She loved that he was hers, all hers, forever.

"But when the time came to put the bride and groom to bed, the groom rose from the feasting table with a wild look on his face.

"'I cannot stay the night,' he said, his voice as forlorn as the sound of a tree falling after lightning has blasted it. 'I have an appointment elsewhere.'

"'Elsewhere?' thundered the baron. 'Where else should the groom be this evening but in bed with his bride? What cheating game is this you play?'

"'The only cheat is that I was here at all,' said the groom, his words turning all the colors in the room to gray.

"The bride felt a fist clench around her heart.

"'My appointment is in St. Anselm's Church, some twenty leagues away from here,' said her groom. 'I must return to my bier and prepare for my burial. I was murdered in the forest.'

"Oh, the sorrow in his eyes, in his face, for groom loved bride as well as bride loved groom, and he wished more than anything in life or death to stay by her side. But he could not. 'Come,' he said, offering her his hand. 'Say farewell.'

"The guests were frozen with horror and perhaps with a bit of magic as well, for no one moved or protested as the bride put her hand in the hand of her corpse groom and walked with him into the garden, to make their farewell.

"'I came for you,' he said, 'And now that I have seen your face, know that I will return for you.' He turned her hand over, placed a cold kiss on her hot palm, and disappeared into the green and black darkness of the forest."

"Oh, I've got shivers!" Mrs. Avery rubbed her arms.

All the chairs on the porch had stopped rocking,

and the crickets were even louder than before. The air had become heavy and still. A clap of lightning illuminated the night and Mrs. Avery gave a little shriek of fright.

"That story was told to me by Edith Wharton herself," I said. "One summer night at the Mount, when a storm was coming and we felt uneasy. Beatrix was most moved by it. 'A specter bridegroom,' she said. 'Ghastly.'

" 'To some extent, all bridegrooms are specters,' Edith told her. 'We never marry the man we believe ourselves to be marrying.' That was after Minnie's divorce, and a few years before her own."

"There is such a thing as a happy marriage," protested Mr. Hardy. His wife had died ten years before, and I had noticed that the more distant our spouses are, the more saintly they become.

"I did not say there was not," I said. "I was only telling a ghost story, upon request."

"We will need to go in soon. I felt a drop of rain," Mr. Hardy said, holding his hand out to test for more.

"I could talk all night," I said, and laughed.

"I noticed," said Mrs. Ballinger.

The piano player in the hotel's front parlor stopped tinkling halfway through "At the Devil's Ball," and a moment later we heard him shut up the piano. People had been singing along, and now they fell silent, but the tune finished itself in my head.

"Never approved of that song. It's blasphemous," declared Mrs. Ballinger, as if Mr. Irving Berlin needed her permission.

"It's merely whimsical, and funny, if you think about it. Good for a laugh," Mr. Hardy said. "The soldiers enjoyed it."

Rain started to fall then, though "fall" wasn't quite the word. It came down like a curtain, thick and noisy, a light, eerie blue against the blackness of night. We jumped from our chairs and cowered against the porch wall trying to stay dry.

"I think we must go in," Mr. Hardy shouted over the heavy pattering of the rain. He ushered us into the doorway as men do, as if herding sheep or ducks, his arms making a semicircle. I have always loved that particular gesture. Inside, we shook ourselves and raindrops spun from our heads.

Mrs. Avery yawned. "I'm going upstairs. It's been a long day. And tomorrow I'm going to the afternoon concert at the pavilion with my daughter and her children. She's coming in on the train."

"Of course," I said. "Sleep well, Mrs. Avery." We were silent until long after her heels had clicked down the hall. Mrs. Avery's daughter had, yesterday, telephoned at the last minute to say she couldn't make it; we feared she might repeat this inconsiderateness tomorrow. The telephone had much to answer for. When people had to take the time to write notes and send them out through a footman or the post, people were more obliging.

"Poor soul," sighed Mrs. Ballinger. "Children can be so ungrateful. If my Evie kept breaking her promises to me . . ." She left the sentence unfinished and went upstairs to her room.

"She'd tan her bottom," Mr. Hardy said, when we were alone in the hallway. "Will you take a drink with me, Daisy? Before you go up for the night?"

We went into the hotel's barroom, where the young people had set up a gramophone and were dancing. We sat at a little table as far away from the dancers as possible, though once in a while a particularly vigorous couple would jump in our direction, their arms and knees going off at all different angles.

"I could barely waltz. If I had to do that dance, I would have given up on socials after my first party." Mr. Hardy ducked his head the way shy children do.

"I waltzed divinely," I said. "When Mr. Winters and I took to the dance floor, people stopped to watch. I'll have a brandy," I said.

We sat in silence, watching the dancers, listening to how the rain sometimes overpowered the thumping recorded music, and I thought of the first time I had waltzed with Gilbert, on the little dance floor of the Hotel Eden, in Rome. It was two days after he had found me with Giovanelli at the Colosseum, two days after he stole the first kiss, or thought he had stolen it, though I had been planning that kiss all along. "I believe you are a flirt, Miss Cooper," he said, pulling my chair out for me and extending his hand. "Someone will have to watch over you and keep you out of trouble." We whirled to Strauss' Treasure Waltz, one-two-three, one-two-three, around and around. He waltzed well.

"Was Mrs. Nevill a flirt?" I asked. That was the name that had been associated with his.

Gilbert stopped dancing so suddenly I almost lost my balance. "You will never say that name again," he said. "We had an association, and now it is over. You need know no more." He took me back to the table where I had been sitting with my mother, and the three of us sat in awkward silence. He wouldn't dance with me again that evening. But he asked to see me the next day, and the day after.

Mrs. Nevill was never mentioned again. My mother carefully explained that single men often form attachments, and some married men as well, but brides and wives simply look the other way and hope the attachment ends soon. I was luckier than many women in that I had met Gilbert after Mrs. Nevill was no longer a part of his life. She had found richer game.

"Terrible weather," said Mr. Hardy, interrupting my thoughts.

"It is," I agreed.

"You were very far away, just now."

"I was in Rome. Again."

"I've never been to Rome," he said. "But I did go to the world's fair in Chicago. Saw Little Egypt dancing on the midway." He chuckled. "Have to admit, went back several times to see her. The missus wasn't too pleased with me, but that girl could really shimmy, and her costume, all spangled and sparkling, was a sight to remember."

He smiled and even blushed a little, and there was something in his face, a kind of innocence, a reminder of other times, that made me weak with nostalgia. I thought again of that yellow barn against a blue sky, the row of hollyhocks, and had a sudden and overwhelming urge to return to the farm outside of Schenectady, to see if that barn was still there, even though my grandparents had died years before. Perhaps new owners had painted it a different color, or even torn it down.

"Well," Mr. Hardy said, when I had finished my drink. "It's late."

"Sleep well, Mr. Hardy."

"Walter. Call me Walter, Daisy, if you don't mind."

"I don't mind at all, Walter. Good night."

I climbed the stairs slowly to my room, exhausted yet still unwilling to be alone. Solitude did not come easily to me.

In my room, I flicked on all the lights and out of habit checked to see if the maid had left any mail or messages. No. There was, of course, no letter from Mr. Winters. Again, that terrible pang of loss and regret. I should be used to this by now, I thought. But I wasn't. I tossed and turned for most of the night, and when I did sleep I dreamed of dark catacombs and a formal Italian garden where all the flowers were black.

The next morning dawned sunny and mild. The heavy rain had broken some of the roses in the garden, but those with the stronger stems looked freshened, pleased with themselves.

"They needed a good soak," said the gardener, looking up at the sound of my footsteps. He was clipping off the spent flowers and I remembered something else Beatrix had once told me about her childhood. Her first garden lesson had come from her grandmother in Newport, who had taught her how to deadhead the garden, remove the spent blooms so that new ones would come. The first thing Beatrix had learned was how endings lead to new beginnings, and that was a lovely thing for a child to understand.

"There will be a fresh set of buds, after that rain," said the gardener, turning back to his work.

It promised to be a pleasant day, so I decided to walk downtown and look into shop windows. I tried on a hat, a little white crocheted cloche, so much more practical and comfortable than the wide-brimmed, silk-flower-bedecked cartwheel hats of my girlhood, but decided against spending the money. I had lunch in a little café and then sat in the park, reading, or trying to read. By dinnertime I was ready to retreat to my little inn and to my porch companions.

We gathered again for the evening on the hotel porch, and Mrs. Ballinger was her usual complaining self. There had been fried haddock for supper, and she did not like fried fish.

Mrs. Avery was even more timid than usual, shrinking in her rocking chair as if she needed, wished for, someone to hug her. As we had anticipated, her daughter had called at the last minute and canceled their afternoon outing. Walter, who seemed to feel keenly the pain of others, had pushed his chair closer to Mrs. Avery's and patted her hand every so often.

I was growing fond of Walter. He was not a progressive thinker, that was true, but if you turned your back on all those who clung to older ways, you could grow very, very lonely. He was kind, and a good listener. I noticed that evening he wore a different jacket, a new and more stylish one, and kept his collar buttoned. Once in a while he caught my eye and smiled at me.

"I'd give her what for, if my daughter didn't keep a date with me," said Mrs. Ballinger, taking a lump of green knitting wool from her bag and beginning to wind it furiously.

"Feed her to the lions," I said, "like the Christians in the Colosseum. I have always felt sorry for those poor beasts, chained and maltreated, that were forced to eat humans, who, I've heard from a South American explorer who lived for a while with cannibals, taste like pork, when the lions would have preferred a little deer or hen."

Mrs. Avery gasped and began to rock so quickly her chair gave off mouselike squeaks at the pace of a quick polka. Mr. Hardy frowned and gave Mrs. Avery's hand another little pat of comfort.

Mrs. Ballinger did not miss that gesture. I think she had rather been hoping that Mr. Hardy might develop a certain tenderness for her.

"You go too far, Mrs. Winters," she spluttered. "I don't see why I sit here, taking this abuse."

"It is not abuse. It is only after dinner chatter," Mr. Hardy protested, turning Mrs. Ballinger more enthusiastically against me, but then men rarely understand the subtle malice of female competition. "Although we could do without further references to cannibalism," he said. "Mrs. Avery might have a delicate stomach."

"Don't know how the subject came up at all," Mrs. Ballinger said.

"The lions in the Colosseum and the ghost of Nero," I said. "Rome."

"I'm sure my daughter had her reasons," Mrs. Avery said with a sigh.

"Blazes," said Walter. "Look at that sky, will you?"

Yet another thundercloud moved in sullen, inky shadows over the horizon. It was a week of storms, as if some angry god had been awoken and would not go back to sleep. There was no breeze, and we all, Walter included, fanned ourselves vigorously against the humming attack of mosquitoes, the ladies with lace and gilt paper Japanese fans, he with the morning copy of the newspaper.

"The afternoon was so nice. But tonight it's like a hothouse," I complained, wishing I could take off my stiff leather shoes, but one does not sit barefoot in a public place. Oh, go ahead, a voice whispered in my head. Minnie. She was a proper lady, well-bred and well-mannered, yet once in a while she had felt an urge to break the rules. Henry James had seen it in her, that tuft of rebellion as soft as a feather, yet also as enduring. Feathers last a very, very long time. Coward, said Minnie's voice in my head, laughing.

"Did you know that the word 'orchid' comes from the Greek *orchis*?" I said.

"Of course," lied Mrs. Ballinger, springing to the bait. Stupid women are always overeager to show off how much they know, which is very little.

"And that *orchis* means 'testicular,'" I continued. "Ground-growing orchids tend to have twin tubers that look like—"

Walter jumped in before I could finish. "Some iced tea, ladies? Should I ring for the bellhop?" He gave me a little look of reprimand. Poor Mrs. Avery had stopped rocking entirely and seemed about to spring up and run away.

"Perhaps, Daisy, you should continue the story," he suggested.

"I'll never be able to enjoy my Easter corsage again," muttered Mrs. Ballinger.

I slipped off one shoe and then another and wiggled my toes, enjoying their freedom. Mrs. Ballinger pretended not to see. Walter winked at me.

TEN

Amerigo was out of sight but not out of Beatrix's mind as she and her mother journeyed from the land of noodles and bright sunlight and *stornelli* songs on the Spanish Steps to the land of Schubert *Lieder*, schnitzel, and dark forests surrounding medieval towns.

As they traveled ever farther north and east, the sun dimmed and the vegetation grew lusher, thicker, more intimidating. On the days when they went by carriage after dark, they could hear wolves calling to one another. Shadows lost their contrast and the difference between day and dusk was not as strong as it had been in the south. Time felt different, too. Beatrix had been warned by her aunt Edith that she would feel this change, and it would mark the moment when she knew she was entering a different reality.

Rome had ghosts, of course, but for the most part they had been talked of as naughty children, wanderers who refused to stay in the grave but had no power over the living. Even Nero's ghost, wailing its way through the Piazza del Popolo, had a clownish rather than frightening quality.

The ghosts were different in Germany. More powerful. More omnipresent, especially if one listened to downstairs gossip and read the more lurid type of travel book. In Germany, one slept with the covers pulled tight to one's chin, and not just because it was cold at night in the late spring.

Beatrix thought often of ghost stories as she and her mother toured the houses and gardens of Berlin, places where Edith as a child had been told those frightening tales that had haunted her ever since. Edith still refused to sleep in a room where there was a collection of ghost stories or even a suspicion of a haunting. She believed in them, you see. That's why she wrote her own series of ghost stories: to try to tame her fear of them.

Beatrix was more pragmatic. She believed in fevered imaginations and unexplained thumps in the night, the moving shadows and moaning winds that are the beginning of the imagination's overpowering of the mind's logic. She did not, however, believe in ghosts, though she loved a good ghost story, that raising of the flesh on the arm, the momentary sense that some unseen presence stands behind your chair. I suppose in her heart she was a bit of a pagan. Most gardeners are, and they know that life has forms both visible and invisible. The new rosebud is there, hiding in the stem, invisible to the eye but there, nonetheless.

It was decided that I would join them in Berlin. Mr. Winters had insisted I take another week of vacation, away from family worries. What many men don't understand is that mothers worry more, not less, when they are away from their children.

Even so, after a quick trip back to Paris to see that all was well with the children, I went on to Germany, to rejoin Beatrix and Minnie. I had not yet learned to stand up for myself, or even to argue back.

Since leaving Rome, Beatrix and Minnie had toured the Boboli Gardens in Florence, the gardens of Villa d'Este and Hadrian's Villa, the public gardens of Milan. In Bavaria they had visited Nymphenburg, the Grosser Garden in Dresden, and the conifer collection in Pillnitz.

Beatrix had filled several journals with sketches, measurements, and notes. When she slept, she dreamed of parterres and fountains; awake she reminded herself constantly of Mr. Olmsted's advice to hunt for beauty in the commonplace, in the rustic.

"I think it is difficult to accomplish what Mr. Olmsted and Mr. Sargent have recommended," she said after our first day of sightseeing in Berlin. "To make gardens a place of joy rather than an extension of court and palace. The Italians cling to the formal past as if they would drown without it, and the Germans seem inspired mostly by grandiosity," she said.

"It does all make me rather long for Maine," Minnie admitted. "Some of the gardens feel as formal as Mrs. Astor's drawing room. The world needs gardens where children can play."

"I have seen only one such garden." Beatrix stared at the sprigged wallpaper.

She hadn't stopped thinking about Amerigo since leaving

Rome. I could see it in her face, a combination of dreaminess, worry, and longing.

"The garden of the young Italian who came to your hotel room," I said.

Minnie shook her head, a half smile on her mouth. "The poor man no longer has a name, it would seem. He is just the man who importuned my Beatrix. I have heard sly remarks from a dozen and more people about that evening."

Amerigo had been right about that. There had been gossip. Minnie hadn't minded much. She trusted her daughter. But in those more innocent days, the world took a dim view of young unmarried girls receiving men in their hotel rooms.

"A garden for children sounds a delightful thing," I agreed, trying to turn the conversation away from Amerigo.

Beatrix rose and tapped her damp walking shoes, which she had placed on the window ledge to dry. It was much too warm for spring, and the three of us had been sitting as still as possible, fanning ourselves occasionally and sighing over various concerns. Minnie had had another letter from the Paris lawyer about the divorce settlement; Beatrix looked lost between two worlds, that of maidenhood and that of passion; and I wondered what Mr. Winters was doing that evening back in Paris, with whom he was playing cards, for playing cards he assuredly was.

The remnants of our own supper, soup and sausage and boiled potatoes, still littered the huge round table positioned in the center of our room in Pension Grindelwald. Berlin was inferior to Rome and London and Paris in that it did not yet have any grand hotels, and this one proved the point. The street floor was a tavern with a sawdust-covered floor, and while there was a separate room where unescorted females might dine, we had decided to take our dinner upstairs, in privacy.

The owner of the little hotel must have been an avid hunter, for boar and deer heads abounded on the walls, and the candlesticks were made of antlers soldered into pewter bases. One particularly disgruntled-looking boar looked down on us from the corner of the room, and a snarling stuffed wolf crouched in the hall. It was, on the whole, too much like being stuck in a fairy tale. We had all dreamed of wolves the night before.

"Wasn't it strange? My wandering there like that?" Beatrix asked. The sound of shouting, singing, and accordions came up to us from the street. It was the Whitsun holiday, and all day, brass bands had marched through Berlin. Crowds of young people filled the plazas, the boys wearing caps of all colors, the girls in their white blouses and dirndls. Many of the young male scholars had dueling scars crisscrossing their faces, worn proudly as badges of honor.

"You mean that young Roman's garden?" Minnie asked. The heat had disordered our imagination, and the conversation twisted and turned on itself, coming back to Amerigo.

Minnie studied her daughter's face, which was a blank. Perhaps too blank. Beatrix was learning to hide her feelings, and that of course meant she had feelings. For this man, this Amerigo.

"Yes. So strange, I think."

"No stranger, really, than my running into Mr. Winters at the Colosseum," I said, and then almost bit my tongue, for Mr. Winters had followed me; there had been no coincidence about it at all. "I did not mean it like that, dear Beatrix," I quickly amended.

Beatrix laughed, but Minnie looked as if she wanted to ask something but could not with Beatrix there. Minnie often talked to me in a very entre nous manner. I was ten years older than Beatrix and only fourteen years younger than Minnie, which gave me an extraordinary position in their household, an intimate of both mother and daughter, as need and situation required.

"It's so warm tonight." Beatrix leaned out the window to look at the revelers below.

"Finish the story. About wandering into Amerigo's garden," I said, at a loss to suggest another topic of conversation. She hadn't really talked about it in detail, not until the gossip began.

"Amerigo confessed that he had seen me in his garden, speaking with his housekeeper, but he hadn't come out to greet me. He said he was in the middle of a discussion with his father."

"I would guess a heated discussion, if it preempted his sense of courtesy," I said.

Minnie was no longer looking at me but staring at the stuffed boar head on the wall. She had removed her stockings, and her feet, so white and narrow, looked like calla lilies resting on the green velvet ottoman.

"I wonder what they were quarreling about," Beatrix said, closing the window. A particularly loud brass band had begun playing.

"That is between father and son," Minnie said, "and nothing to do with us." I hope it has nothing to do with us, her little sigh added.

We sat fanning ourselves.

"Did you know Mrs. Haskett is also here, in Berlin?" I said.

"Oh, Lord," sighed Beatrix.

"Is she planning on purchasing the Prince of Brandenburg's art collection, or perhaps all the old shields from the mercantile board for her garden gazebo?" There was venom in Minnie's normally sweet voice.

"Not that I have heard. Something about a cousin of a cousin studying here for a year, and she has come to inspect and support. He has been keeping odd company and she's been enlisted by his parents to usher him into some better drawing rooms. He has gambling debts and Mrs. Haskett is to try to imbue some sense into him."

"How much we learn about almost strangers." Minnie sighed again. "How people do talk."

Reprimanded, I shrank into the horsehair cushions of the sofa.

"Mrs. Haskett seems to be everywhere," Beatrix said. "A most unpleasant woman."

"Impossible to avoid her, I'm afraid," I said. "She knows you are here and has already planned a musical evening for your enjoyment."

"Oh, Daisy! You didn't tell her!"

"No, dearest Beatrix, she already knew. I ran into her this morning at that little milliner's shop." Her comment stung me with its suggestion of blame. In fact, Beatrix had made herself somewhat notorious by receiving Amerigo in her hotel room in Rome. The American community abroad was keeping its collective eye on her, just as it had once kept its eye on me.

"We'll have to go." Minnie sighed. "It would look strange, otherwise."

"For my sins, I assume." Beatrix was laughing.

At that very moment, there was a knock on the door. Minnie's maid came in with a card on a salver. Mrs. Haskett had extended a formal invitation for the very next evening.

I was with Minnie and Beatrix the following day when they toured Berlin's Tiergarten. The peonies were in bloom but the strange heat of the season made them look as blowsy as a woman of questionable reputation who has not been properly laced up. There was a sensual profligacy to them, with their big, scented pink petals, the deep green leaves, the stems not quite strong enough to support the full flower heads.

"They need backbone," I said with a sniff.

"Cooler weather," Beatrix corrected. "Peonies do not like the heat. Walk on, Daisy. I want to see the iris beds. I've heard they have some varieties we do not yet have in the States."

Because it was a holiday, the gardens were thick with people, some of whom—the young people especially—looked as if they had celebrated to excess the evening before. Hats were worn crookedly; faces were red; some seemed to stumble rather than walk. A group of young men lurched into us by the rose garden, almost knocking Minnie over. They apologized and bowed several times, then lurched off in the opposite direction, shouting back and forth and waving invisible foils at one another in pretend dueling challenges.

Minnie walked blindly, clinging to her hat, sighing often. The heat made prickles of perspiration run inside my clothing.

Berlin, with its premature heat and festive mood, agreed with me, though. Compared to Paris and especially Rome, it was a very new city. For the past decade or so they had been busily replacing medieval streets and ancient houses with new avenues and strong, tall buildings. The Chicago of Europe they called it, and it did indeed remind me of Chicago, especially the Chicago as it had been during the world's fair, loud and brassy and busy and so filled with newness it fairly gleamed in the sun. It smelled of new paint and fresh sawdust. Rome had been all ghostly ancient ruins and Renaissance villas, and Paris was so well satisfied with the moment it had no need of a future. Berlin seemed the city of tomorrow, being constructed even as we watched.

"I don't think I can spend much more time here in the garden, Beatrix," Minnie complained. "It is simply too warm." She tipped her hat to an exaggerated, even rakish angle, to get the sun off her cheeks. Her face was florid and damp.

"Let's sit. I'll see if I can find a lemonade seller." Beatrix ushered us to a free bench and then went off in search of cool drinks. Minnie and I sat fanning ourselves and watching the throngs of people go by. Some looked the worse for wear, after the long celebrations and the license that masks and free-flowing alcohol provide.

Whitsun is a holiday situated between the hard days of winter and the busy planting of spring. Much as it has been given its proper religious overtones, it still maintains its pagan undertones of resurgent fertility, to match the season. That day in the Tiergarten the blond, rosy-cheeked German girls looked particularly blooming; their young men looked properly mettlesome. It made me think of June weddings and March christenings, of Mr. Winters alone in Paris.

Minnie's thoughts wandered along similar lines. "I think Beatrix has changed," she said when we were alone. "Have you noticed a change?"

I had. There was a tension in Beatrix's movements that hadn't been there before Rome. Sometimes she left her sentences unfinished, and Beatrix had never been one for leaving anything unfinished, certainly not a thought.

"Perhaps the tour has been too demanding," I said.

"No. She is physically stronger than ever. It is something else, something more subtle than mere exhaustion."

"You think it is the Roman, Amerigo."

"Perhaps. Such a complicated age, twenty-three. Last winter one of her New York friends teased her about being a spinster, did you know? A spinster, when she is still so young! And I am almost useless on this matter. Here I am, entering into a divorce settlement just as my daughter is facing decisions about the rest of her life. I don't want her to rush. There is no need to rush. Yet if she never takes a chance . . ."

Minnie looked as if she might weep. I saw the difficulty, of course. You'd have to be blind not to: a mother on the verge of divorce with a grown daughter on the verge of . . . well, we didn't know, and that was the problem, wasn't it?

"The heat makes you worry," I said. "Beatrix has more common sense than anyone else I know. She won't rush. She won't be unwise." But I had had a vision of Beatrix in a travel costume, tiptoeing down a hotel staircase late at night. A vision of an elopement. She wouldn't. She couldn't. But then, perhaps that was the chance she needed to take?

"Gardeners love order and control," she had admitted to me that day at Holms Lea, when we first met. "But before there can be control, a certain amount of risk has to be taken. Will that peony get enough light? Will that tree, full grown, cast too much shade? You must be willing to take chances."

"Daisy, you of all people should know," Minnie went on. "Sometimes one doesn't make the decision. It is made for one. It is why young people are so fond of the words 'fate' and 'destiny.' They still believe in it. A Roman! She would be so far from home."

Beatrix came back before I could answer, carefully carrying three glasses of fruit punch. There was a half smile on her lips. Minnie and I looked at her.

"Is something wrong?" Beatrix asked. "Do I have a smudge on my face?"

"Let's go look at the lion," I proposed. "I hear he is a particularly sweet old thing, all yawns and big yellow eyes. If I don't go to see the lion so I can tell her all about it, Clara will never, ever forgive me."

But even the lion was overcome by the heat and refused to do anything more amusing than swish his tail at the flies, so we returned to the hotel, and the stuffed animal heads peering at us from all the walls and corners, to rest for the evening.

ELEVEN

Mrs. Haskett's residence in Berlin was on the newly fashionable and expensive boulevard Unter den Linden. There, she had rented a large town house for several months to avoid the summer heat of Rome, though Berlin did not seem much cooler. The owners had obligingly moved into the back rooms so that Mrs. Haskett could enjoy the front rooms—and they could enjoy the undoubtedly large rent she paid them. They pretended to be cousins, to avoid the stigma of a crass financial arrangement, but unless one searched back to Adam and Eve's extended family, I don't think a blood connection could be found between Mrs. Haskett and the Baumgartens.

"Must we?" Beatrix was still protesting when our carriage pulled up in front of the house that evening. The Berliners kept marvelous horses, large and white and as clean as porcelain, so unlike Rome, where one might end up being forlornly pulled about by a single horse with its ribs showing, or even donkeys.

That evening, the carriages with their liveried coachmen and footmen and magnificent plumed horses filled the wide boulevard.

"Yes," Minnie said, smiling. "We must. For your sins in Rome."

"It is a high price to pay for a few minutes spent in moonlight in the Colosseum."

"Beatrix, don't forget the hotel room," I said.

She shot me a scalding glance. "If I could go back in time, I would never open the door to his knock," she said, but I didn't believe her. Nor did Minnie, judging by her expression.

Beatrix wore a red dress that evening, dangerously close to scarlet. If she was going out to be seen, then she would ensure she was seen. She wore a little tiara of pearls, and two larger pearls dangled from her ears.

To my eyes, and to others as well, I assume, she looked decidedly American: tall and healthy and full of confidence. When she stepped up the stairs to the entrance, her movements were filled with athletic grace and ease, the result of a childhood spent on horseback and swimming and besting even the strongest boys at tennis. It was as if the Americanism of this young woman declared, "The nineteenth century might have been Europe's, but the twentieth will be ours!"

I walked between mother and daughter, our arms interlinked. Heads turned in our direction as we entered the ballroom. Minnie was small and dark, precariously balanced between her mature beauty and the inevitable, mortal loss of it. Beatrix was all youthful strength and radiance. I, in the middle, blond and average in size and height, was the young matron. The Three Graces, we had been called when we went out together in New

York. Conversation ceased when we stood at the top of the stairs to be announced. The footman, dressed in a Louis XVI costume, as were all the other servants, barely had to raise his voice.

The room was ablaze with candelabras and huge urns of white roses. Mrs. Haskett, resplendent in a tawny spangled Worth gown and with diamonds at her throat and wrists, broke free from a circle of friends, more likely sycophants, and rushed forward to greet us.

"I'm so glad you could come," she said, putting her arm around Beatrix's and Minnie's waists in an overly intimate manner. This seemed a bad omen. She was condescending, and only people who believe themselves to be superior can be condescending.

"Good evening, Mrs. Haskett. You have a lovely rental here in Berlin." Minnie managed to look down her nose though her hostess was four inches taller than she. Mrs. Haskett's patronizing familiarity was too much. Minnie was a warmhearted and generous woman, but she was also a member of one of the oldest families in the East, and she preferred that people not forget it, especially not when her daughter's reputation was at stake.

"It is rather quaint, isn't it?" Mrs. Haskett said, making it seem as if she had rented a hut, not a huge town house. "I was tempted to take a castle in the Odenwald for the season, you know, one of those airy, ancient places that look down on the river . . . which one is it? I don't remember . . . but it seemed just too, too beyond the pale. All trees and wolves, from what I heard. And there was dear cousin Harold to consider. He does need me."

Harold, six feet tall and looking as though his teeth pained him, came to her side as soon as she beckoned and gave us a stiff, unhappy greeting. It was obvious he would rather be elsewhere, perhaps the nearest tavern or gaming table.

Mrs. Haskett dismissed Harold with a wave of her hand, and he slunk away to find the nearest punch bowl.

"Will there be a tour of the house?" I asked. Mrs. Haskett, if she heard the derision in my voice, ignored it. I had once offered a tour of my new home on Fifth Avenue and learned the hard way that only the nouveau riche did such a thing. I had been laughed at, behind my back, for weeks.

"My footman can show you around, if you want. Don't miss the picture gallery on the mezzanine. I've had my Vermeer and Van Dyck installed. The David sketches haven't arrived yet." Mrs. Haskett still had her arm around Beatrix's waist.

"Is there a solarium?" Beatrix asked, always eager to see orchids and other exotics. She managed to disengage herself from her hostess and put several feet of empty air between them.

"Of course!" Mrs. Haskett seemed to think better of her response and quickly added, "Not in good repair, however. Nothing of interest, I fear. You would be much happier seeing the picture gallery." She turned Beatrix halfway and pointed to an arched doorway. "Through there. All the way to the end of the hall and up the stairs."

There was malice in Mrs. Haskett's face, hidden under the forced smile, the feigned gaiety. I often wondered what had so embittered her, that she must spend the rest of her life purchasing what had once belonged to others and making trouble whenever possible. When I spend time with people such as she, I remember we are a species that once threw our neighbors to the lions for amusement. Mrs. Haskett reached out as if she would forcibly restrain Beatrix, then thought better of herself. She wasn't smiling any longer, though.

The band had started playing a lively polka, and a swirling mass of people took to the dance floor. Beatrix threaded her way through them, heading away from the gallery and toward the opposite arched doorway, into the solarium.

"I warned her," Mrs. Haskett said.

"What was the warning?" Minnie asked, her voice colder than the sherbets on the buffet table. At least I assumed there would be sherbets and a buffet.

"She'll find out." Mrs. Haskett's angular face was fierce in its intensity.

Minnie took my hand as if she suddenly needed support. We had both guessed. Neither of us knew what to do. Stop Beatrix, warn her? Wouldn't that suggest we still thought of her as somewhat childish, in need of protection?

Minnie decided. "Come, Daisy. Let us look at the pictures. Perhaps we will visit the solarium later."

Beatrix was already out of sight. She had passed through that arched doorway and was on her way.

T his is how Beatrix later told it to me. I believe she gave her mother the same version, but there is no guarantee. Minnie and I did not exchange notes. Somehow, what had happened had taken on a life of its own and we became mere bystanders.

Amerigo was there, of course, bending over a pot of orchids.

He heard her footstep and turned, his mouth slightly open in surprise.

"You!" he said.

"Indeed," she agreed, equally startled. As soon as she saw him, she understood her combination of fatigue and restlessness of the past weeks. It was, she said later with a smile, like Eve encountering Adam in the garden, as if she had been waiting for this moment without knowing she was doing so. There was pleasure, yes. And fear. And that sense of inevitability that accompanies the great passions of life.

"What are you doing here?" Amerigo asked. He sounded a little anxious, and that reassured her. She couldn't stand bullies of either sex. If he had rushed forward, embraced her immediately, taken advantage of the moment and her surprise, she would have fled. Instead, they stood in the solarium, surrounded by heat and green and the earthy smell of humus and loam and flowers, not moving toward each other, only looking, enjoying this last moment of separateness either of them would ever know.

"I was invited to come hear the music. And you?" She stood in the doorway, enjoying those dozen steps between them, knowing that as soon as she closed that space there would be no turning back.

"A little family business. Look," he said softly. "Do you know she has bought a Vermeer?"

"So I've heard." Beatrix fanned herself. It was humid and warm in the solarium. Perfect conditions for an orchid but not for a young woman already flushed with emotion.

"Shall I get you a glass of water?" he asked.

"No, thank you. Has the Vermeer been hung among the ferns?"

He laughed. "Not even our hostess would make such a mistake. No. But she wished me to see her orchids first."

"Ah. I was to view the pictures first."

"Perhaps she was trying to prevent our meeting. There are so many people here."

"Indeed. We could have spent the night and never encountered the other."

"But you found me."

"It seems." Somewhere water dripped, measuring the seconds. Time! It called to them. Never forget time. It will not stand still. Amerigo took the first step. She took the second. They alternated, like children in dance school. When they were within arm's length, Amerigo took her hand and repeated the kiss he had given her in Rome, on her palm.

"I am happy to see you," he said, not releasing her hand. She saw in his face it was more than happiness he felt. She imagined her expression echoed his own.

"And me, to see you." There was no coyness in her, no dishonesty. She knew there was no need, and no purpose for it. They were the only two people in the world, and they were in a garden. An artificial one, certainly, but a garden nonetheless.

They moved slowly, side by side, down the rows of tables, afraid to look at each other for fear of revealing too much.

Because it was the fashionable thing to do, Mrs. Haskett had assembled a large collection of exotics in her Berlin house, and Beatrix and Amerigo toured the solarium, exchanging quiet opinions and comments on the flowers for the pleasure of hearing each other's voice. Silence, Beatrix felt, was to be avoided. It was too full of possibility.

"A *Cattleya labiata*," she said, stopping in front of a large pink flower. "First found in Brazil by Mr. Swainson. It is a favorite among collectors. I find it a bit too showy."

"Yes, you are right," Amerigo agreed. "It reeks of a stuffy ballroom, a too-large corsage on the wrist."

"The color is much too florid," Beatrix said disapprovingly of a purple freckled *Phalaenopsis bellina*.

"It should be paler. This looks as if an artist has overpainted it," he agreed, happy to discover that they agreed on such a simple thing as the color of a flower.

"And look, she has an *Orchis spectabilis*. It is a North American orchid, and now she has brought it to Europe. There was a whole shelf of these at the Chicago fair."

The flowers of the *Orchis spectabilis* are an inch or so in size, and of a shape that makes them suitable for imposing thoughts on them, much as the shape-shifting clouds are. It is a delicate plant easily found growing in leaf litter but easily overlooked because of its diminutive size. In the solarium, surrounded by the huge, flamboyantly colored tree orchids of Brazil and Colombia, it seemed even more unassuming.

But Amerigo, who could tell the brushstroke of a Fra Angelico from that of a Fra Lippi, saw more in the plant than many people see.

He bent to examine it more closely. "It looks like a ghost in a white hooded cape," he said.

"I never thought of it that way, but yes, it does, doesn't it?" Beatrix lowered her head for a closer look, and a coppery lock of hair fell over her forehead. It was all Amerigo could do to leave that lock in place, not to reach over and tuck it back.

Beatrix thought perhaps his Roman religion shaped his thoughts on this orchid, but it didn't matter. In New York, that hint of superstitious Catholicism would not have offended her, for Minnie had taught her better, but would have required her to reconsider some previous opinion of him. Here, in Berlin, it seemed all of a piece and even appropriate. A monk, then. A ghostly monk.

"Have you seen white-hooded ghosts often?" she asked.

He knew she was jesting, but he answered seriously. "My palazzo is said to be haunted. I myself have never seen the ghost, but the housekeeper has. On all the saints' holidays she puts out a plate of food for it, and once a year we open the chapel where his bones are kept and have a mass said. He was an old monk who was persecuted by one of my ancestors centuries ago."

"Why? Why was he persecuted, and what happened to him?" They had reached the end of the orchid tables and Beatrix let her shawl drop off her shoulders. It was warm, as any orchid room should be, but the heat was making her dizzy. She could hear the dancers laughing as the musicians played the opening notes of a mazurka.

"It was over a painting that had been acquired by less than legal methods. A holy relic the monk wanted returned to the church." Amerigo leaned against a table. There were only inches between them.

"Not *The Wolf of Gubbio*?"

"The same. It was stolen from Sassetta's studio in Siena before it could be delivered to the church in San Sepolcro. For a certain amount of money, it was delivered to us instead. We are a family known for our love of art and questionable, if traditional, methods of acquiring it."

"What happened to the monk?"

"Brother Leo was sent to the palazzo to bring back the painting, but my ancestor would not give him an audience or even speak with him. The guards at the gate treated him poorly. Brother Leo slept by the gate in all weather, good or bad, for many weeks, waiting for the painting to be handed over to him. He refused to eat and grew thin. He refused to move, so all visitors had to step over him. Most inconvenient. But one night he had a dream about the painting, and the wolf spoke to him. 'Tell the signor that if he returns the painting, he will get something else in its place.' It's the story of St. Francis and the wolf all over again, you see. Give up one thing—marauding and killing—to get another—free meals for the rest of your life. So the duke of the time, my ancestor, gave up the painting and received for it something even more precious: Sassetta's study for the painting of *The Wolf of Gubbio*. Sassetta destroyed all the studies, preferring his reputation be based solely on finished works. How this one study survived is probably another tale of theft."

"And the monk?"

"The duke waited a suitable amount of time and then had Brother Leo thrown out a high casement to his death, for the embarrassment he had caused. Such a death can never be proven as murder, of course. It looked at it was meant to look, like an accident. But the family knew. Knows. And they say Brother Leo has never really left the palazzo, but moans up and down the halls, especially on nights of the full moon, when he howls in loneliness for his brother monks, whom he never saw again in this life."

"Such a strange history!"

A commotion began in the doorway of the orchid room. Another couple had found their way there and stood at the entrance, locked in an embrace, her white arms pale against his black jacket, his hands pressed tightly against the yellow silk of her gown. Amerigo cleared his throat; they heard and fled, laughing.

Beatrix looked at Amerigo and smiled, hiding her own embarrassment.

"Are there no scandals, no murders in your family?" he asked. "In Italy we all have what you call the skeleton in the closet."

"Most of my family money came from banking. There may have been a certain laxity there. And an ancestor helped throw tea into Boston Harbor, and my great uncles abandoned a widowed sister to poverty. But no ghosts I've heard of. There have been marital irregularities," she finished.

"That is where we have the advantage over you Americans." Amerigo turned abruptly and walked to the next table. "We accept certain conditions, and what you call 'irregularities' become very regular."

"You mean mistresses." Beatrix followed him.

"Yes."

"My father has had a mistress for many years, and now he is divorcing my mother."

"That would not happen here," Amerigo said solemnly. "In Italy the husband would not be so cruel, and the wife not so narrow-minded."

Beatrix's face blazed red. She could not bear any criticism of her mother, but she knew from the quarrels she had witnessed in childhood that her mother could be judgmental and distant; she could be preoccupied. She was not entirely blameless.

Her mother and father had been ill suited to each other; she saw that now. Mr. James had sent her a note a year before, warning her against seeing too much in this dissolution of the marriage. The scandal of divorce would eventually die down, he had written, but to live locked together in misery would be worse.

"Whenever I see the little *Orchis spectabilis*, I will think of your monk," Beatrix said.

"I hope you will think of me as well."

"That would mean I had stopped thinking of you." She was, you see, free of coyness, as brave in her words as in her emotions. Amerigo perhaps had never before met that kind of girl.

They moved down the aisle of the next orchid tables, their feet crunching over drainage gravel, and when Beatrix was admiring a yellow lady's slipper orchid, Amerigo again took her hand and would not release it. There is a stage, in love, when mere touch sends such thrills of ecstasy through you that no other gesture is needed than to hold hands and feel that current flowing from one to the other.

They walked slowly, hand in hand, bending at the same moment over the same flower, commenting on the color and form and fragrance of individual blooms.

After half an hour of this, Amerigo took her in his arms and kissed her. She would not describe the kiss to me, of course. But she smiled at this part of the story. Beatrix had made the first leap. She had taken her first chance.

"Did you enjoy the flowers?" Mrs. Haskett asked when Beatrix and Amerigo joined the other dancers on the floor, an hour later. "You have been uncommonly long about it."

"Cattleya should not be potted with fern root. The fungus will kill them. You should speak with your plants man," Beatrix said, gliding away in Amerigo's arms as the band played a waltz.

Mrs. Haskett watched them dance, her face frozen into its usual smile. There was pain in her eyes, in that slight twitch at the corner of her mouth. She fluttered her fan vigorously and moved away from us.

Minnie, standing next to me, grew even more tense. "I don't like this," she murmured. "We should not have come."

"Too late. But judging by Mrs. Haskett's expression, I suspect she also wishes we had not come. Look at how she watches Amerigo."

There was already an undercurrent of gossip buzzing around us like mosquitoes on a breezeless summer evening. Too many eyes looked away from their dance partners' faces and watched Beatrix and Amerigo instead, with those sly, sideways glances that boded trouble.

Mr. James, in his little novel in which I am the namesake, exaggerated the gossip I endured after my evening in the Colosseum. But there had been gossip and I had come perilously close to losing my reputation, and reputation was a woman's most important possession.

Perhaps, I thought that evening, it would have been better if the American girl and the Roman man had never met, after all. Soon I would be absolutely certain that their meeting had been ill-starred.

TWELVE

"Did Amerigo say why he was in Berlin?" Minnie asked Beatrix the next morning. "It does seem an odd coincidence."

After the splendid, glittering rooms of Mrs. Haskett's town house, our own rooms in the Pension Grindelwald seemed even rougher than before, with their mostly bare floors, small-paned windows, and all those taxidermic animals glowering at us.

Impressed by the difference in settings, we had rather let ourselves go, as if in retaliation. Minnie was still barefoot. Beatrix was in her gown and wrapper, her unbrushed hair falling in reddish clouds over her shoulders and back. I had propped my feet up on an ottoman and leaned back into an overstuffed chair with all the unladylike abandon of childhood.

Beatrix was starry-eyed and distracted, as all maidens in love are said to be. "He is trying to sell her a painting, and it seems she is leading him on a merry chase, saying yes one day, no the next, and never bringing the price up to what it should be, even when she says yes. I understand it is very old and quite valuable."

"Sounds just like her. Manipulative, greedy, and . . . and common," said Minnie, who rarely said anything nasty about anyone. She poured milk into her tea and gave it a furious stir with her spoon. "If she must collect and own the best of Europe, she should at least pay a fair price."

"It is even more complicated. His father doesn't wish to sell the painting, and legally, his father is still the owner." Beatrix sighed and leaned her chin into her hands as she gazed out the open window. From a distance, we could hear the sounds of hammering and banging and shouting, the protesting creaking of girders, all the noise that accompanies the rise of a modern building, as Berlin soldiered on in its determination to replace old with new.

"Which painting?" I asked. I had been to the Louvre several times and was wondering if I might not try a little still life painting myself.

"It's a study for *St. Francis Taming the Wolf of Gubbio*, by Sassetta. Part of a fifteenth-century altarpiece showing the life of St. Francis. Most of the original altarpiece has gone missing, sold off to various collectors. His family owns a rare study for it."

"I wonder if that fellow out in the hall might have been a model," I said, having grown to detest the stuffed, ready-to-pounce wolf I had to pass each time I visited Minnie's rooms.

"Gubbio is in Italy, silly," Beatrix said. "In the saint's time, a huge wolf was gobbling up the citizenry of the town and countryside of Gubbio. Francis, being a gentleman's son long before he became a saint, struck a gentlemanly deal with the wolf. The townspeople would feed the wolf all the chicken and fish he wished, if he would leave them alone."

"Not quite fair to the chickens of the town," I commented, and Minnie gave me a little kick.

"The wolf agreed. The study that Amerigo owns—rather, his father owns—shows Francis and the wolf shaking on it, much as dogs and owners shake hands. He has promised to show me the painting before he sells it."

Minnie was all alertness. Plans had been made. Their meetings would no longer be accidental. Her daughter had a lover, and now that it was definite, the mother was no longer certain that a leap into the unknown was just what her daughter needed.

"He will sell it without his father's permission?" Minnie put down her teacup and buttered a slice of toast.

"He is certain he will win his father's approval before the purchase is made."

"And when will this private showing occur?" Did I hear a touch of wariness in Minnie's voice? If Beatrix did, she ignored it.

"When we are in Paris. He doesn't have the painting with him, of course. It's much too fragile. But if Mrs. Haskett doesn't meet his price, he will offer it to other potential buyers in France who have expressed interest. He does so need the money."

Minnie did not like this at all. Meeting in a solarium was one thing. Speaking of money and commerce—that was another. Even most married couples, for better or for worse, rarely spoke of money. And they had agreed to meet in Paris. Paris, where the lawyer and the estranged husband with his mistress were waiting to confront Minnie, to buy her off with a divorce settlement. This seemed unwise, the confluence of what certainly appeared to be a beginning love with a dead one.

"He speaks very freely of his circumstances," Minnie said, latching onto the one concrete element that a mother could criticize, and this time the wariness in her voice had turned to acid. "Is he desperate? Does he mistakenly believe you are wealthy?"

"Quite the opposite. I have told him that when I return to New York I will work as a landscape designer."

From outside the window we could hear laborers shouting. A flock of chattering birds rose in alarm from the linden tree opposite the hotel.

"You are angry," Beatrix said. "I should have asked you."

"No. You are not a child anymore. You don't need my permission. I just . . ." Minnie twirled a lock of her hair, a childhood habit she had never broken. "I worry. I do so want your happiness, more than anything in this world."

Beatrix smiled. "And if my road to happiness leads me to Rome?"

Minnie and I both sighed.

"In Italy, you wouldn't have a chance of establishing a professional reputation," Minnie reminded her. "You might redesign the gardens for your husband's home; you might achieve a name as a woman with a good eye for color in the garden. And that would be that."

Beatrix laughed. "You should not buy the wedding gown just yet. We have had no such conversation. Nor do I intend to."

Minnie shook her head. It had become painfully obvious that Beatrix did not yet understand the workings of the heart.

What we plan for ourselves so often has little to do with what the heart commands.

We spent that afternoon again in the sunny Tiergarten, with Beatrix making little drawings of the various waterways and statuary. She often sighed and muttered to herself as she rubbed out faulty lines and tried to capture difficult perspectives.

The Tiergarten was as crowded with Americans as the Borghese gardens had been in Rome, and as each separate group passed where we sat, Minnie reading, I knitting, and Beatrix sketching, we received long, intrusive glances. We overheard— were meant to overhear—snatches of conversation. Hotel room. Colosseum after dark. The orchids . . . An Italian! We all pretended not to hear, though Minnie's face grew a little stormy. She continued to smile vaguely as ladies do in public, but a crease appeared between her eyebrows and deepened as the afternoon lengthened.

When we went to supper that evening at a fashionable inn famous for its cuisine, conversation ceased as we passed already filled tables. Gossip spreads quickly, even more quickly than usual among travelers, but there had to be a guiding hand, and it was Mrs. Haskett's, of course.

"I think we shall leave Berlin soon. It is too warm on the continent," said Minnie after we were seated, studying her menu. "It is time to go to England and Scotland, don't you think, Beatrix?"

"In three days," Beatrix said, and that was how we knew Amerigo would be in Berlin for three more days. "Where will you go, Daisy?"

"Back to Paris. I miss the children. Everything is so quiet and orderly without them."

"Will Mr. Winters be there?"

"I'll have to check the racing papers and see if the horses are still running," I said.

Minnie and Beatrix sighed.

"Don't!" I said. "Don't you dare pity me. He is a scoundrel. We all know that. But I wouldn't change a thing about him."

That wasn't completely true, but one must put on a show. I only hoped I would get back to Paris and discover he hadn't used our entire quarter's income during my absence.

The next day we went to Potsdam to see the Charlottenhof Park, Beatrix busily making notes and drawings all the while, vigorously pursuing her studies of the plantings and the landscaping. Minnie's frown grew deeper.

To be a female landscape designer in America was one thing. America was new, its cities and parks were new, and in the whirlwind of novelty there was occasionally even room for a novel idea: working women. But Europe was ancient, as root-bound as any plant needing, and not receiving, a larger pot. In Europe, Beatrix would be no more than an eccentric, an amateur, frustrated and perhaps growing a little silly as she aged.

Could Amerigo come to America? It says much of the situation that none of us even considered such a plan. He had family, an estate, ties. Men did not readily give up such things, and when they did they were often scorned by the New York Four Hundred as nothing more than fortune hunters.

There were rules about such things. Women took their husbands' names. They lived where their husbands wished, kept company with those of whom their husbands approved. They gave themselves and their lives into their husbands' keeping, for better or for worse. No. If there was to be a union, Beatrix would have to stay in Italy.

Minnie felt a touch of betrayal. She and her daughter had planned a professional life for Beatrix, independence. Was she on the verge of giving it all up for something as unpredictable as love?

At some point during those next two days, Beatrix met again with Amerigo. When we napped in the pension? The summer heat felt oppressive and Minnie and I spent hours indoors, fanning ourselves and pressing cool compresses to our foreheads. Or perhaps it was after dinner, when Beatrix went for her walk and left us behind.

We knew she had seen him because she was able to tell us that Mrs. Haskett had not met the price for *The Wolf of Gubbio*. She was still leading him on.

"That is an ugly phrase, leading him on," Minnie said.

"The truth is often unappealing," Beatrix said.

"So he goes to Paris now, to meet with other buyers."

"He will be there when we are, after England and Scotland."

"I see," said Minnie. And she did.

Before we all left Berlin, Mrs. Haskett invited us for a luncheon. The three of us would rather have been dosed with castor oil than attend, but we felt we must, else the gossip surrounding Beatrix would only grow worse. Mrs. Haskett had put us in that kind of position.

The silly woman served English-style roast beef and potatoes on one of the hottest days of the year, with a warm steamed pudding for a sweet. The conversation, talk of bankers and investment ventures and who had purchased what, was as bad as the food. Some dozen people sat at her table, overwhelmed by all the crystal and silver and lace and courses of food, when all we wanted was a simple cold plate of salad.

Mrs. Haskett's three daughters were dressed alike, in sunny yellow muslin and with orchids in their hair, and the four young men who had been invited, second sons of the minor aristocracy, studying or pretending to study law, had been seated among them like so many sacrificial lambs awaiting the slaughter. Their manners were excellent, their conversation drivel. They ate with a steady concentration that suggested actual meals were spaced well apart in their lives. I knew the signs. Their allowances went elsewhere. They would be behind in the rent for their rooms, and a bill collector made regular rounds to them. They gambled, I imagined. It was a common enough fault.

I assumed the fourth young man had been invited for Beatrix, but she would have none of this blatant matchmaking over charred beef. She addressed her comments, few as they were, to the women at the table.

"You leave Berlin tomorrow, I hear?" Mrs. Haskett asked after the custard sauce had been passed around. The meal had been so heavy and the air in the dining room so warm and humid I thought I would melt, but Beatrix looked as cool as ever. She had Minnie's ability to persevere through conditions that would drive other women to distraction, and to stay as fresh as my namesake flower.

"Yes. Time to go to England, and then on to Scotland. I hope it will be cooler," Minnie said, although we all knew the question had been meant for Beatrix.

"Such a shame your special friend could not come to lunch today," the terrible Mrs. Haskett said, this time turning physically in Beatrix's direction so that there could be no confusion as to whom she was speaking.

"Friend?" Beatrix asked, wisely leaving off the adjective that had preceded it.

"Signor Massimo. I invited him, of course, but he declined. I hope you haven't had a falling-out. Such a charming man." Her voice dripped venom. Mrs. Haskett's three daughters tittered behind their handkerchiefs.

Minnie slowly, with exaggerated calm, put her dessertspoon down and wiped the corners of her mouth with her napkin. She swallowed once, twice.

"Signor Massimo is a friend of the family," she lied. "I don't know what you meant by 'special friend,' but if it is as I suspect, Beatrix has none." She rose, again slowly, majestically.

Beatrix and I rose as well. "Such a lovely lunch," Minnie said. "We have overstayed, however, and must leave. Thank you, Mrs. Haskett."

The whole table stood and began to disperse to various corners of the room. Minnie had that kind of authority. If she said a luncheon was over, it was over.

"Do give my regards to dear Mrs. Wharton when you see her," Mrs. Haskett said, blowing us kisses as we made our way down the hall and out the door.

"Horrid, horrid woman," Minnie muttered all the way back to our hotel. "It won't stop here, Beatrix. She means you harm. I see it in her eyes."

"It's because she can't marry off those three daughters," I said. "They're like the evil stepsisters in a fairy tale."

"No," Beatrix said. "It is because we didn't remember her name when we met in the Borghese gardens."

"It may be more than that," Minnie said. Her sweet, pale face was dark with emotion. "Have you not yet wondered why Mrs. Haskett, certainly no longer young but not quite yet old, has been stringing along—I believe that is the phrase—Signor Massimo? Perhaps she is interested in more than the painting."

We shrank back into the upholstered cushion of the carriage, our mouths rounded in horror. And then, after a silent consideration of Mrs. Haskett in Amerigo's arms, we gave her the greatest insult possible. We laughed. If she had been there to hear us she would have done us physical violence, I am certain.

THIRTEEN

Beatrix disappeared during our last evening in Berlin. She shared a supper of sauerbraten with us at our hotel, went out for her evening walk, and did not come back till sometime after Minnie and I had gone to our beds. In the morning, we did not ask her where she had been, or with whom, and she did not speak of it. Her face glowed and she seemed to walk on the very air.

She even patted that terrifying stuffed wolf in the hall, as if making a fond farewell to it.

I returned to Paris, to my husband, who greeted me at the train station with roses, two dozen of them, and a smile much too similar to the children's when something had been broken.

"Where are the children?" I asked, feeling a moment of panic as mothers do when their children are not where they are expected to be.

"Clara and India are in the Bois de Boulogne, riding, and

Athena is napping. I thought we might have a quiet afternoon together."

"Athena hates to nap," I said, disappointed that he hadn't brought our offspring. "How much have you lost?" I turned my face so that he kissed me on the cheek, not the mouth.

"Not so much that I can't win it back next week," he said.

There would be far fewer gamblers in the world if we could learn to control optimism. But then, it was optimism that kept me going back to Mr. Winters.

"I have had a letter from a Mrs. Haskett," he said, helping me up the steps of the carriage. He badly tipped the porter who promised to have my trunk delivered to the hotel. "Who is the blighted woman? Have we ever met?"

"We were introduced in New York, but she was not one of our set. Unfortunately, the Joneses and Whartons and I met up with her in Rome and she forced her acquaintance on us. She is making trouble for Beatrix. What does she say in the letter?"

"She will be in Paris and would like to call on us. She has a matter upon which she would like my advice. Something about an old painting." He preened a bit. People rarely asked Mr. Winters' advice on any serious matter.

"We will pretend we never received the letter," I said. "Throw it away immediately."

"As you say, dear." He twirled his mustache for a moment, thinking. "Mrs. Haskett. Widow of Reginald? Tall woman, wide shouldered. Great head of streaky hair that looks like fur. Greedy eyes." His faults were many, but Mr. Winters had a fine memory, at least for remembering what was not necessary to remember. "Beatrix can handle her, I suspect. What kind of trouble?"

The driver folded up the steps and closed the carriage door. My husband sat opposite me, giving me the full benefit of his smile, his face, his impeccable suit and tie. He looked just what he was: an American raised abroad by adoring aunts; a man who never really had to do that much thinking for himself, who certainly had never worried overly much about money, unlike my father or brother. Even his marriage proposal had come after much prompting by me, much to Mr. James' delight.

"He will disappoint you," Henry had warned me. "Forced to dance attendance on his aunts, and much tired of it I should think, he will, henceforth, refuse to listen to any feminine advice, especially his wife's." Henry all but chortled with glee when he gave this assessment. Then he had pushed aside the tea tray, taken my hands in his, and grown solemn. "I warned Minnie," he had said. "And look how that has turned out. And now, dear girl, I warn you."

"Is that why you murdered my persona in that strange little novel?" I had asked him. "Roman fever. Malaria. Indeed." The year after my marriage, Henry had published *Daisy Miller*, the novel in which poor Daisy takes fatally ill after an assignation in Rome.

"Death or marriage. Often there may not be that much difference to a woman, if the marriage is unsuitable," Henry had grumbled. "Women are better off married, if married well. Otherwise, spinsterhood is a wiser choice."

Tell that to a young woman, just released from the school-room, who is seeing Europe for the first time and encounters her first love in the process. There is no choice in this matter. Wisdom comes later in life.

"Mrs. Haskett is determined to ruin Beatrix's reputation," I said, sorry already that I had refused his kiss. I took his hand. "For some reason, she has taken against her and is making her the subject of the summer's worst gossip."

"Jealousy," said Mr. Winters, taking back his hand.

"What?"

"The woman is jealous. Beatrix is young, pretty, and of a much better family. Of course there's no comparison at all, on the matter of breeding."

There was a hint of malice in his voice. He came from an old family. I did not, as Mr. James had made quite clear in his little novel. Mr. Astor's great-grandfather may have been a fur trader who blew his nose on the tablecloth, but with me the family origins were closer and therefore more shameful, since my own grandfather had raised livestock and kept a general store till he and his son, my father, grew lucky at speculation. At certain times Mr. Winters enjoyed reminding me of this, and that was when I knew he had lost greatly at the races. He was going on the offensive.

"There is a man involved," he deduced.

"Yes. An Italian. Beatrix has been walking with him. They visited the Colosseum in the evening."

"And was she kissed?"

"She was."

"She'll have to marry the fellow. Is he presentable?"

"Good-looking, but poor as a church mouse, I suspect, and in the process of selling off the family heirlooms, or trying to."

"Uh-oh," said my husband. He grew thoughtful and looked out the window.

"Remember that evening?" he asked as the carriage bounced us down the Champs-Élysées. There was romance in his eye. I knew the hotel suite would be filled with roses, and in our bedroom, on my pillow, there would be a little red jeweler's box. The size of the pearls would suggest how much he had lost. And soon he would have to pawn that bracelet or collar to pay off a debt. I had tried to explain to him that he lost considerable sums on these transactions—the pawnshops never paid the full value—but he had lifted his well-bred chin and refused to discuss the matter with me. A husband had given his wife a gift. What right had she to complain?

"Do I remember the evening in the Colosseum?" I said. "Of course I remember." He had arrived unexpectedly, he had thought, though I had planted several clues in his path, should he choose to follow. Hansel and Gretel could not have asked for a better bread-crumb trail leading to the Colosseum, to me, walking in the moonlight with the beautiful Giovanelli.

"How much?" I asked again. He would not answer, but sat up straighter in protest, all manly indignation that I had been unwomanly enough to question him about our finances. "A dangerous place, the Colosseum after dark," I said.

We were home by then, and I jumped out of the carriage without waiting for his assistance, a habit that always made him glower and clear his throat with disapproval, but my little Athena was waiting for me in the nursery—lamplight shimmered through the curtains—and I couldn't wait to see her.

I stopped in the hall long enough to unpin my hat and toss it onto the table with my wrap. The French nurse we had hired (less expensive than traveling with a set of New York servants) greeted me with a warning. "She has sneezed. She has a small fever," she said, her voice making it somehow clear it was my fault. I dashed up the stairs, Mr. Winter clearing his throat even more loudly. A lady moved slowly, he often told me. Even in a crisis.

Athena was curled up under her favorite blanket, hugging her teddy bear. Her forehead was warm, not hot, and she did not shiver. I took a deep breath and tried to calm myself.

"Can I have a bonbon?" she asked. "Daddy won't let me have any candy."

"Later," I promised. "When I come for the good-night tuck, I'll sneak some in."

"Naughty Momma," she lisped with approval.

When Athena was asleep again, safely watched over by the nurse, I made the required inspection of our apartment, housekeeper at my side, running my finger over mantelpieces, checking the sweetness of the milk in the larder, and in general making it clear that I was the general, the housekeeper and her staff the troops. This inspection was a complete waste of time since the household ran perfectly well without me. Sometimes I missed working in granddad's general store in Schenectady, the merry ring of the register, the friendly gossip with the customers. A so-called lady of leisure was a creature who had little purpose except to produce children and be decorative at dinner parties. I missed feeling useful.

By the time I had finished the completely unnecessary inspection, Mr. Winters was already in his study, buried behind the evening paper. I knocked before entering.

"There are letters for you," he said, pushing a tray in my direction.

The letters from Gil and Robert had already been opened, though they had been addressed to me. Gil was hard at work at the bank, but he had spent two weeks in Newport, sailing. Robert was in New York, working with a private tutor so that he could begin his law studies at Harvard in the autumn.

"They are men, no longer children," Mr. Winters had said when I had first complained about leaving them behind. "Would you raise them as farm children are raised?" I had boasted once that my father had not left the farm, for even a single overnight, till he was nineteen and moved to town.

It was true: both boys encouraged me to shake their hands rather than kiss them, and they towered over me. But that did not ease the echoes in the empty places of my heart.

The new, unopened correspondence on the tray was topped by the invitation from Mrs. Haskett. I tore it into quarters without even reading it. Underneath was a letter just arrived that day from Beatrix. This letter I opened gently and settled into an armchair to read.

"On our way," she had written. "Tomorrow we cross the channel and begin a tour of England. Fingers crossed that Miss

Jekyll will receive me." She was referring to the famous landscape gardener, with whom she had arranged to meet.

"Does she write of her Italian?" Mr. Winters asked.

"She does not," I said, not liking his tone of voice. I put the letter back down on his desk and, doing so, clumsily knocked over a pile of his correspondence, opened and flattened so that when I picked them up they were easy to read.

"I'll get them," he said, jumping to his feet, but they were already in my hands.

Bills. Tailor bills, florist bills, the quarterly check for the governess, made out but not signed, not delivered. Copies of IOUs.

I sat back down, feeling as if an invisible hand had knocked the air out of me.

"I will not discuss it," he said, grabbing them and ushering me out of his study. I stood in the hall, leaning against the wall, for a long time, thinking.

> Dearest Daisy,
>
> I hope the children are well. Please give my warmest regards to Mr. Winters. (Has he wagered and lost much this season? Don't tell him I asked.) The channel crossing to England was rough but well worth it, now that I have seen London, and the young London ladies, their skirts tucked up to their knees, bicycling through Battersea Park. Remind me, Daisy, should I forget, to install bicycle paths in my

future gardens. They are not allowed here in the royal parks and gardens but are springing up all over the place in the public gardens.

As soon as we had recovered from the travel and settled into Symonds' Hotel, Mother insisted we take the train to Surrey to visit Mr. Strachey, for a literary afternoon on the terrace and a good catch-up with her old friends. They talked of poor Mr. Wilde, who had been sent to Wandsworth Prison and hard labor for "the love that dares not speak its name." Mr. Strachey blushed when he said this, and looked shyly at me, but Mother tsk tsked at him to indicate she had not raised me as a foolish innocent, and I already knew as well as any the sad and strange history of Oscar Wilde.

One younger man, I have already forgotten his name, jested that during the trial there had been a large migration of young London men to Paris to avoid similar prosecution. This was a little beyond what Mother was willing to gossip, so she asked how Mr. James' new story, "The Middle Years," was being received and the conversation was guided into calmer waters.

I spent much of the afternoon gazing out the window across the beautiful Surrey hills.

It seems to me that air and its quality of

light, and the soil itself, are the essence of any garden or landscape. The plants and trees, that part we call the garden, are the intermediary between the two essences of soil and light. The garden is the earthy part, the temporary part, and therefore the human part. Remember, God first placed us in a garden, so that we might delight, and so that we might gently work.

The light and air in England are as gauzy as a veil, soft and temperate without the hard edges of challenge of the Roman sun. I find them very agreeable.

I have met Miss Gertrude Jekyll, who is not quite so agreeable as her garden. I had written, introduced myself as a novice in her own field, and asked to make her acquaintance so that we could discuss gardens. She sent a trap and driver to the station to pick me up and bring me to her home, Munstead, in Surrey. Mother stayed behind in London, visiting old friends.

Meeting Miss Jekyll, Daisy, was too much like looking into a mirror that foresees the future. There was I, twenty-three, a former musician now turned gardener making her first tour of Europe to study gardens. There was she, fifty-two years of age, a former musician and artist, showing off her garden after her many tours of Europe, her many turns and twists in her own path. When she shook my hand in greeting, she spent a careful moment assessing me, and I, her.

I think we both agreed, instantly, that we would be colleagues but not good friends. She perhaps had moments in her youth that she regretted, moments of which I reminded her. And she threatened me with a solitary future, a woman struggling to be herself, to make her name, without a man at her side.

The decision is not always ours, is it? I wonder if Signor Massimo is in Paris yet. If you run into him, you will let me know? I am worried about his well-being; he seemed disheartened when we parted. There is much on his mind, more than he can share with a casual acquaintance. Am I just a casual acquaintance? I wonder. It feels . . . I will not write how it feels, except to say I think I know how flowers feel when they turn to the sun.

Miss Jekyll has grown fat. (Please do not show this letter to anybody. I write freely when I write to you, but others might harshly judge, and rightly so, my lack of charity.) She has the mannerisms of one who no longer seeks to charm. She slurps her tea and chews cake hurriedly, as if eager to be elsewhere. Indeed, we almost took our tea standing, so rushed was she. When she walks her head juts forward like a laborer's, and her very round cheeks shake like a blancmange being carried to table.

Oh, but her garden! I had been warned by Mr. Strachey that Miss Jekyll did not like to speak to strangers of her earlier artistic efforts, before she began this garden. As a young woman, Miss Jekyll had been a painter, and one of considerable talent, had been the general consensus. But eye trouble had forced her to give up close work in order to preserve what was left of her failing sight. That was when she began gardening. Daisy, I remember that night at the fair, when my voice failed, that terrible sense of betrayal by one's own body. It does seem telling that both Miss Jekyll and myself, disappointed in other arts, turned to gardening. I never think of it as a second best, but as my true course in life, found after other experiments failed, and I'm certain she does as well. "A living painting," she called her garden. Her garden is a delight. No other word will do.

In it, the artist has come back to life. There is such a miracle of color, such a temptation of texture, such a delight of shape! No oil canvas could have created the majestic delight she has constructed here at Munstead. In this garden the viewer does not stand before the art, as one does in a gallery, but in it, surrounded by joy.

Miss Jekyll currently lives in a newly built

and temporary house she calls a "hut," designed by Sir Edwin Lutyens, since she and her mother have decided to live apart, and the mother, of course, occupies Munstead House.

"After Mother is gone, the house will go to my brother, Jekyll," she told me, a touch of acid in her voice. "I need my own home. Do you have a brother, Miss Jones?"

When I answered in the negative, I thought I saw a glimmer of jealousy.

The hut is a sweet little cottage, and the tenement dwellers of the Lower East Side would think themselves deceased and in heaven to occupy such a place, but Miss Jekyll eagerly awaits the completion of her own house. It is being designed to suit her own needs: windows will minimize light to avoid the pain that glare causes her; passages will be wide, and there will be a sheltered place to sit in the courtyard; all the cupboards are to have glass doors so she can admire her collections.

"My house is to have an overhanging gallery, somewhat like a cloister," she said, and there was a twinkle in her eye. "Single women belong in a convent, or a house that reminds one of the convent, don't you think, Miss Jones?"

"Not at all," I said, knowing that I was being tested. "Marriage is no requirement for a fully lived life."

We paused as she plucked a beetle from a vine and crushed it between her fingers. "A garden is not for the squeamish," she said.

But Daisy, it is when Miss Jekyll speaks of gardens that she comes to brilliant life. She seems young again when she talks of plans for borders of pansy, fern, and geranium, of lily ponds and orangeries, and woodland trails she calls "road poems." Her eyes shine.

Her garden is still young, but she has designed it brilliantly, so that every time a corner is turned, a curving path followed, the eye is delighted anew. The lilies were blooming during my visit, and I saw she had planted them so that, during blossom time, they would be surrounded by greenery, not other flowers.

"It is a great mistake in the garden to plant so that different flowers bloom at the same time," she instructed me. "They must be situated to their own best advantage; otherwise, you end up with a busy hodgepodge of color and shape and fragrance, like a disordered closet."

I pretended to jot this down in my notebook, but I had already come to that conclusion myself. Gardens fail when people expect too much of them.

"You have just come from Italy, I understand," Miss Jekyll said to me, poking at a weed with her walking stick. "It is disconcerting, isn't it? All those straight lines. Too much geometry and not enough nature. And some of the villa gardens haven't a single posy in them. They are all box hedge and stone walls and fantastic fountains. Avoid straight lines, Miss Jones. They do a garden much harm. Color. That's what a garden needs. And a sense of mystery rather than grandeur."

"I agree," I said. "They should be a place where children can play."

"And where young women can fall in love."

I must have blushed.

"Oh, dear," she said, smiling. "Italy has much to answer for, hasn't it? Is he a penniless nobleman?"

"You are mistaken," I said.

The Surrey soil, I was delighted to find, has much in common with our own soil at Bar Harbor, and Miss Jekyll grows many of the plants I grow in my Reef Point garden, ferns and whortleberry, hosta and delphinium. The blues she achieves in her garden are magnificent, not faded or anemic but as bright as the Madonna's robes in a medieval altarpiece.

When I described this to Mother later she raised an eyebrow. She worries that Rome has softened me toward papist viewpoints; Rome, or my friend there.

He was on his way to Paris. Daisy, have you heard anything of him? My mail has not yet reached London.

The meeting with Miss Jekyll was informative, but not a great success, I fear. It was that initial impression we shared of each other, for as I found her old and unattractive in a decidedly spinsterish way, she must have found me over-young, perhaps flighty. We parted as fellow gardeners, but not as friends. It would greatly surprise me if she wrote to me, as she promised.

Mother and I returned to London, a little weary, a little anxious. We go to Scotland next, but after that . . . Paris. Father, the lawyers, the divorce. I will have to be very attentive to Mother, for she will surely be in low spirits. There will be no time for leisurely walks.

If you hear anything of him, be sure and write me, Daisy.

Be well, dearest friend. I remain your own,

Beatrix

Dearest Beatrix,

I have had no news of Amerigo Massimo, but Mrs. Haskett leaves her card almost daily. So far, I have ignored her. The children are well, though Athena had a slight fever for a day or two.

Mr. Winters and I are not on the best of terms at the moment. Yes, it is the old problem. When you are in Scotland, you might ask your uncle for advice on my behalf.

Always your loving friend,

Daisy

FOURTEEN

I n August, there was a great migration of English folk and their visitors to the north, to the Highlands. After visiting London and Surrey, Minnie and Beatrix joined this migration. They took the overnighter to Scotland and then a local coach to Loch Earn. They spent a few days hiking and golfing, and then continued on to Millden Lodge in the lovely, wild heather–scented Glen Esk, where Minnie's cousin, the famous New York lawyer John Lambert Cadwalader, rented a shooting lodge for the season.

Ever since Minnie's husband had abandoned the marital home and relationship, John Cadwalader had been her adviser, and guardian to Beatrix. It was Mr. Cadwalader who had declared, years before, that Beatrix had the intelligence and temperament to make a success of whatever she wanted to do with her life. He had meant it, and even the very young Beatrix knew that such praise was not to be dismissed as mere flattery.

Mr. Cadwalader was a bachelor, one of those elderly gentlemen who appeared never to have been young or reckless. I had met him only once but felt an instant respect for him. He had fine white hair, a high-bridged nose, curling white mustaches, and a habit of thinking long and hard before answering even the simplest of questions. I wondered what Beatrix would tell him, and what he would say.

"Lovely weather," Beatrix wrote in her next letter. "Spending days and days roaming over the moors or following the guns in the field. The house is full of a hunting party, most of the male persuasion, stomping around on the gravel, torsos crisscrossed with hunting bag straps, unloading rifles."

> I had thought in Scotland he would seem quite distant. This place is as far from Rome and its moods as I could imagine. The only ruin is the old gatekeeper's cottage, and there are no fountains but natural springs, no topiaries or other forced contrivances, only wild meadows and forests. Yet Amerigo still seems with me, somehow. That day in the catacombs, in Rome. I thought he was there, that he had somehow followed us. I saw something, Daisy. Something that, even as I saw it, I knew it wasn't real. Yet there it was. A shadow, a form, and it was him, as if a part of him had left his body and stayed with me.
>
> Perhaps it was astral projection. I read about

it in theosophist tracts from Madame Blavatsky. Projection is probably no stranger than seed germination, which is the most wondrous miracle I can think of. But why would such a thing happen? I do not know him well. Despite that, he has rooted in my mind. He grows there, steadily. The acorn will be an oak soon, and I will never be rid of him. What do I wish? To be free. To continue to be free. To pursue the path I have chosen. Yet there he is, standing before me, on that path. What do you think of his smile, Daisy? You saw him there, at Mrs. Haskett's soiree in Berlin. It is a good smile, isn't it?

Uncle says under no conditions are you to leave Mr. Winters. If you do, you will lose the children. He has made inquiries through his banker and various friends in London and Paris. He believes you should ask Mr. Winters to deed the New York house to you. He has lost a considerable amount, and to keep the children safe you should own property outright. Will he agree to this?

Daisy, I have become sunburnt, and somehow fond of both boiled oats and overcooked venison. It is almost as if each landscape creates of us a different person. Yesterday I was on Black Moss moor, flat on my back and looking up at the clouds, finding cows and sailing ships in their ever-changing shapes. Imagine me thus in the Borghese gardens. I would have been carted away to an asylum for loose women.

If the landscape creates the person, and in a garden the person creates the landscape, then it is to be considered a true relationship, not only a pastime.

Dearest Daisy, all will be sorted out properly. I feel it. Both for you and me. Be brave, and believe and trust your loving friend,

Beatrix

Mr. Winters had taken me to Monaco for our honeymoon. On our first evening there he had, for the first time, approached a gaming table. "Amusing," he had said after an hour. The next afternoon, he had sat for two hours. And every day after that, till we returned home, poorer than when we had left.

My husband was by nature of a generous disposition, despite the early training of his aunts in Switzerland, who counted the sugar cubes as you put them into your tea. But to deed property? It didn't matter that we had purchased the Fifth Avenue house with money from my trust. A wife did not financially separate herself in this way.

But I would. For the children. A woman should possess her own little corner of the world, I thought. Else she is little more than a servant in her own home, unprotected from any disaster. I had chosen Gilbert for my husband, and looking back on my marriage it seemed that had been the last choice I had been allowed to make, that I was excluded from all serious discussion about finances or politics. Whenever Gilbert and his male friends wished to discuss William McKinley, or the Dreyfus affair, or coal miner strikes in Pennsylvania, or the failures of some of their investments because of the depressed economy, they did so behind closed doors. I and the other women, left behind in the drawing room, spoke of fashions and children.

We were legally not much better off than children. How could we be, since we had no say in the running of our households and certainly no say in the running of our country?

I had six children and a husband who could no longer control his gambling. I would own, at least, the house purchased with my father's money.

Mr. Winters balked at the proposed arrangement and then sulked. He did not approve that I had spoken of our financial situation to Beatrix and Minnie, that they had in turn spoken of his gambling losses to Mr. Cadwalader.

"Unheard of," he said, turning white and pushing away his plate. The maid who had been serving a dessert of peaches and cream backed out of the room, sensing the storm to come.

"But, Gilbert, many wives own property," I protested.

"No," he said, banging his fist on the table. He repented of that. A gentleman does not show temper. "We will discuss it no longer," he said more quietly.

Mr. Cadwalader sent other letters to his lawyer, my bank, and my husband. I have no idea what was in these letters—a touch of blackmail, the threat of scandal—but they achieved their mission. Mr. Winters finally agreed to deed the Fifth Avenue house in my name, on condition that he would still manage my financial affairs. Fair enough, I thought. What husband would give up that right? What wife would demand it? Mr. Wharton managed Edith's finances; Minnie's divorce was more about the ultimate separation of finances than the emotional separation they had agreed upon years before.

I took my first steps to becoming a self-determining person, even though only a woman.

Gilbert's bad temper continued, so as I waited for Beatrix and Minnie to arrive in Paris, I occupied myself with outings for the children, which pleased their governess greatly. I often passed her little closet and saw her, feet up on an ottoman, napping or reading a popular novel.

With the girls in tow, I visited exhibits about the wireless telegraph and Mr. Diesel's combustion engine, went riding in the Bois de Boulogne, took long walks down the tree-lined avenues of Paris. My daughters were all like me, fair-skinned blondes who liked to get their own way. That was charming in children, but dangerous in matters of the heart, and I was already worried about Jenny, knowing in advance she would choose an inappropriate gown for her debut and make a questionable marriage. Our children do tend to repeat our own mistakes, despite how much they design to do the exact opposite.

I wished with all my heart that Robert and Gil were with us as well, but as Mr. Winters said, they were no longer children but young men who must begin to make their way in the world.

Little by little Gilbert almost, but not quite, forgave me for requiring that the New York brownstone be put in my name. He even accompanied me to the private party at Princess Esterhazy's to see the moving pictures of Louis Lumière. They were short, only a few minutes each, but how amazed we were to see moving photographs! One was called *The Gardener* and it showed a young rascal stepping on a hose and drenching the gardener. Beatrix would have found it amusing and I thought I might try to wrangle another invitation to the princess's once Minnie and Beatrix had arrived.

Mrs. Haskett continued to leave her cards with us on a daily basis. It began to feel almost threatening. I knew she wished to know when Beatrix and her mother would arrive in Paris, but I could not guess why.

And then one afternoon I ran into Amerigo Massimo at the Louvre. He was standing before one of da Vinci's paintings of the Madonna, his hands behind his back, peering wistfully up at the winged angels surrounding the Virgin.

"How marvelous to have wings," I said, breaking into his silence.

"Truly," he agreed. "One could simply fly away. How good to see you, Mrs. Winters."

"And you, Signor Massimo. Are you in Paris for long?"

"A week or two. Business matters. Don't you think this Madonna looks a little like our Beatrix? The hair, the complexion."

"A little," I agreed. "She would prefer a larger landscape in the background, though. She prefers paintings of gardens."

"Yes. When we looked at the Caravaggios in Rome she said that to me."

We stood for a minute, pretending to study the painting, wondering what else could be said that would not open some floodgate. "Will you take a cup of tea with me in the café?" I finally asked.

"I can't stop thinking about her," he said, once the little serving maid had brought a tray with tea and biscuits to our table. "Normally, you see, I do not care for American girls. They are . . . What is the word? Silly. Or grasping. Italian girls are better brought up, better mannered."

I nodded. Giovanelli had said the exact same thing to me, years before. And then he had tried to kiss me, in the moonlit Colosseum, before Mr. Winters had finally caught up to us to interrupt that kiss.

"Beatrix—Miss Jones, I mean—is different. She has—what is the word?—gravitas."

"Yes," I agreed. I declined to specify what made her different, that childhood of cold silence between mother and father, the father openly appearing with his mistress in New York, defying the convention not of faithfulness, for many broke that vow, but of discretion. Beatrix was more serious than other girls, and for good reason.

"Does she speak of me?" he asked.

The table next to us filled up with a family: husband and young wife, and a row of little boys in sailor suits who clamored for ice cream. I was glad for the distraction—the rattling of chairs over the floor, the wails of the youngest child—because Signor Massimo had asked a question I should not answer.

"Can you tell me what brings you to Paris?" I asked. He understood immediately. His face shifted, like a door being closed. The pleading left his eyes; he sat up straighter.

"I am negotiating with clients about a painting I wish to sell. A very old painting. One of Sassetta's studies for *The Wolf of Gubbio*. Mrs. Haskett has shown interest but will not make up her mind about it."

"The St. Francis legend," I said, finishing my tea.

"You know it?" He showed surprise. Charmingly, only one eyebrow rose, not both, giving him a mischievous look.

"The story is in one of my little boy's schoolbooks, along with the fables of Aesop."

"Yes," he said with a tight smile. "That is very American, I suppose, placing the saints alongside the fable writers." There was disapproval, and I wondered if Beatrix had considered how the two might mix in a single household: European Catholicism and New England Protestantism. It did happen. Plenty of American girls had married Old World Catholics, but their fathers often required, by way of their bankbooks, that the children not be raised as papists. It made for an unhappy situation when one of them, as one must, breaks the marital agreement or the parental promise.

"Has the painting been in the family long?" I asked gently.

He laughed, but it was not a happy sound. "Very long. Since it was painted, and it is my father's favorite. But you see . . ."

"I understand." I reached over the table and touched his hand.

"Thank you. Between you and me, Mrs. Winters, I do not have my father's blessing in this venture. He wishes to raise funds in other ways."

I should have been more alert, paid better attention. But I thought Amerigo simply meant they might sell land instead of art.

"If I can help, please call on me," I said.

"You are kind. Perhaps when Miss Jones is in Paris you will allow me to take you and her, and her mother of course, out for a luncheon, or to the opera."

"Perhaps," I agreed.

We rose, and he took out his wallet to pay for our tea. He counted out the coins very carefully, and when he walked away, after that courteous little bow required of well-bred men, there seemed to be a hint of despair about him. He was, as my grandfather would have put it, between a rock and a hard place, needing to sell what should not be sold.

FIFTEEN

"Have you seen him?" was the first thing Beatrix said to me when she arrived in Paris. Her time in Scotland had not dulled that longing.

"I ran into him at the Louvre. He was standing in front of a Madonna that he thought looked like you." Cleaves took her hat and coat and I led her by the hand into the sitting room. Jenny was in there, curled up in a window seat with a book, and when she saw us, she closed her book and came to give Beatrix a hug.

"She's so grown up," Beatrix said when Jenny left us to chat alone. "Even taller than when I saw her last." I could tell she did not wish to discuss Amerigo, not yet. There are times when all we want to do is talk about the beloved, say his name over and over. And there are other times when even his name must be kept close, guarded like a secret.

"I think Jenny has a beau," I sighed. "The governess says she's awfully eager to walk in the same area of the park every day, where medical students from the Sorbonne gather. I can't imagine where or how she met him, but notes have been exchanged, or so I've been told. I think it is time for us to return to New York, but Mr. Winters . . ." My voice trailed off. Mr. Winters wished to stay in Paris.

"You look tired," Beatrix said. "I have been selfish. Tell me how you are." She sat by the window and looked out over the boulevard, at the passing nurses pushing perambulators, the young girls in their convent school uniforms of white collars and broad-brimmed hats, marching in a single row under the chestnut trees. Soon it would be autumn, my favorite time of year, and those leaves would drop, carpeting the ground with red and gold.

"There was a protest on that street yesterday," I said. "Laborers demanding higher wages, but Mr. Winters wouldn't tell me any more about it. We had to stay in all day. Other days, though, I have been busy. Museums, concerts, an evening spent watching a new contraption, a moving picture. It was about a gardener and a watering hose. Very amusing."

"Then we will continue the amusements," Beatrix said, leaning forward with excitement. "On Sunday I will take you, or you will take me, since you know your way around better, to Versailles, to see the play of the fountains and Nôtre's gardens and the orangery. They still have one of his tree-moving machines there, I believe. Imagine moving a fully grown tree."

"Is that all you plan for your Paris visit?" I asked. "More gardens?"

"No. It is not." She grew serious, her eyes half closing. There was a conflict in her face, a decision that had to be made that did not make sense to her. Gardeners like things to make sense. If you plant a peony, you expect a peony. You don't expect irises to grow in sand or apples to fall from pear trees. She had come to Europe to study gardens. She hadn't planned on meeting Amerigo, or anyone like him. Such things happened to other women. Not she, who had danced through several seasons without showing a preference for a single partner, who had learned how to end a conversation just as a gentleman was making it a little too earnest. And now apples were falling from pear trees.

"Amerigo sent a note to my hotel, asking to meet with me," she said, looking out the window again. "I said yes."

The next day Beatrix arrived for lunch, bringing her exhausted-looking mother with her. "The doorman is not looking well," Minnie said by way of greeting. There was accusation in her voice. "He needs bed rest."

"He has too many children to be a man of leisure," said Mr. Winters, who had appeared in the doorway. "Don't encourage him, Minnie. He is a malingerer and always looking for tips. How was the channel crossing?"

"Tolerable. How are you, Mr. Winters?" Minnie was always formal with my husband. There was a distinct lack of warmth between them, and the lack of warmth had turned to a chill since the announcement of Minnie's divorce proceedings. Mr. Winters didn't approve, and she knew he didn't approve.

When a woman marries according to the truth of her heart (which is not the same as wisdom, unfortunately), when she then raises an excellent daughter born from that marriage, and when the marriage fails and she turns to good works rather than dissipation or despair . . . that woman neither expects nor deserves disapproval.

Mr. Winters disapproved, of both her independence and the upcoming divorce.

He saw Minnie's situation only from a husband's point of view, the one that said a wife must endure all for the sake of the vows made, that a wife is a form of property to be managed and maintained. That a wife must always put her husband's happiness above her own, even when the form of that happiness is a mistress with unnaturally colored hair and a too-loud laugh when she is in public with him. His was a common enough viewpoint.

"We were not born to merely suffer," Minnie told me once. "And I will not. There is too much that needs to be done in this world for intelligent women to sit back and weep the days away. There is work to accomplish." She herself, in New York, worked in Bellevue, Presbyterian, and the Hospital for the Ruptured and Crippled, providing not just the usual crocheted shawls that society women provided at Christmas, but real labor, helping to train nurses in sanitation techniques and bringing in teachers for children with tuberculosis and poliomyelitis who were away from their studies for months at a time. "It gives them courage to know they have to work at their schooling, even if they are ill," she always insisted.

"You are looking well, Mr. Winters," Minnie said now, drawing off her gloves. "How was the racing season?"

He grimaced. Polite conversation is a dance around things

that must not be said aloud, but everyone in hearing distance already knows the silent conversation. How much did you wager this year? Minnie was saying. When will you stop?

"Pleasant," Mr. Winters answered. Mind your own business, he was saying.

"Well," I said. "What shall we do today? Are you tired, or would you like to walk?"

"Walk," said Beatrix.

"Rest," said Minnie at the same time. The very next day would be her first meeting with the lawyers. We decided she should stay in my apartments for the day and put her feet up, gather her thoughts, and make notes for the morrow. "Gird myself for battle, you mean," she said. "For battle it will be."

Mr. Winters gave them a tight little smile, the look of offended patrimony. "I, alas, cannot join you," he said, turned, and left us. It was difficult to love such a man. Understand, I did love him. There were afternoons alone with him, early evenings in bed when he played the lovelorn knight and all was as it should be between man and wife, or close enough.

Such times were scarce that season, but love, for me, was not a seasonal thing. There are things between a man and a woman that are not easily spoken of, but my passion for him was as strong as it had been when we first met. When we were alone, in bed, we were in complete harmony.

"Mr. Winters will be out most of the afternoon," I reassured Minnie. "If he does come back early, he will probably stay in his study."

"The rift has not healed, then." Minnie eyed me sadly.

"It will," I assured her. "In time."

Beatrix and I began her tour of Paris with a walk in the Bois de Boulogne, comparing the gardens there to the ones at the Villa Borghese in Rome.

"Still formal, but better maintained, more pleasant for walking," she decided. "The lines curve and meander. Straight lines are so like a military parade, aren't they?" She hitched up her skirts slightly so as not to sweep over a marble that had strayed into our path. Children shrieked on the lawn and one young little fellow, debonair in his sailor suit with a rim of jam around his mouth, came to fetch his toy. He looked up at Beatrix, a long way up, and smiled at her, sticking his thumb in his mouth.

We stopped like that, in the middle of an alley of plane trees, and waited for his nanny to fetch him safely back to the circle of children playing on the lawn. She was busy, though, with another child.

A breeze caught the leaves on the trees and shifted sun and shade together in a moving mosaic. There were those who thought the new painters—the Impressionists, they were called—were untalented charlatans, but I liked their work, how they made light and its workings on our eyes a character on the canvas as well as their ballerinas and water lilies.

"Athena no longer sucks her thumb," I said.

"You sound sad. Surely that is a good thing."

"She is my last baby, and soon she will be all grown up."

"Not that soon," Beatrix argued back. "There are mumps and multiplication tables and the first afternoon dance to be got through. It will be a while yet before she packs her trunks."

"You are making fun of me."

"Never." She slipped her arm through mine. "I am trying to cheer you."

"I thought I was to cheer you. You are seeing Paris under trying circumstances."

"There will always be trying circumstances. The point is to take a good look around, get your bearings. Soldier on." There was a softness in her smile that made me think Paris would not simply be a matter of soldiering on for her. Had they met yet, she and Amerigo?

The jam-mouthed child in the sailor suit picked up his wayward marble, made a clumsy little bow to Beatrix, and scuttled up the little hill to his friends.

"When I saw Signor Massimo at the Louvre last week, he said he would like to take us to the opera. Minnie as well," I told her as we walked on.

"Yes. He told me in his letter."

"I doubt he can afford a party of that type," I said. "He is here to sell a family heirloom."

"*The Wolf of Gubbio.* A pretty little painting. I'm sorry he has to part with it."

"You've seen it?"

"Yes."

So. There had been a second visit to the palazzo on the Via dei Serpenti. Perhaps a third or fourth?

"You know, Daisy, there was something in the painting, some expression in the wolf's face, that reminds me of Mrs. Haskett."

"She is here as well," I said. "In Paris."

Beatrix stopped walking. "Mrs. Haskett seems to be everywhere I go," she said. "It can't simply be bad luck."

"It seems to me she is everywhere Signor Massimo goes."

"We do seem to have made some awful threesome."

"Perhaps Edith can write a short story about it."

"Now you are making fun of me, Daisy. Let's have a look at the greenhouses," she said. "They are quite, quite large. Did you know that when the British were chasing Napoléon all over the continent and beyond, they camped here, in the *bois*? Thousands and thousands of trees were cut down to make tent poles and firewood. Most of the trees you see now have been planted in Mother's lifetime. They are doing quite well. Paris takes its gardens seriously."

We turned down a little gravel path, shadowy with large trees touching branches overhead.

"The original plan for the park called for all straight lines," Beatrix continued. "But the designer forgot to measure elevations and ended up with two streams at different altitudes. Haussmann decided to use curving paths rather than straight lines. Much more pleasant, don't you think? The problem with straight lines is that you see the ending of the path too quickly, so the journey is not worth the while. With a curving path, the garden keeps its mysteries and surprises. The ultimate ending stays hidden and therefore worth exploring."

She began to hum under her breath, something she rarely did. She often said that humming, rather than singing, felt like trying to run with your ankles hobbled together. But she hummed that day, and if I'm not mistaken, it was an Italian love song.

. . . .

When I saw Beatrix two days later at her hotel, she was no longer humming. She and Minnie had met with the lawyers and with Mr. Jones.

"It was a nightmare," she said. "The lawyers sneered at Mother. And Father . . . I can barely say the word . . . Father read a letter from Grandmother, blaming everything on poor Mother. It was, she said, even Mother's fault that he took a mistress. If she had been a proper wife, none of this would have happened."

Minnie and I had sometimes discussed this penchant for mothers to prefer sons above all others, but especially above daughters. My mother had done so, placing my brother, Raymond, on such a tall pedestal that I could not, in her opinion, even touch his shoes. Minnie's mother had done the same, and her mother before her, back through time. It was one of the many reasons Minnie had encouraged her daughter, her only child, to be independent, to be more than a woman standing obediently at a man's side.

"Nonsense," I said, though we knew many would agree. It was the price of divorce in those days, that irrational judgment and condemnation from people who really were themselves in no position to judge.

Meanwhile, there was the divorce to be gotten through.

"The letter was ridiculous." Minnie stood in the doorway of her room, immaculate in a white frock and white pearls, her dark hair brushed into a tidy chignon. "We all thought so, even if not everyone said it aloud. I'm only surprised that Freddie didn't bring his mistress to the meeting as well. But it is finished. The divorce has been settled."

She came to join us where we sat at a lace-covered table and poured herself a cup of coffee. If her hand trembled, Beatrix and I pretended not to notice. "Now," she said, "I get on with my life and my work. Wife no more." She lifted her chin. "Lovely words. I shouldn't speak like this in front of my daughter, but we have no secrets, have we, Beatrix?"

Minnie smiled and sat straighter than ever, but her eyes were bright and damp. Much as you might look forward to independence and ending painful relationships, that parting, almost as final as death, is a type of failure, a turning away from a dream you once had, a dream lovely enough to carry you into the future.

Frederic Jones had Paris and his mistress and his set of friends. Except for Beatrix, Minnie was alone.

Poor Beatrix, I thought. First love is difficult enough to navigate, but when one must choose between a lover and one's mother, between different continents . . . impossible.

After the meeting with the lawyers, Minnie stood even straighter, though there was a suggestion of wariness and pain in her face. "A lady does not give way," I heard her say to herself more than once. There were no more damp eyes, no trembling hands, yet the grief was visible.

"Not today, dear ones," she said when Beatrix and I tried to persuade her to attend some Parisian diversion with us, an afternoon concert or event at the Louvre, and she sounded so like a woman in mourning that I found myself tiptoeing in her presence, afraid of making a loud noise.

Beatrix and I made our rounds alone, inspecting, it felt to my feet, every tree and plant and parterre in the area. She no longer made notes or sketches, but sometimes brought her camera with her, relying on that and her memory to record anything that needed to be recorded. We spent long days at Versailles, walking the impossibly straight allées. "Much too grand and formal for the New World," Beatrix commented. At Parc des Buttes-Chaumont, Beatrix admired the way an old quarry had been planted as a pleasure garden, and at Parc Monceau we stood under a huge mass of exotic banana trees and pretended we could hear monkeys chattering.

On Beatrix's fifth day in Paris, we returned from our investigations to find Minnie at her desk, feet propped on a stool, pen in hand. She looked up and smiled at us.

"I've had a letter from Edith," she said, waving it at us. "She has begun writing a collection of short stories and wishes me to help her find publishers. I'm to be her agent. Beatrix, we will return home. I've made our bookings. I think we have both had enough of Europe."

Minnie was again engaged in active labor. That was all she asked of life. That, and her daughter's happiness.

Beatrix, though, was a study in conflict. Her face clearly reflected her great relief that her mother's good spirits had returned. But to leave Europe meant leaving Amerigo. How could she leave what had not yet truly begun?

We none of us had the answer to that question. Maybe she would not leave with Minnie. Was that the likely outcome?

The next day, I had arranged to take Beatrix and Minnie to meet Princess Esterhazy and to see the moving pictures of Louis Lumière. This time Mr. Winters chose not to accompany me—rather, us—saying that the carriage would be too crowded, he would crush our skirts, and it was better to let "the ladies" have the afternoon to themselves.

There were plenty of gentlemen at the princess's salon, however, and Beatrix caught many an eye. Oh, how she bloomed that season. When we took our chairs and the red velvet curtains were closed to dim the room, many heads turned in her direction, observing her under cover of the semidarkness.

The moving picture had just started with a strange crackle and whirring noise when there was a larger commotion in the foyer, a woman's voice, the giggle of young girls, apologies being offered, the soft, noncommittal voice of a servant. Princess Esterhazy rose and went out of the room and came back a moment later with Mrs. Haskett at her side, the three daughters trailing.

"So sorry," Mrs. Haskett apologized several times. "Mary couldn't find her new gloves." She waved a heavily ringed hand at the tallest of her girls.

Minnie, Beatrix, and I avoided looking at one another. The impossible woman had managed an invitation to the princess's salon. We knew then the depth of her ambition.

We watched the moving picture several times . . . it was only a few minutes in length, and quite funny, but it was also very thrilling to see that something once completely static, a photograph, now could move. It had time in its makeup as well as light and shadow.

"Like the difference between a silk flower that never changes and a rose that buds, blooms, then wilts and leaves a hip," Beatrix whispered to me. "How marvelous."

Over my shoulder I twice caught Mrs. Haskett staring at the back of Beatrix's head, and I knew Beatrix had a dangerous enemy in this woman. I was more certain than ever that she had schemed to have Amerigo for herself. She wouldn't have been the first wealthy woman to purchase a younger lover. So many things were for sale.

SIXTEEN

This part I must tell as a re-creation, based on many intimate conversations over the past years. Beatrix was and remains an intensely private person, yet even the person who is strongest in solitude occasionally needs to voice sentiments and emotions. That is especially true when speaking of one whom one has loved. Memories must be voiced now and then, or they begin to fade away, as pale as any ghost. It is a form of grave visitation, I suppose, another way to leave flowers or a memorial wreath, even if only imaginary, in salute to a lost one.

The Sunday afternoon of her reunion with Amerigo, Beatrix could neither sit nor stand still nor eat, knowing a decision would be made that day that would affect the rest of her life, and she still did not know what that decision should be.

She did not wish to leave her mother alone. Nor did she wish to give up Amerigo, to sacrifice him and their feelings for each other on the altar of custom and family duty. She was, after all, an American, an American from New York, where self-determination is one of the highest virtues.

The people of the New World were not accustomed to bowing meekly before the standards of the Old World.

Beatrix herself was constitutionally unsuitable for bowing and blind obedience to custom. She was not like her father or her uncle Teddy, who would have been happy to live just as their fathers and grandfathers and great-grandfathers had lived. Why change? such people seemed to say. The scheme of things as they are has worked well enough for me. Leave well enough alone!

And then there are the Minnies and Ediths of the world arguing back: No, the scheme works only for a few. What about the rest of us? Why must we be silent, in the shadows? A new century was coming. Beatrix cast her vote with the new century, not the old one.

So now you must imagine. An elegant, passionate twenty-three-year-old woman who is experiencing for the first time the kind of emotion that requires one to defy sense and tradition. And believe this, Beatrix was passionate. She knew how to dress, how to serve a tea and guide a dinnertime conversation into safe lanes, avoiding the quicksand of religion, politics, and money. She attended church and wore gloves and hats and sat a horse perfectly. But none of those qualities interfered with her natural disposition, which was a wonder with the world and all its pleasures, a determination to be fully in the world. To love.

This passionate young woman, as new to love as a just-fledged bird is to the sky, sits alone on a café chair in the Bois de Boulogne, waiting. The chair is strangely identical to the one on which she sat in the Borghese gardens, and just as in the Borghese gardens, there is a weed taunting her from the middle of the gravel path.

After months of travel and touring, she has learned to stare down that weed, hands folded calmly in her lap. For this, too, she must wait, to be at home in her own garden, where she is master and keeper and worker, all in one, and no one can eye her askance when she takes off her gloves and plunges her bare hands into the soil to tug away what is not wanted.

A group of children with their nurse pass by. Some women on horseback, their habits spread like blankets over the glistening chestnut flanks of their horses. A balloon seller, tipping his hat and tugging at the confetti-tailed strings of his wares. A quartet of young people, arm in arm, laughing, showing off their stylish summer clothes, followed by an elderly couple, walking so closely together, side by side, they seem a single entity.

The last, Beatrix eyes with some envy. The number of times she has seen a married couple so obviously content with each other can be counted on her fingers and toes. Perhaps simply her fingers.

She wonders if she will be coupled, and if that coupling will last. She thinks it strange to be sitting in a Parisian park on a late-summer day, thinking coolly about couples lasting or not, as she waits for the man she so patently loves. It is as if she is two people, not one. This happens sometimes in plants, especially in hybrid trees and shrubs. Something will stir underground; perhaps lightning runs through the soil or there is too much or not enough sun. The hybrid becomes aware of itself and the fact that it has been manipulated. It snakes up through the ground a new shoot that refuses to follow the rules bred into the parent plant; it changes color or shape and the plant has, in effect, twinned itself.

If she were rude enough to take the little pocket mirror out of her purse, she wonders if she would see two reflections, not one, the passionate girl and the coolheaded one.

He's late.

Another couple, one she recognizes though she can't remember their names, strolls by. They nod at her but do not stop to chat. As they pass, she hears that one word, "divorced."

Beatrix and Minnie understand there will be a required period of punishment. And then, if all goes well, they will eventually be welcomed once again, not in all parlors, not at all events, but at enough of them that they will not suffer permanent or complete exclusion. When a woman takes her destiny into her own hands, as Minnie has done, there is a price to be paid. But because Minnie is of good family, the price will not be more unbearable than the marriage itself had become. There is some justice in that, though Beatrix, who yearns for the new century, wonders why there need be a price at all.

In the garden, when you make a mistake, you dig it up and throw it on the compost pile. Just like that.

Still, he does not arrive.

Her chest begins to ache with a warmth that is not unpleasant yet makes her eyes itch, as if tears were starting. She wants to jump up and leave, quickly, pretend this afternoon did not happen, but she knows she cannot. She is here, waiting, and she will wait.

Twenty minutes past the agreed-upon time, he appears, walking so quickly his coattails flap as if in a wind. His hat is askew, his face flushed. He has dropped a glove somewhere on his path and clutches the other so tightly the tawny kid leather has creased itself into pleats.

"Beatrix." He doesn't bow or tip his hat. Instead he throws his arms around her and kisses her, on the mouth, a long kiss that dances her head in sensual circles, a waltzing kiss that leaves her dizzy.

She should say no. Not here.

She doesn't. She kisses him back, putting her arms around him as well.

People walk wide circles around them. Some pause and stare and chuckle. A woman harrumphs with disapproval, but the kiss goes on, ending only when both of them are panting for air.

"Come away with me," Amerigo says. "Now. Leave a note for your mother, take an overnight valise, and come away with me. It is the only way."

She knows what he is saying. This is not an improper proposal but a request that she become his wife, now and without family approval.

Her mouth opens to say yes. But the word won't come. She lets herself drown in his gaze, but something holds her back from giving him that one simple word. She wants this more than anything, this vision of a quick flight followed by a lifetime together. Yet she cannot speak that word.

Instead, she closes her eyes and leans even closer to him. She wants another kiss, like the first one, his mouth on hers, warm and moist, sending shooting stars into her veins.

"Maybe tomorrow," he agrees, when they are sitting again on the bench, calm, admiring the fine day like any of the other hundreds of couples strolling and talking in the park.

The moment has passed.

"Not tomorrow," she says. So calm, so cool, scheduling her elopement as well as possible around already made plans. "I must prepare her. I will not simply disappear."

"You will tell her?"

Beatrix has never, before this tour of Europe, before Massimo, kept anything from her mother. Their conversations have been almost sisterly, open and intimate and trusting.

"Yes. I must. And are you telling your father?"

"I cannot."

She thinks about this for a moment and all it implies. The space between them, those two or three inches of open air required by good manners in public places, now feels like a mile of distance. The sun blazes down, yet Beatrix shivers. A price must always be paid. What would hers be? "All the more reason, then, to tell Mother. We must have someone on our side," she tells him.

"And she will be?"

"She wishes my happiness. And I think you are it. Amerigo." She takes off her glove and reaches for his hand. Sometimes, at the Bar Harbor garden, she has been able to put a leaf between her palms, close her eyes, and feel the living vibrations of the plant, judge its vigor and determination to thrive. She places Amerigo's hand between her two palms and closes her eyes. She feels the blood flowing through his veins, the warmth of his living self, the mystical combination of flesh and spirit in the way his hand rests quietly between hers. Acceptance.

What does it mean? Is he accepting all he has required her to accept? To live among strangers, to brave the disapproval of those whose approval her safety and happiness most depend upon. Or is his a more passive acceptance, more responsive to commands than to choices?

A garden path is most interesting when one cannot see the end of it but must walk through the twists and turns and make the discovery, footstep by footstep.

The next day, Beatrix and Minnie were resting in their rooms when a page boy brought them an envelope on a silver-plated salver.

Minnie looked at it with dread. "I am quite tired of unexpected notes," she said. "Let's tear it up without reading it. What if it is from your father? What if he wants another meeting for some reason or other?"

"It's not Father or the lawyer." Nor Amerigo, Beatrix thought. "I believe it is from Mrs. Haskett."

"Ignore it." Minnie had a presentiment.

"Can we do that?"

"I can," Minnie said, tearing the envelope and its single interior page into long strips and crumpling them.

They sat for a while, drinking tea, breaking their morning roll into crumbs, but neither of them eating.

"He has asked me to go away with him," Beatrix said. "An elopement."

Minnie looked at her daughter, at her radiant face, feeling that tug at her heart that mothers feel, wanting to love and protect, yet knowing they must set their child free, all at the same time.

"I think I expected this," was her response. "What was your answer?"

"I told him he must meet with you first, that we needed your approval and goodwill."

"You know that I wish only what brings you joy and fulfillment." What else could a loving mother say? She had not forced Beatrix to marry when she came of age, as most mothers did. She certainly would not now require her daughter to stay unmarried. They sat in an even longer silence as mother and daughter adjusted to the new reality, the old dreams on the verge of being abandoned, all sureness evaporated as surely as the sun dried up the dew in the hotel garden.

"Does he have his father's approval?" Minnie asked, realizing they must now discuss practical matters.

"I think not."

She is the daughter of a divorced woman, Minnie thought. This is terrible, terrible timing. If only they had met a year or even six months earlier. If he were Protestant American rather than Catholic Italian, they might have had a chance. Now there would be no approval from the father; they would begin with a black mark against them.

"You could live half the year in New York and Maine, and the other half in Rome," Minnie said. Both of them, in their thoughts, had moved on to the next difficulty.

"That would give me only half a year for my work, wouldn't it? Even if Europe were ready for a female landscape designer, my languages aren't good enough for me to be able to discuss plans with clients." Beatrix put down her teacup and leaned her chin into her hands, looking young and lost.

"Do you love him enough to risk that?"

"Yes."

"Then all other plans must start from there. You will work it out. I have faith in you." But Minnie was heartsore, thinking that from now on her daughter would be lost to her for much of the year. Ceres herself could not have been sadder, thinking of Persephone, gone from her to the other world. But it must be borne.

Amerigo, realizing that the only way to win Beatrix was to also win Minnie, asked to meet with them, and Minnie agreed. I saw him the day before, when I was walking in the park with my little girls, and he looked like a man about to jump from a ledge.

"Have you slept?" I asked, worried about the shadows around his eyes, the feverish quality of his complexion.

"Not much," he said. "I see Beatrix tomorrow. And her mother."

"Ah." What else could be said? Wish him luck? Great matters were at stake.

On Thursday, Beatrix and Minnie stayed in their hotel, waiting for him, as arranged. The best tea service had been sent up, flowers put in vases, lamps lit since it was a cloudy and dark day. Beatrix was nervous about so many things. What if he was late, as he had been that day in the park? Minnie admired punctuality. What if he behaved too informally or, worse, too stiffly? It was imperative that Minnie like him, approve of him.

Minnie was exhausted and worried. She looked often at Beatrix, opened her mouth to say something, but then closed it again upon a confused and anxious silence.

At a quarter to three someone knocked at the door and was admitted. Early? thought Beatrix, confused. Why has he come early?

But it wasn't Amerigo. Their maid ushered in Mrs. Haskett.

Beatrix and Minnie shared the same thought: something was about to be stolen away from them. A perilous journey had led them to this one single moment, and there would be no turning away from it.

Minnie tried, though, for her daughter's sake. "I can't ask you to stay," she said, rising and politely offering her hand. "We have an engagement."

"You will want to hear what I have to tell you," Mrs. Haskett insisted. Uninvited, she took a chair by the window so that she was backlit. A dim, fuzzy light seemed to emanate from her so that she seemed otherworldly, more ghostly than angelic. Her hat had two bows on it and they stuck up like monstrous ears.

Beatrix sat, too. As soon as she had seen Mrs. Haskett at the door, she had had a presentiment of something important, something vital being stolen away from her. The tea tray sat on the little table in front of the settee where Beatrix sat. Beatrix stared at the teapot but did not pour.

"He is already engaged," Mrs. Haskett said. "May I?" She didn't wait for a yes; she reached for the pot and poured herself a cup. "To the Princess di Cosimo. A pretty young thing. Wealthy family, of course."

Minnie, who had been standing in the doorway, hoping Mrs. Haskett would leave, sat down. She did not, could not, look at Beatrix.

What could they say? Any answer they gave would allow Mrs. Haskett the knowledge that Beatrix had been lied to, by omission if nothing else. Or they themselves could lie, say they already knew (and neither of them had doubted it as soon as the words had been spoken; they believed the woman though they couldn't trust her motives), but if they pretended they already knew, why would Beatrix have allowed herself to be seen with him? They were well and truly trapped.

Beatrix was heartbroken. He had let her believe he was free to give his heart, but he had not been. He had involved her in a triangle, a bitter contest, and she hadn't even known. He had deceived her. She wanted to weep, to hide her face with her hands and let the tears stream through her fingers. But she could not, not with Mrs. Haskett sitting there, watching so closely.

Minnie passed Mrs. Haskett the plate of sandwiches and petit fours. Only their visitor ate and drank.

"Everyone seems to have known of the engagement but you," Mrs. Haskett said. "An arranged match, of course."

"Are you enjoying your stay in Paris?" Minnie asked. "I've heard there is a wonderful exhibit of floral paintings at . . ." She paused, unable to remember the name of the gallery. But they could not, they must not, have this conversation. They must go back in time, weeks back, months back, to the Borghese gardens, and Beatrix does not leave her chair, does not go for a walk alone, does not meet this man. But it has happened.

"I know the one you mean. Everyone is talking of it. Courvier. He's showing Monet's work," Mrs. Haskett said. "Atrocious."

Beatrix sat, straight-backed, smiling, revealing nothing of the interior storm that had uprooted trees, flooded streams, washed away rose beds and destroyed the garden of her trust. Calmly, she discussed Monet's paintings, the wonderful colors, so like a garden when seen through a glowing dawn light. Minnie was never prouder of her daughter than she was that afternoon.

Amerigo arrived promptly at three and was shown in by the same maid that had admitted Mrs. Haskett. Like all young men in love, he required his eyes to find the beloved first in that room, and to be blind to all else. So it was without awareness of what had already occurred that he went to Beatrix, took her hands, and kissed them.

"My darling," he said, still blind to that awful figure seated in the chair by the window.

Minnie stood. Her voice was like ice. "We have not been introduced." She recognized him as the young man who had waltzed her daughter away from her at Mrs. Haskett's Berlin soiree and saw with some regret that, had he arrived before Mrs. Haskett, before that terrible announcement, she would have liked him, would have been prepared to welcome him. Now she saw only the man who had harmed, perhaps broken, her daughter.

In turning to face Minnie, Amerigo saw the other visitor. His face became ashen; the light in his eyes dimmed.

"I see," he said, and his voice might have been announcing a death or a bankruptcy.

"Good day," said Mrs. Haskett, rising. "I will leave you three to your private conversation." She was smiling.

"We were affianced when we were still children. Neither of us wishes the marriage to go through. She, too, loves someone else. Yet our families insist. I had hoped to pay our debts by selling art, and in that way free myself from this family burden. Mrs. Haskett made offers. Never high enough, never enough that my father would agree to them."

Amerigo refused the chair that Minnie had offered him. Manners above all else, she had been taught. This man has just broken your daughter's heart, but you must offer him a chair or, the alternative, ask him to leave, immediately, and never come back. That she could not do. The look on Beatrix's face would not allow that particular finality. An explanation was needed.

So Amerigo paced, back and forth, back and forth, between the seated girl and her mother, trying to explain. He ran his shaking hand through his hair, ruffling away the fierce brushing that had tamed thick black curls. He tugged at his high collar, loosening it so that his throat and the vein that corded his neck showed. He resembled, Beatrix thought, the David who had slain

Goliath in the Caravaggio he and she had stood before just a few months before . . . beautiful, and a murderer.

What explanation could argue away the problem he had created, being engaged to one woman and offering elopement to another?

"What more is there to say?" Amerigo asked. "I have broken your heart, and mine as well. Yet if I had been more open, would you have consented to see me? I would have been a good husband. A loyal husband. And so I took the only chance I saw."

"That you could marry Beatrix before she found out. The marriage would have been based on a lie," Minnie accused.

"I see that now," Amerigo said. Finally he sat, and it was an admission of defeat.

Beatrix, who had been staring out the window and looking at him in quick sideways glances—it was the only way she could control herself—reached over and took his hand.

"I do understand," she said softly.

"Do you?" There was a note of hope in his voice.

"Yes. But you must understand, we can never meet again."

"If you had gone away with me that day . . ."

"It still would have come to this moment, except then we would be trapped forever in the dishonesty. Don't you see, Amerigo? My mother has divorced. Your father would never approve. And you have humiliated your fiancée and lied to me. There is no future for us, unless we wish to be alone, completely alone, moving from hotel to hotel seeking the company of other outcasts. Could you live like that? No. I thought not. Neither could I."

When Amerigo left a few minutes later, Beatrix felt the way a garden appears after it has been destroyed by storm and flood. She went to her room without another word to her mother, closed the door, and fell to her knees.

Minnie, on the other side of that door, heard the sobbing and knew she must let it run its course.

A Garden for Second Chances

A garden in which one can reconsider past decisions must be more than a garden in which one feels regret. If simple regret is to be the theme, then a bed of rue will do nicely. Rue is a plant of insignificant flowers, of loose form unless grown in strong sun, and with no fragrance. But a single plant does not constitute a garden, any more than a single decision constitutes a lifetime.

No. A garden of second chances must contain fragrant plants and strong colors interspersed among shrubbery. Hyacinth in the spring, of course, and roses, roses, and more roses in early summer, especially Rosa moschata. *This climbing rose grows so vigorously it can be fiercely pruned back yet will still, in the following season, cover an entire wall with blooms.*

In back of the roses, like a curtain in a theater, a thick planting of tall false indigo, and to the side of the false indigo, a bed of Cheiranthus cheiri, *English wallflower, which if sown in summer does not bloom until its second season.*

The flower beds should be edged with sweet alyssum, and the alyssum must be cut back every few weeks to keep it blooming till frost, just as hope occasionally has to be trimmed back to allow the unknown to flourish. Other flowers should include pansies for thought, heart's ease for regret, bleeding heart for pain, and autumn-blooming crocus to represent that just when we think all is lost . . . it is not. New fresh blooms arise when and where we least expect them.

The bordering hedge, representing the cutting off of yesterday from today, should not be excessively neat; rather than trimmed, it should be plucked, leaving a lacy and uneven edge.

The lines of a garden for second chances can be straighter and more formal than the lines for a garden of first meetings. This is, after all, a garden in which one looks over the shoulder as well as straight ahead. Garden structures should include a bench nestling in a small glade of ferns, where one can sit and reconsider. The ferns should be Osmunda claytoniana, known more familiarly as the interrupted fern.

In the center of this more formal garden there should be a sundial to remind us of time and its passing.

SEVENTEEN

"Poor, poor girl," said Mrs. Avery. "Oh, poor thing. To have to endure such heartbreak . . ." In the early-evening light her face was as white as the moon that hadn't yet risen. She looked as if she would weep.

"Young men often do not speak plainly enough," said Mr. Hardy. "Still, to not tell her of a previous attachment was very, very wrong."

"But don't you see? He was in love, and people in love often do wrong things. I myself . . ." I stopped in time. I had never told another soul, not even Beatrix, how far along that attachment with Giovanelli had gotten when I was still trying to convince myself I was in love with him and not Mr. Winters.

Mrs. Ballinger did not sit with us that evening after dinner. I was glad of that, since I thought that stiff-backed, righteous woman's judgment of Beatrix and Amerigo would be less than generous. It was just Walter and Mrs. Avery and myself, and a friendly threesome we made of it, though we were almost strangers. For two years, other than the time I spent campaigning and marching for women's suffrage, other than a few parties for my young grandchildren, I had been alone.

One year for formal mourning. A second year if you actually loved your husband. That had been my mother's formula when my father died. She had stayed in formal mourning for three years.

"It did not end there," I said. "Neither the love, nor the complications. When Minnie went to the door the next morning, determined that she and Beatrix would book passage home that same day, she found that Mrs. Haskett had left a note on the little table, leaning up against the vases of roses the hotel had sent up the day before, sent by Mr. James to Minnie.

"'When we are in residence in New York, this autumn, I would be so pleased to visit you,' she had written. 'Of course, when I return I will be speaking with a journalist from "Table Topics." They are always so eager to print news of Americans traveling abroad.'

"It was a threat, you see. Blackmail. Invitations into Minnie's inner circle would be the price for not talking of Beatrix's affair with Amerigo."

"Dastardly!" said Walter.

Such a sweet and old-fashioned word!

"Exactly," I said. "Thank you, Walter. She did have those three daughters to marry off. Enough, perhaps, to make any woman desperate. And Minnie, practical and good-hearted woman that she was, knew she would help Beatrix, and Mrs. Haskett, even though she had asked for help in such a nasty way.

"When they were back in New York that winter, Minnie

invited the woman to a few salons, and soon other people were inviting her as well. 'A friend of Minnie's,' they would say. Perhaps it was blackmail, but it was practiced commonly enough in those days, when a single misstep could ruin a woman forever. Do you know, one of Mrs. Haskett's daughters eventually married an English lord? Imagine. All because Minnie invited her to her salon a few times, and then Henry James agreed to have tea with her as well."

"Never had much regard for the so-called nobility," said Mr. Hardy. "By the way, has anyone heard anything yet about the suffrage vote in Tennessee?" He gave me a teasing glance, letting his eyes rest on my suffrage rosette.

"No politics. Not tonight, Mr. Hardy, if you don't mind," declared Mrs. Avery, who seemed to be growing less timid. "I'd like to hear the completion of this story. You can't leave it there, Daisy. Broken hearts must be attended to. It is, I suppose, something like that story you began with, about the specter bridegroom. Her Italian lover wasn't a specter, but he did disappear, I assume?"

The piano player inside temporarily ceased his tinkling repertoire of Irving Berlin tunes. He seemed to have a very limited musical education, and two nights in a row of Berlin was making me restless.

"Disappear is the very word," I said.

So much in life disappears. That's why, when we pass an old farmhouse where ancient peonies and daylilies still bloom among the weedy ruins, we are so touched by their beauty. Sometimes the most fragile things are all that survive.

Beatrix's choice to become a designer of gardeners was about creating beauty that outlasts the seasons—and the years. Walk a garden path and you walk in a kind of eternity where love is always a possibility.

Nine years later, in the autumn of 1904, Henry James came to visit Edith Wharton at her new home, the Mount. Edith, as my interpretation of her stay in Rome years before had indicated, had previously been impatient and unhappy with domestic duty. Acquiring land right there, in the Berkshire hills, and designing and building her own home on that lovely land, elevated her attitude. She was mistress of all she surveyed, from lake view to china cabinet.

It wasn't domesticity that had caused Edith's health problems years earlier, but that kind of social Newport domesticity that requires a woman to spend her waking hours visiting people one does not particularly like and, in turn, being visited by them.

"All that driving up and down Bellevue Avenue, just to show off new frocks," I had heard her comment once to Minnie. "Can you think of a worse waste of an afternoon?"

Edith and Teddy were still married in 1904, but Teddy had less presence in her life. It was as if he were becoming a ghost, something seen on occasion, a presence one knew was there but didn't particularly bother with. Edith's "scribblings" had, by then, turned into a successful literary career, earning both acclaim and royalties. Teddy had some of his own money, but he had begun to creep around his wife's house in a disconcerting way, sometimes mumbling to himself.

"Teddy is in charge of the wines," Edith announced at each dinner, and because the wines were excellent, Teddy would smile and puff up a little, and then just as quickly deflate once actual conversation started, since the talk was literary and Teddy was not.

He was still a handsome man, still admired by his friends at least for his charm, dwindling though it was. All I will say of Edith is that as soon as she acquired her own bedroom down the hall from Teddy's, her nervous depression lifted considerably.

Beatrix, who had not married, had carefully, diligently built her career as a landscape gardener. When she returned from the European tour, she set up an office in her mother's New York brownstone and let it be known that she was open for commissions. Many people were skeptical: a female landscaper? Thanks to friends and connections, and then word of her skill and creativity, commissions trickled in: she drained swamp for cultivation, tamed forty acres of wild forest into a pleasant grove, and laid out a small cemetery. ("Full of light and attractive views," she wrote to me. "Remember those terrible catacombs in Rome?")

Three years after opening her design office, Beatrix was so well known and well thought of that she was chosen as a member of the new American Society of Landscape Architects—the only woman so honored. "Earth-shaker!" Mr. James called her in his letters.

Beatrix was totally absorbed by her chosen work. I rarely saw her without a reference book or a trowel or a sketching pad in her hands. She forged ahead, determined, and only once did she falter, and that just for a day. She and Mr. Sargent quarreled.

She had come back from her European tour full of ideas

about garden design. When she had returned to visit the Sargents at Holm Lea, she had talked enthusiastically about how American gardens, while acknowledging the debt to the past, to those formal European gardens, should also look forward to the future and pay due respect for place. New York is not Rome, she said. Boston is not Versailles, so our gardens should not mimic those.

Mr. Sargent had nodded and absentmindedly poked at the fire in the hearth. Who would not agree with such an argument? He had done worse than disagree, though. He had grown bored. "My dear," he had said, a little too softly, putting his feet up on the fender. "Are you ignoring your research and your studies in botany? There is more to gardens than prettiness."

The rebuke stunned her, and she saw that she and her mentor had come to an intellectual parting of the ways, saw that men and women often approach the same problem from different angles.

"Of course I will continue my studies and research," she said quietly, watching embers like fireflies dance over the flames. "And I will design gardens that others may find pretty."

Mr. Sargent and Beatrix remained the best of friends and colleagues, and he did all he could to aid her career, but after that bored comment from her teacher, Beatrix realized she was breaking ground in many ways: she had entered a career dominated by men, and she had chosen a path different from her mentor's.

"Daisy," she wrote to me after the tour, "I sometimes feel like I am the only one of my species, something rare and isolated. A specimen plant, unclassified and stared at in curiosity. Oh, dear one, tear up this letter when you have finished. Throw it into the hearth and turn it to ashes. I am close to complaint, close to loneliness. And you know that I will not give in or give way. Onward."

She gave an interview to the New York *Sun*, defying the convention that a lady have her name in the newspaper for only three occasions: birth, marriage, and death. In the interview she was described as "comely" and "majestic," and I think that helped her career, but it also made her even more of a curiosity to some.

Completely disappeared from her life was Amerigo Massimo. He had written twice to Beatrix after she sailed back to New York. The first was an apology, signed with "all my heart, all my regret, to my darling Beatrix." I don't know if Beatrix wrote back. She received a second letter, a year after her arrival home, saying that he had married his princess and both families rejoiced at the match. He left it at that. No complaints, no hints of bitterness or anger at the forced arrangement. He was, after all was said and done, a gentleman, and I imagine he did all he could to make his little princess happy, once the inevitable had arrived.

There were no more letters after that, and if Beatrix thought of him, longed for him, she gave no sign of it. She made almost yearly trips to Europe with Minnie, to continue her studies and explorations, but when in Rome she avoided certain places and explored only gardens and villas she hadn't visited before.

What was her state of mind? Cheerful, usually. She had her work, and a good job she was making of it. She had independence and had found her way in the world, had swum against the current and landed on a pleasant shore. If she was lonely, she gave no sign of it.

Not till that autumn of 1904.

It was a wonderful season of mild days, chilly nights, and nature's finest colors as far as the eye could see, and at the Mount one could see very far. Edith had had a busy summer, writing every morning, working with various village committees, and motoring through the New England countryside in a little auto. When that beautiful autumn arrived, she had even more cause to rejoice, because it brought friends: Henry James, Howard Sturgis, Walter Berry, Minnie, Beatrix, and myself. Few things made Edith happier than a house full of friends who knew to leave her alone to write in the morning, but in the afternoon accompanied her on motor trips through the countryside.

Henry, who had a secretary (he had permanent cramping of his right hand by then and dictated his work), housekeeper, maid, and little else, pretended not to be slightly awed by the staff Edith had hired for the Mount: her beloved housekeeper, Gross, shared the running of the house with Arthur White. There were maids, footmen, a cook, and kitchen boys. The gardener, Reynolds, had a small army of male assistants, and there was a chauffeur with the incongruous name of Cook. There was Anna Balmain, who had once worked in Minnie's household, who now worked for Edith, as her secretary.

I caught Henry sometimes running a fingertip over the always dustless furniture, sighing over the exquisite meals, stroking the collar of a freshly pressed shirt, and there on his face, plain to see, was the sixth deadly sin, envy.

Edith was assisted by one other whom Henry envied above all else: her sister-in-law, Minnie, was acting as her agent, and doing that with as much efficiency as she completed all her other work. Minnie had, by then, published a book of her own, *European Travel for Women*, a travel guide of useful information that Murray and Baedeker hadn't thought to include: how to tip in London, the correct teatime in Paris, how much it costs to rent a steamer chair during the crossing. Because of her many literary contacts, she was well positioned to help Edith in her own career. Because of her divorce, she appreciated the extra income Edith paid her.

Divorce hadn't damaged Minnie: her character was too strong, her virtuous reputation too stainless. It helped that she had powerful friends, Henry James and Theodore Roosevelt among them. The divorce had, though, brought changes. Poverty was far, far away, but the velvet drawing room curtains in the brownstone were not replaced even though they were faded; there were fewer expensive dinner parties and more informal lunches; she dressed as beautifully as she ever had but wore her gowns more seasons than others might have agreed to do.

Those small changes did not worry her. Minnie walked through life with the confidence of one who makes all her own decisions. Others might say, "I'll have to speak with Tom or Lawrence to see if we can come," or, "No, I can't come; my husband doesn't enjoy music," but Minnie could give a simple yes or no, depending on her own preferences. She answered to no one and if she occasionally remembered that demeaning afternoon in the lawyer's office in Paris, that castigating letter of accusation from her mother-in-law, she did not mention it.

I was studying Minnie, to see how it was done. Mr. Winters

and I had separated. Not officially, of course; there were no announcements. India and Athena were still at home and a few years short of marriage age, so we had to keep up appearances for their sake. But Mr. Winters spent more and more nights at his club, and sometimes entire weeks went by when I didn't see him at all.

My life and house felt empty without him. I had hoped that a formal ultimatum from my lips would produce the desired result: me or the gambling. Oh, how I had posed in front of the hearth, hand to heart, other hand to forehead, just like an illustration in *Harper's* called *The Gambler's Wife*. He had smiled and put his arms around me and assured me, again, it was just a run of bad luck and his luck was bound to change. But neither luck nor attitude changed. Thank God Mr. Cadwalader had encouraged me to put the New York house in my name.

That autumn of my visit to the Mount, Clara, already married and expecting her first child, was in New York, in her own home; the younger girls had gone to visit friends in Newport. Gil Jr. and his wife were busy doing up a brownstone on Madison Avenue, Robert was working in a law office in Boston, Jenny was carrying her second child, and Mr. Winters was avoiding me in order to avoid any conversation about finances. I had been left to stew in my own bitter regrets, and it did not agree with me.

"Lenox," Minnie had said, the day she found me weeping in my dining room, alone, into a bowl of soup. "It is time to visit Edith."

Beatrix took a week off from work to make the trip, to help Edith with her gardens. Beatrix had been working too hard.

There were shadows around her eyes and she was thin, so she let her mother coax her into taking a small vacation.

But when you are ambitious and essentially healthy, and passionate about your work, there really is no such thing as a vacation.

Every morning Beatrix walked through the grounds of the Mount with the head gardener, Reynolds, pointing out which bushes should be trimmed, where spring bulbs would be best placed. Their meetings were often somewhat loud, since Beatrix had grown from girl to woman, and a woman with very strong views at that.

She was not shy in criticizing some of Edith's ideas for her gardens. Edith wanted an Old World Italian feel to the grounds, with long walkways and closely trimmed hedges; Beatrix urged her to consider the more natural English style that Gertrude Jekyll was still perfecting and that Beatrix herself preferred.

"Suit the plant to the place," she repeated often, "and the garden to its locale. Plant an American garden, Aunt Edith, not an imitation Italian garden." Mrs. Wharton would nod, tilt her head slightly to one side, and then continue sketching straight-lined paths and formal parterres. They quarreled over the gardens, and Beatrix did not visit her aunt often at the Mount after that autumn. The disagreement over the gardens wasn't the only reason she avoided the place.

"It reminds me of Rome," she said. "Why should a good American garden remind one of Rome?"

I often went with Beatrix on her walks in Lenox, and one day, when we had ventured into a woodsy area with a gravel path strewn with gold leaves and huge oaks towering overhead, she stopped to look at a seedling that had sprouted between two rocks. An acorn had wedged there and sent up a four-inch stem with two sickly pale leaves.

She peered hard at this little plant, and a look of great pity came over her face.

"Poor thing," she sighed. "It will not thrive. There isn't enough soil or light." She bent over and pulled it from its cradle between the rocks.

This seemed ruthless to me. But, of course, she was right. Leave an oak to grow in that place and it would either die quickly or grow large enough to do harm when its roots pulled loose from the gravely hillside.

When she plucked that sapling I understood what had happened to her in Italy. Despite her passion for Amerigo, she had not been able to stay there, had not eloped with him that afternoon he asked her to. She had called it a "hesitation," but it had been a resistance, a foreknowledge of disaster to come if she tried to plant her very American sensibilities into an Italian setting. Some women thrive in foreign situations. Beatrix would not have. So she had pulled herself free of it, despite the pain. Mrs. Haskett's cruel visit and gossip about Amerigo's engagement to another woman had been the deciding factor, not the initial one.

"Walk on, Daisy," Beatrix said, giving the uprooted sapling a little caress before she tossed it to the ground. There is life, and there is death, and in between we try to make the best of it, her expression said.

Mr. James, who was that year visiting the land of his birth

for the first time in two decades, was enamored of Edith's new home, and of the splendid autumn weather, and he was pleased to get to know his fellow bachelor Walter Berry.

Before Edith had married Teddy Wharton, she had been in love with Walter, and she had married Teddy when she realized Walter would not have her.

She never knew why their friendship had not progressed down the path it seemed to want to take but was perceptive enough to realize that it was not entirely her fault. Walter Berry, tall, handsome, aristocratic, and intelligent, had expensive tastes and a penchant for chorus girls. Such men do not do a favor to the women they marry, and he was honest enough to know that and to act upon the knowledge by not acting. He and Edith began as friends and remained friends, with no hint of flirtation in the relationship. Walter flirted only when and where he could make a hasty exit with no backward glance; with friends he was true and stable.

Howard Sturgis was also unwed, but unlike Walter he had a nature more feminine than masculine, and often more childlike than even feminine. When Howard came into a room, that room took on the aura of a child's birthday party, full of merriment and pleasure.

And so our days passed at the Mount, with card parties, walks, drives through the countryside, vivid discussions about literature and plants. I was often distracted from my problems with Mr. Winters, but they nagged at me like an unremitting pain. I had, years before, taken a step in the direction of self-determination by requiring that the New York home be put in my name. Now I was wondering what it actually meant to be a wife, if marriage was necessary, and if necessary, what a woman should be willing to endure. There were the children, of course, and any sacrifice was worth their well-being; there had been the splendid intimacy with Gilbert, the social status of being wife to a man with an old family name. But when children were grown and gone, intimacy turned to dust, and the name was not gilded enough to pay debts—what was left? I had no answer.

The evenings at the Mount had a different atmosphere from the pleasant days. Sunset brings out doubts and regrets, and autumn does as well; the days may remind us of summer and sunshine, but the evenings look ahead to cold and snow and isolation. Tensions rise; old fears come to the surface; anxieties about the future cloud conversations. Autumn challenges your expectations, makes you aware of your limits. In the evenings our laughter was briefer, with longer moments between. We would all of us, that week, feel a cage of loneliness separate each from the others, once the sun went down.

"Read to us, please, Henry," Minnie said after dinner one night when we sat before the blazing hearth. A wind whispered around the house and there were occasional bangs and taps that made us jumpy.

Edith sat quietly, stroking the dog in her lap, thinking. Minnie was knitting tiny baby caps to donate to one of the homes for unwed mothers in New York. Beatrix was thumbing through plant catalogues, planning a new spring border for Edith. I listlessly shuffled and reshuffled a deck of cards and laid out hands of patience on the side table.

"*The Turn of the Screw*. Again?" Henry asked with a little sigh, pretending to be a little irritated though we all knew he was flattered.

"A perfect choice," handsome Walter Berry agreed, and Henry puffed up a little.

Mr. James was a great literary success, of course, but his earnings were modest. I had overheard Edith complaining to him that her anticipated royalties from *The House of Mirth* would barely cover the cost of the new automobile she had purchased. Mr. James had replied that his earnings that year would barely cover the old wheelbarrow he needed to paint.

"I'll get the copy from the library," Minnie said, rising.

"No. You stay there. I'll get it," Beatrix said. She was thirty-two that summer, and strikingly lovely, with her athletic gait, coppery hair, and direct, unblinking gaze.

I sometimes saw Mr. James watching her too closely, studying her, and I later wondered whether it was Beatrix he had in mind when he created that tall, amiable, peacemaking daughter, Rosanna, in *The Ivory Tower*.

"How is her occupation going?" he asked after Beatrix had left the room to fetch the book. There was a hint of admiration in his voice.

"Such a stern word, *occupation*," said Howard Sturgis, grinning.

"Splendidly," Minnie said. "She is in demand since she designed the plantings for that little development outside of Manhattan." The "little development" was Tuxedo Park, a new community of summer cottages for Manhattan's wealthiest, men who wore the new tailless evening jackets from London that would soon be named "tuxedo" in honor of the community.

"Put in some roses, did she?" Mr. James inquired, shifting his bulky figure in his chair.

"Certainly, roses. As well as viburnums, spirea, and lilac," Minnie said with pride. "After she had graded the lawns and created a screen planting for the entrance lodges. Mr. Garrison was especially pleased that she was able to create the gardens without sacrificing the oaks and birches already there."

Mr. James shifted again. "It is rare for a girl to be so fond of trees, I think. I always picture her with a little watering jar in her hand, fussing over a bed of pansies."

"Yesterday that girl, as you call her, lifted an eight-foot-tall maple into the hole she had dug herself. Even Reynolds, who is not impressed by much, was impressed by that." Minnie grew thoughtful and put down the striped cap she had been knitting. "I think," she said softly, "Beatrix was dismayed by some of those gardens we visited in Italy, where all the trees and shrubs had been laid waste to accommodate a foolish statue or unnecessary fountain."

"They have a different aesthetic," Mr. James agreed. "Beatrix, don't you agree, they have a different aesthetic?"

"Very different," she agreed, having just come back into the room. When she felt my eyes on her, she gave me a little smile.

"I should think Italy hard to forget," said Mr. James, who wrote very clever books—certainly the sentences were a test of endurance and sophistication—and was known to be attuned to the dramas going on about him.

"One should not dwell in the past," said Minnie, picking up her knitting and clacking the needles at a furious pace.

"But the letter you sent me when you were in Rome in 'ninety-five has become a constant reminder of your travels there. Your description of the Borghese grounds was particularly effective."

"We had time enough to study them," Edith said. "Beatrix had gone off and left us sitting for quite a while."

Minnie, Beatrix, and I grew suddenly absorbed with the ceiling. Edith did not know the story of Beatrix and Amerigo because Minnie had never told her. "What if she used it in a story?" Minnie had said to me when we decided to never openly speak of it. "That would do Beatrix such harm, and much as I love Edith, one should never trust confidences to a novelist."

The novelist, sensing the unspoken narrative swirling above, on the ceiling, studied us with curiosity.

Mr. James, seeing that we did not wish to pursue a conversation about Rome and the Borghese gardens, picked up his book and turned the pages, looking for a passage he wished to read aloud for us.

"Paris, of course, has superior gardens," said Walter Berry, meaning, I believed, that Parisian women were more amiable.

Howard, playing cards with Teddy at a corner table, slapped his hand down and said gleefully, "You win again, old man." Howard often made sure that Teddy won, to sweeten Mr. Wharton's moods, which were often quarrelsome.

It was dark by then, an early, humid autumn dusk having turned into a dark night shadowed by clouds over the moon. The wind rattled the French doors and we thought we heard a squeal from some small animal, followed by the whooing of an owl.

For a moment I grew nostalgic for autumns past, when just such a wind would have set candles and gas lamps flickering. Edith had installed electricity and plumbing and all modern conveniences at the Mount, even a little elevator between floors.

And just as I was growing nostalgic for flickering candles, the lights went out completely. A stronger wind blew shut the French doors that had been opened onto the terrace and the warm autumn evening.

"What the blazes?" Mr. Sturgis shouted. Mr. Wharton, increasingly unpredictable, laughed.

"A fuse," Edith said. Her little dog began to yap furiously, jumped down to the floor, and pranced in anxious circles at her feet.

"Perhaps that wind has caused some sort of damage to the system," suggested Beatrix, who knew about such things.

"Oil lamps!" I cried, excited. "Do you still have some, Edith, or were they all given to charity?"

"I think candles," Minnie said. "Especially if they are perfumed."

Edith's housekeeper appeared a moment later, carrying candles and matches. The wind was picking up and we could hear leaves rustling and that strange sighing of nature that emerges on dark autumn nights. "Do you want a fire?" the housekeeper asked, all concern for her employer.

"No, it is still too warm, and the wind might cause a downdraft. We are fine, Gross. Go back to bed," Edith said. "Thank you," she added. "Can you read by candlelight, Henry, or must we sit in pensive silence till the electric problem is solved?" Edith placed three of the candlesticks on the table next to him.

Edith pretended to be gay, but her nerves were showing in the slight tilt of her head. She was uncomfortable in darkness and refused to be in a dark room if it also contained a book of ghost stories. It was an old fear dating from her childhood.

I suppose because she was not alone, she allowed Mr. James to go on with his reading from *The Turn of the Screw*.

He read from the beginning in a lovely, clear voice, and we three ladies and three gentlemen sat transfixed by the story. We all knew it well. I myself had read the novel at least half a dozen times, yet it still tethered my imagination so that my thoughts could not wander as he read, not even to wondering what Gilbert was doing that evening. We passed a very pleasant hour that way, Henry pausing occasionally to refresh his throat with a sip of brandy.

When he came to one passage the atmosphere in the room changed.

"'It was plump, one afternoon, in the middle of my very hour: the children were tucked away, and I had come out for my stroll,'" Henry read, his voice deep and beautifully modulated. "'One of the thoughts that, as I don't in the least shrink now from noting, used to be with me in these wanderings was that it would be as charming as a charming story suddenly to meet someone. Someone would appear there at the turn of a path and would stand before me and smile and approve. I didn't ask more than that—I only asked that he should *know*; and the only way to be sure he knew would be to see it, and the kind light of it, in his handsome face.'"

Beatrix, who had been leaning deeply into her chair, eyes closed, all the better to see the story in her mind's eye, sat up as straight as if she had heard a fire alarm.

"Let's stop the reading there," Minnie said, understanding instantly the memory that had jolted Beatrix. Amerigo, in the Borghese gardens.

Teddy, who had sunk into a light sleep as soon as Mr. James began to read, came to with a start. "Edith," he shouted, as if she were several rooms away. "What has happened?"

"Nothing, Teddy. Just the wind. Don't you remember?" Edith asked gently.

"Of course I do," he grumbled, but it was obvious he didn't. "The damned lights went out." Mr. Wharton rose unsteadily to his feet—he had drunk a considerable quantity of wine at dinner—and took the book from Henry. "That old chestnut again, my fellow? I should think you'd want something more lively." He tossed the book in the air, caught it, then threw it into a corner. It landed, spread-eagled and spine broken, like a wounded animal.

"Bedtime, I think," Edith said, rising.

EIGHTEEN

It took me a very long while to fall asleep. I missed Gilbert and the happy promises of my early years with him. That first time I had seen him in the garden at Vevey he had been all American confidence combined with an Old World charm and sophistication—an irresistible combination to me, who had known only naive younger men with little experience of the world.

And the way he had looked at me, there in the garden. Knowingly, admiringly, with a kind of amazement, as if he had never before seen such a pretty girl. He turned my head. He made me feel special, wonderful.

And now we were broken—that was how it felt—we'd become as broken as a vase that falls from a table and shatters into pieces. Was this how Minnie had felt when she first knew she must separate from her husband? Was this how Edith was feeling, this same night?

When I did sleep, I had uneasy dreams of being chased through darkness by some unseen monster, my dress torn ragged by sharp branches, my hair fallen loose and streaming behind me.

I woke in darkness sometime around three in the morning, startled awake by a noise that ceased as soon as I came to full consciousness. I was no longer used to being awakened at night. When the children had been small it had happened frequently. I would creep from bed so as not to wake Mr. Winters, who could have slept through an earthquake, and then step around the snoring nurse to check on my babes.

That hadn't happened in years. The youngest, Athena, was already twelve. I was used to sleeping through.

Even so, this noise had been different from the accustomed nightmare moans, snores, and coughs of a household. Like the monster in my dream, it avoided identification.

I sat up and waited for it to resume. It did. A man's voice talking lowly, slowly; pausing, then starting again as if the speaker were in conversation with another person I could not hear. Was that Beatrix's name I heard?

The hair on my arms rose on gooseflesh. It was a stranger's voice. In the house.

I rose and found the candlestick Edith had given me for the night. When I struck the match, the voice ceased, as if I had startled it.

I went to the door, meaning to peek into the hall, but just as my hand touched the knob, the door swung forcefully open.

"Beatrix! You frightened me."

She stood there in her white nightgown, candle also in hand, forefinger pressed to her lips in the "shh" gesture.

"No one else is awake," she whispered. "You heard it, too? I think someone is in the house." She frowned and in the eerie candlelight her eyes looked even larger than usual. "I rang for a servant and no one came."

When she said that, I realized how strange the atmosphere was. Were we awake, or was this part of my nightmare? We felt isolated from the other people in the house, and for a chilling second I was tempted to call out, to rouse the other sleepers to end this terrible isolation.

Beatrix seemed to intuit this and again put her forefinger to her lips, warning me to be silent. We made our way down the hall, our movements as slow and laborious as if we passed through water. The moonlight shining through lace curtains shimmered in ever-changing patterns over the floor.

Beatrix leading the way, we crept down the stairs, pausing at every twist and turn and doorway to make certain no one lurked behind a chair or around a corner. She picked up a heavy bronze statuette to use, I assumed, as a weapon, should the need arise.

Still, no one else in the house woke or moved but us.

Our search seemed to take years, not minutes. We tiptoed silently through the house—the den, the library, the dining room, the gallery, all the lovely rooms that ran along the outside terrace. Edith had built a strong house. The floors did not creak, nor the stairs squeak. The voices had stopped and the only noise in the dark was the rustle of our nightdresses and our occasional murmurs to each other. I bumped into a table and Beatrix whispered, "Are you all right?" A leaf from a potted plant brushed her cheek and she jumped back two steps.

The silence grew unbearable, worse even than the muffled sound of conversation that had awakened me. I could hear my heart beating, the pulse roaring in my ears, as we tried to discover the source of that overheard conversation.

In all the downstairs rooms the windows were latched shut, the doors unopened. Nothing seemed amiss; certainly there were no prowlers, though every shadow seemed somehow ominous.

"No one," Beatrix said after we had peered into the corners of the drawing room where we had sat, hours before, listening to Mr. James read from his ghost story.

"I don't believe we imagined it," I said.

"Nor I. Yet aside from those who belong here, the house is empty. Let's go outside, into the gardens," Beatrix said. "I don't think I'll sleep anymore tonight." She looked shaken, in need of air.

We opened the French doors and walked through them, across the terrace, down the stone steps to the lawn. By unspoken agreement, we headed in the direction of the walled Italianate garden, with its conical topiaries and trimmed hedges, its insistent reference to Old World formality. The bushes made sharp-edged shadows on the grass and the wind made those shadows dance.

"The voices were speaking Italian," Beatrix said, sitting on a stone bench. "Is that what you heard?"

"Yes. And I think . . . I think I heard your name in the conversation."

"I know. That was what woke me up. Someone calling my

name." We sat in the moonlight and waited without knowing what we waited for. My heartbeat had slowed down; it seemed less frightening outdoors than it had been indoors.

The night around us was silent. We could hear a gentle breeze stir the bronzing leaves on the trees, a faint rustle like a skittering mouse when a leaf fell to the graveled path, but nothing else.

"Strange, the voices spoke in the house, but not here," Beatrix said, shivering. "We must have dreamed it."

"The same dream for two people? I don't think so."

"I suppose not."

"Are you warm enough?" I asked, wishing I had brought my cashmere wrap. My slippers were wet through from the walk over the dewy grass. They'd never be the same.

"I'm fine. Are you feeling chilled?"

We sat in silence, each wondering at the significance of what we had heard. One person might have been accused of being overimaginative or mistaking a dream for an actual event. But when two people experience the same event, it is more than imagination or restless dreaming.

"How curious this night feels, Daisy. Before I woke up, if I did wake up, I was dreaming a different dream, in which I was singing a song I heard after we went to the Borghese gardens that year in Rome. 'My destiny is written in your heart.' That was the opening line, and when I first heard it I wanted to find the sheet music and learn it myself. Amerigo told me later that most of those songs have never been written down. They are passed from father to son."

After those years of silence, she had said his name.

"Perhaps Henry's reading stirred something. Opened some doorway," I suggested. "Athena and her friends were playing about with a Ouija board last week, and all the girls were convinced some spirit by the name of Gray Wolf came through to instruct them."

Beatrix smiled. It was a very patient smile; even thin moonlight could reveal that.

"Are you growing superstitious, Daisy?" she asked with a tilt of her head.

"Well, the spirit did tell them that one of the girls, Chloris, should be careful going down stairs. And the next day she fell down three stairs and sprained her ankle."

"Coincidence is not the same as guidance from beyond," she insisted, unconvinced. "Coincidence can be very strange, though."

Gardeners are direct people. They know the ground; they know the plant. Beatrix knew the ground of our conversation and the words that would suit it.

"I recently had a letter from him. Amerigo Massimo," she said.

I didn't bother to hide my astonishment. "What did he say?"

"He will be in New York in December and would like to meet with me. He intends to visit the gardens in Central Park. His wife will be here as well. He has three children. Two sons and a daughter. Imagine."

Beatrix rose from the bench and paced, wringing her hands.

"Have you thought of him often?" I asked, beginning to shiver. Amerigo had contacted her. Was this why we had heard that voice, had that strange shared dream of words in Italian?

"I've been too busy to think beyond the work of the day, the week," she said. "I never determined to be an old maid, Daisy. But I will not marry just to prevent people from saying that. I have met so few men one might marry. They are either already with wife and children, or not of a mind to have either. Or, worse, they are the type that one simply cannot, with any honest logic, sit next to at dinner and say, 'I could be happy with this person for the rest of my life.' I will not settle, just to say I have a husband. But to answer your question. Yes, I have thought of him often, and wondered what my life would be if I had gone away with him, as he proposed. I can't say I have no regrets. Sometimes . . ." She did not finish the sentence.

"Even a great passion for a man does not guarantee happiness when you are finally married to him."

She took my hands in hers. "Your unhappiness makes me sad," she said.

"It may come out right, yet," I said. "I haven't given up."

My thoughts kept wandering back to that whispered conversation that had awoken us. We had sat pleasantly in the autumn evening listening to Mr. James read about that sad, confused governess, that young woman aching for a love she would probably never know, imagining the secret delights of meeting a handsome young man around the next turn of the path, setting off a desire so strong, so frustrated, she would lose herself in it and endanger those innocent children in her charge.

The atmosphere had changed once Mr. James began to read, had become oppressive. We had all changed from relaxation to alertness. And then Teddy had made that scene, not the Teddy who had been charming at dinner, talking of wines and Mediterranean cruises, but the other one, wild-eyed, his movements hasty and ill-judged, his conversation worrying.

Bedtime, Edith had said, and so we had gone to our solitary beds.

"Do you think it was his voice?" I asked. "Amerigo's?"

"How could it be? There are too many questions with implausible answers." She bent down to pluck a little round clover that had sprung up in the grass. It glowed white in the moonlight. "In Berlin," she said, studying the clover, "in Mrs. Haskett's solarium, I saw an *Orchis spectabilis*. The flowers were not much larger than this, but they were pure white and had a strange hooded shape. Amerigo thought it looked like the ghost of a monk. Which monks are the ones that wear white rather than brown? It couldn't have been his voice," Beatrix said decisively. "Besides, it was just a dream, wasn't it? We should go in. Let's not speak of this to the others, nor think of it again."

Shadows chased ahead of us as we walked back up the lawn and stone steps. Things moved. I saw them in the corners of my eyes, but when I looked there was nothing there.

Minnie was in the hall outside Beatrix's door when we went back upstairs. She looked worried, and her hands holding her dressing gown together at the throat were white-knuckled.

"Where were you?" she asked. "I woke up and thought I heard something, maybe a prowler, and came to make sure you were safe. And you were gone!"

Beatrix could have been a mere child of ten, Minnie looked so frightened for her. But Beatrix was not; with the passing years, strength was flowing from mother to child, and it was Beatrix, now, who put her arm around her mother to comfort her.

"All is well," Beatrix said. "Come, go back to bed. You need your rest." She kissed her mother on the forehead and walked her back to her own bedroom.

NINETEEN

In the morning we gathered around Edith's breakfast table for tea and eggs and ham, and we all moved a little slowly, it seemed. There wasn't the usual joking and teasing. The atmosphere remained changed somehow, and we felt like toy figures being pushed about by unseen forces.

At least, that is how Mr. James expressed the strange lethargy we experienced, as a sense of weakened volition. "It began when the lights went out," he said. "This modern age gives you a false sense of being in control, when a simple wind can cause such havoc," he complained. "I wonder if all these modern amenities really add much to our quality of life. I, for one, do not trust that little elevator she has had installed."

"Edith loves the modern age because as a writer she can inhabit any era she chooses," Minnie said. "Why not also be of one's own time, not always looking back?"

Edith was not with us. She spent her morning hours in bed,

writing, her work tray spread over her lap, and no one interrupted her work schedule, not even special visitors from England. I peeked in once when her maid had left the door slightly ajar, and there was Edith, awash in white linen bedcovers and nightgown, surrounded by pages filled with cursive blue lines of her most recent story. It was like a fall of autumn leaves around the elegant tree of her own figure.

Henry understood this schedule and perhaps was even a little glad for it, because it gave him some time away from her presence. They truly admired each other, Henry and Edith, but there was always a slight tremble in the atmosphere when they were together.

That autumn, Edith was working on *The House of Mirth*, that story about poor Lily Bart, who aims too high in marriage and ends up falling very low. It is one of my favorites, and my well-worn copy has underlined passages in which marriage is described as a kind of banking transaction or investment. There are many of those passages. Minnie smiled when I pointed this out to her. "Beatrix and I did the same," she said. "It is revealing, isn't it? The price we are expected to pay, or be paid, to become a wife of a suitable man."

We spoke of *The House of Mirth* at breakfast, trying to guess the ultimate fate of poor Lily, and whether she would ever find a husband.

Minnie, who ate lightly, spread jam over unbuttered toast and looked up at the ceiling, as if she could see Edith through it, as she said, "Lily's mistake is in refusing to consider possibilities other than marriage before it is too late. So many women make that mistake."

"Other women don't have your resourcefulness," Henry said. "And you have not been completely without error in your relationships. If a woman as intelligent as yourself is badly caught, what could less intelligent poor Lily expect?"

Minnie did not mind when Mr. James made the rare reference to her failed marriage; she knew he meant no malice.

"Gertrude Jekyll and I have found a different path," Beatrix said.

"Yes, well, poor Miss Jekyll. I fear finding a husband for her would have been extremely difficult. But you, Beatrix. Don't smile at me like that. I know there have been offers, and all turned down. Will you not eventually regret that?"

Henry turned a gimlet eye on her, waiting.

"Why, Mr. James, must men believe women are incomplete without them?" Beatrix finished buttering her toast and spread some raspberry jam over it.

"I thought I heard a noise last night," Mr. James said, turning the conversation into a different path. "Did anyone else? Were you restless last night, Daisy, and wandering about?"

Beatrix and I looked at each other over our coffee cups.

"Slept like a log," I lied. Beatrix and I had agreed not to reveal what we had heard, especially not if Edith, who was already afraid of supernatural occurrences, could overhear. She had just come into the breakfast room, announced by the little dog barking and dancing at her feet.

"You have finished your morning's work early," Henry said to Edith. "Have you plans?"

Edith also had dark shadows under her eyes that morning. What had been in the atmosphere at the Mount that night? Had anyone else heard voices and decided not to speak of them?

"Reynolds asked for a helper, so I've hired a young man and I am going into town to fetch him." Edith fidgeted with a ribbon on her blouse. "The man is new to Lenox and doesn't know his way about." Edith was irked, as well she should be, since she was now running an errand during her morning writing time.

"I will go for him," I offered, relishing another chance to be driven out in the automobile. That automobile had been one of Edith's cherished modern conveniences, and we were all enjoying the newfound freedom of going where we wished, when we wished, no need to hitch horse and carriage, no railroad timetable to consult and adhere to.

"Why can't Teddy go?" Minnie asked gently.

"He is still in bed. Let him sleep in," Edith said.

"Settled." I stood. "I'll go put on my hat."

"I believe he's an Italian," Edith said. "Do you remember any of your Italian, Daisy?"

"Two or three words. I'll manage." An electric charge had gone through the air. In just a few short days we had become a close-knit group, guests and residents and Edith's staff, moving in and out of the rooms at the Mount, and one another's conversations, with the ease of a formal dance. Now we would have to readjust, even though the newcomer was just the gardener's assistant.

An Italian assistant.

Beatrix pretended to be lost in a seed catalogue but turned the pages so quickly I could tell she wasn't seeing what was on them. Minnie looked worried, as she often did, and Edith, pouring another cup of tea, gazed out the window to where handsome Walter Berry and childlike Howard Sturgis were strolling on the lawn, deep in conversation.

When the car arrived in town, the new gardener's assistant was already waiting outside the inn where the public coach stopped. He must have come in the day before and stayed overnight in one of the attic rooms the inns kept for servants. His suit was travel worn and he badly needed a shave and haircut. He was too tall, too thin. He didn't look at all like Amerigo, thankfully. His eyes were black, not brown, his hair course and straight, not curly. Yet there was something in the way he held his head, the directness of his gaze, that reminded me of Amerigo. Surely he would remind Beatrix as well.

"Hop in," I said, and when he looked up, puzzled, I said more slowly, "Please get into the automobile. We will take you to the home of Mrs. Wharton."

He scowled at me but did as he was told. He sat in the front, next to the chauffeur, long legs jackknifed in front of him. I asked him, in the little Italian I could remember, his name.

"Arturo," he said.

I asked him where he was from.

"Prato. Tuscany."

How long had he been in America?

"One month."

And that ended the conversation. His hands were flat against the dashboard as we careened around corners and down the green and gold autumn roads of the Berkshires. He was smiling, enjoying the speed of the automobile.

When we reached the Mount, Arturo unfolded himself from the front seat and tipped his hat at Reynolds and Edith, who had come to meet him.

"Is he to live here?" I asked Edith, who was shifting restlessly from foot to foot, eager to get back to her writing. Normally, of course, she would not have come downstairs just to greet a new gardener's assistant, but this time she had.

"Yes. Reynolds has fixed up a room for him in the gatekeeper's cottage. This boy seems to bring Italy with him, doesn't he?" she asked, smiling. "Mimosa, spaghetti, church choirs, ancient stone fortresses on hilltops, Renaissance art." She sighed a little.

"Yes." I found myself wishing, for Beatrix's sake, that he hadn't come.

"Well, we need the labor," Edith said, reading my thoughts. "Otherwise, it will be years and years before the gardens are finished."

We spent that afternoon in a leisurely game of croquet, one of the last of the season because frost was in the air and soon it would be too cold for outdoor activities, even on the warmer afternoons.

"I love the change of seasons," Beatrix said, hitting my ball out of the way and skillfully placing hers for a run through the wicket. "Transition. That is when everything seems possible."

"Even the impossible," I agreed, knowing she was referring to the events of the evening before. We neither of us had been actually frightened. Why be frightened of a murmured conversation heard in the darkness? Might as well be frightened of a telephone or concert hall. Unlike the poor governess in *The Turn of the Screw*, we hadn't seen an evil man or a wayward woman, both of them dead, or anything ghostly at all. It had been benign and unexplained, which was to say mysterious in an almost pleasant way.

That's why, when I looked out my bedroom window later that evening after several hours of charades and another reading from Henry, the light I saw in the sunken garden did give me a thrill of fear. Whatever had happened the evening before had taken on substance. It could be seen. The light was small and moved in a circular manner, staying within the same fixed area, as will-o'-the-wisps are said to do until they turn malicious and lure nighttime walkers into dangerous forests or deadly quicksand.

This was a different matter entirely, and though it frightened me, it did not dampen my curiosity.

I put on my slippers, loaned from Beatrix since my little cloth ones were still damp from the previous night, and my cashmere wrap. When I opened my bedroom door, Beatrix was not in the hall. She hadn't seen the light. This was not to be a shared event.

Creeping once again down the stairs and halls of the dark house, I went out into the autumn night, dreading what I might find but knowing it must be explored.

When I got close to that part of the garden, I paused behind a tree and waited. The light was still there, still moving, but now it was attached to a figure, a man's hand and arm moving his cigarette from mouth and down, back up to mouth, back down to knee, as the hand temporarily rested there. He sat on the bench, face always looking forward in the same direction. If he'd had a clear line of view, he would have been looking east, across the ocean.

This was not a ghostly visitation but a clear case of homesickness.

"Who is there?" he said, still staring straight into the east. It was more a command than a question, his voice weary rather than subservient.

I stepped out from behind the tree. "You do not sleep?" I asked.

He had come out in his shirt, no jacket, with the sleeves rolled up, collar open. "No need," he said. "I am not tired."

He had looked older in the clear light of morning than he looked at night, his face in shadow. He wasn't much more than a boy, a boy far from his home.

At that moment, he reminded me of Giovanelli, the boy who had walked with me in the Colosseum by moonlight, the boy from whom Mr. Winters had spent a good deal of effort rescuing me and my reputation, or so he thought. How long ago that had been, before I had become a wife, before my children were born, before love had turned to disillusion.

Poor Giovanelli. Had he really cared for me, and had I hurt

him? When I was young, I hadn't even asked myself that question. All that had mattered was that my plan had worked: I had made Gilbert Winters jealous enough to want to claim me for his own. I missed Giovanelli, for the first time in many years. Like Beatrix, I wondered about that path I hadn't taken.

"You are sad?" I asked Arturo, sitting on the bench next to him.

He turned and looked at me. "Why do you ask?" His voice was hostile, that of a boy used to hardship, who had learned to distrust.

Why *had* I asked? He was a servant, an immigrant. I shouldn't have been sitting with him. But in the cold moonlit night, he was a boy and he reminded me of a boy I once knew. He reminded me of a time when I had other choices, other paths.

"I didn't mean to disturb you," I said, rising. "Good night. I hope you will be happy here. Mrs. Wharton is good to her people."

"I will walk you back to the house," he said, also rising. "There are animals out tonight, hunting. Fox. I heard her. Maybe bigger animals as well. Wolf."

"There are no wolves in Lenox," I said.

"Pity," he said.

"He knows nothing about gardening," Reynolds complained to Edith the next day.

"Then you must teach him, please," Edith replied somewhat

coldly. She did not like her decisions to be questioned, and she had decided to take on Arturo.

"Good chap," said Howard Sturgis, patting Reynolds on the shoulder. "Give him a chance. I like his face."

Reynolds, who stood a half foot taller than Sturgis, managed to cower slightly, as servants are supposed to do, but there was defiance in his eyes.

"So do I, Reynolds," I said, adding my voice to the chorus of Arturo's defense. "He's just a boy, a long way from home and family."

We were all standing in the graveled forecourt of the Mount, where Edith had placed two white statues of youths carrying baskets of fruit. There were cigarette butts in front of the statue on the right, and the gravel had been scuffed into irregular patterns.

"You must tell him he is not to leave cigarettes on the ground," Edith said. "And that is an end to it."

Reynolds, not greatly pleased, tipped his hat and stalked away.

"I would look into this more, if you I were you," Henry said. "A gardener who knows nothing about gardening can be problematic in so many ways."

"Yes, dear Henry. But there is nothing about gardening that can't be taught, and we need more help here with the plantings."

"I agree," said Beatrix, who had been silent during most of this rustic event, the head gardener sending word to the lady of the house that he must have a word with her, all of us tramping alongside Edith like children eager for excitement, the pointing out of the telltale litter, the complaints. "You are right to give him a second chance."

Perhaps Arturo reminded her of Amerigo, just as he had reminded me of Giovanelli, and the memories softened us, brought a hint of Roman sun and umbrella pines into Edith's New England garden.

"It is the third and fourth chance he will obviously require that causes me worry," Henry said. "But it is your house, of course. You must do as you think right."

"I usually do," Edith said drily.

The next morning, I caught Arturo in the library. Edith had made this one of the loveliest and most accessible rooms in her house, with two doors opening onto the terrace, and other doors leading from the den, gallery, and drawing room. Arturo had entered from the terrace and stood before the tapestry dominating the one wall not filled with books.

The tapestry was an Aubusson, a garden scene with a shaggy tree in the foreground and a statue and fountain in the background. Because it was very early morning and the dawn light was still misty, he could have been standing in a real garden, a gentleman with rolled-up sleeves, lost in the pages of his book.

I studied him for a long while, wondering at the accidents by which some men are born to comfort and wealth and others to poverty so intense it forces them to cross entire oceans in search of menial labor. Perhaps that moment was when I first acquired what Mr. Winters called my political consciousness. Arturo was as handsome as any gentleman I had met in Italy. Dress him in evening clothes and put the correct fork in his hand, and he could pass as a gentleman.

But he was not.

"You watch me again," he said after a few silent moments. He did turn to look at me. He did not blush, cringe, or cower as another servant would have, caught out in this manner, being where he should not be.

"Mrs. Wharton will not be pleased if you have tracked mud in here," I said.

"I wiped my shoes," said he, coolly.

"If you want something to read, I will bring it to you. But you should not come in here alone."

He turned to me, his mouth turned down with disdain. "You think I will steal."

"No. But I think that if something should be stolen or even be misplaced, you would then be blamed."

The disdain in his face changed to an expression of curiosity. He did the unthinkable. He extended his hand and expected me to take it.

"What is your name—your given name—Mrs. Winters?"

"Daisy," I said.

"We will be friends," he said.

We heard steps overhead, going in the direction of the staircase. I nodded at the French doors and Arturo disappeared through them, onto the terrace. Moments later I saw him walking past the windows of the library, cap on his head, hands in his pockets. He was whistling. I couldn't tell what the tune was, but it was sad, in a minor key, Italian with a touch of Gypsy or Arabian.

Beatrix came into the room a few moments later, looking for a garden notebook she had left there the day before.

"You didn't sleep," I said, remarking on the dark shadows around her eyes.

"Not well." She yawned and stretched, the lace on her dressing gown falling back to reveal her lean, sunburnt forearms. "I kept having dreams that woke me as soon as I did fall asleep. I dreamed that I was in Italy with Edith and Mother and Teddy, and we were in an open carriage being driven through the countryside. I'm famished. Has breakfast been put out?"

Beatrix took my arm and guided me into the breakfast room as she described her dream. "Wild herbs grew everywhere, popping up in cracks between stones and in the dry, lava-dust soil. One herb had a lovely silvery gray color, but I couldn't think of its name. Grazing donkeys brayed as our carriage passed, their short, thick muzzles opening to reveal yellowed teeth. 'Silly beasts,' said Edith. 'I think they were created just to remind us to laugh.'

" 'Or because they are cheaper to buy and maintain than finer horses,' said Mother. 'The families in Little Italy certainly prefer them.' "

Beatrix took a seat in her accustomed place at the table, facing the windows so she could look out over the lawn. "That is why I look tired," she said. "But tell me, Daisy, why did you seem so startled when I came into the library? I would almost guess you hadn't been alone in there."

"I saw the new gardener in there," I explained.

"Arturo? He really should have asked. I'm sure Aunt Edith would be happy to loan him a book now and then."

"He doesn't seem the kind to ask," I said.

"No. He doesn't. And whoever he is, he most certainly is not a gardener, as Reynolds pointed out. I saw him planting tulip bulbs upside down yesterday. I had to redo the entire bed. Pass the cream."

"Who is not a gardener?" Minnie asked, coming in.

"The new man. Arturo."

One by one the rest of the house appeared in the doorway, Henry, Howard, Walter, hungry for bacon and eggs and strong coffee. All but Edith. We were a full table except for the empty places at the head and foot, because Teddy hadn't appeared either. We were merrier because of that absence, and Howard, before breakfast was finished, had thrown a roll at Henry, who stood and recited a verse in protest of bad manners.

And all the while, I kept looking over my shoulder, through the window, to see if the new gardener's assistant might be passing by.

The first snow fell at the end of that week, large flakes that floated sideways, up, and down, before landing reluctantly on shoulders, hats, eyelashes. It coated Edith's lawn and flower beds and frosted the leaves that had not been raked up yet. Her little dog shivered when she walked it and came in to curl tightly on the sofa blanket.

"Time to return to New York," said Henry, who disliked cold weather. Edith had marble fireplaces at the Mount, as well as a huge rumbling boiler for heat and hot water, but Henry was afraid of overstaying his visit. "Snowed in," he sighed, looking out the window. "Can you imagine a worse thing?" Isolation suited Edith; Henry was less fond of it.

Howard and Walter had departed Lenox the day before, leaving us bereft and at loose ends as their carriage pulled away down the drive. Houseguests, I've always maintained, should leave at the same time. Otherwise that sense of being left behind taints those who remain. It's like waving off people making a sea voyage when you yourself are left alone at the wharf as the ship disappears into the horizon.

Reynolds, I felt, had been even sadder than Edith and Beatrix and I to see Howard go, since for the past two days Howard had been the peacemaker between the gardener and his new assistant. Arturo simply wasn't working out. "He can't plant, prune, or weed. He doesn't know a rosebush from a bramble," Reynolds had complained the day before. "You're wasting good wages on him, Edith," Teddy said, siding with Reynolds.

Edith bristled. She did not want the men of the house questioning her decisions.

"Find something he does know how to do," she said quietly, "and stop bothering me with this matter." She was having trouble with *The House of Mirth*, with painful choices regarding the future of poor Lily Bart, who begins the novel wishing to marry very well, into luxury as well as a good family, and step by step lowers her expectations as men, one by one, let her down.

"Find something Arturo can do," she repeated, and walked away, regal and stern in her bearing, her green skirt trailing over the yellow leaves that Arturo had not yet raked up.

He, meanwhile, had been watching us from a distance, leaning against a tree too far from us to hear what was being said, but the look on his face left me no doubt that he knew. He was laughing at us. I scowled at him. We will be friends, he had said. Friends do not laugh at you. He took the point, grew serious, tipped his hat as Reynolds had taught him, and went off to find the rake he had misplaced the day before.

With the house empty of all Edith's male guests, we ladies seemed suddenly adrift. Gone were Henry's intellectual challenges, Howard's endearing childish pranks, Walter's handsome looks and charm. The rooms felt empty, the lawn too large, the dinner table huge with all those empty places. We packed away the croquet set, accepting the end of autumn pleasures.

On our last day at the Mount, Beatrix and I went for a long walk in the hills, enjoying the crisp air and the feathery snowflakes. Going for a walk with Beatrix was as much about seeing as it was about moving, and we would pause often so she could admire a stand of trees or the way snow frosted the browned wildflowers standing in the fields. When we passed old farmhouses, she would take a little book and pencil from her pocket and sketch the front door gardens.

We talked little, reserving comments mostly for the weather

and the scenery. Since that night of the disturbances, I had felt Beatrix withdrawing more than usual into her own thoughts. She seemed worried, and that was rare because Beatrix did not have a habit of brooding.

"You are wondering if you should go to Central Park and meet him," I said finally, when we were crossing the final meadow that would lead to the Mount and home again.

"No," she said, holding aside a branch for me to pass. "I have decided. If I refuse, he will think it is because I haven't forgiven him." She released the branch, stooped, and pulled a thistle from the hem of her skirt.

"And you have."

"Completely. Because I understand what drove him. He thought . . . we both thought . . . we had a chance of happiness together. He asked me to go away with him. I hesitated, Daisy. Lovers should never hesitate. When impulse is lost, what is left to us but duty?" She crumbled the browned thistle in her glove and let the wind carry it away.

She looked young when she said this, even younger than she had looked in Rome, those years ago. There were freckles on her nose from her work outdoors, and she balanced on one foot, then another, checking her hem for other thistles.

I had an eerie sense that she had somehow stepped outside of time, or at least was immune to it in a way that others weren't. Perhaps it was just the gray wintry day, come so suddenly at the end of a brilliant autumn, or perhaps it was our new sense of solitude at the Mount, but at that moment I reached my hand to take hers, to make sure she was substantial, not just a shadow or one of those strange moving pictures I had seen at the princess's salon in Paris, one-dimensional figures made of points of light and dark.

"Meet with him," I agreed. "End the wondering and worrying." She kept hold of my hand and we finished our walk like that, hand in hand.

TWENTY

When we arrived back at the Mount, there was a great to-do in the front hall. Teddy had found Arturo in the library and was reprimanding him soundly. Arturo stood there, head high, refusing to be subservient, meek, apologetic.

Arturo caught my eye, and I saw such dangerous defiance in him that I felt a little dizzy, the way I felt when one of my children stood too close to a cliff edge.

"It is just a book, Mr. Wharton," I said, placing myself between the two men.

"It is not. It is a principle!" Teddy roared. "Servants do not come into the house unless they are sent for, and they certainly do not come in the front door!" He was so angry he spluttered when he spoke.

Edith, who had been upstairs changing for dinner, heard the commotion and came to the top of the stairs.

"What is this racket?" she asked, obviously out of sorts herself.

When I thought the situation couldn't get worse, Reynolds appeared, hat in hand, face red with anger.

"He's cut the boxwood to the ground," he muttered. "I asked him to trim the bushes, and he cut them to the ground."

Arturo shrugged and lifted both hands, palms up, in a gesture I remembered from Rome, a gesture that said both I didn't know and I don't care.

"You're dismissed!" Teddy shouted.

"Wait just a minute," Edith said, coming down the stairs a pace faster than she normally moved.

"And don't you tell me this is your house and I can't manage the servants!" Teddy roared at her.

Edith smiled her coldest, calmest smile. "Of course I won't," she said, though I thought that was exactly what she had intended to say.

She took a deep breath and looked from Teddy to Reynolds to Arturo and back again at Teddy, and gave up the battle.

"I will give you a month's wages," she told Arturo. "But you should leave tomorrow."

Teddy smiled like a playground bully who has gotten in the last shove. Reynolds looked mighty pleased himself. Arturo, for the first time, looked a little frightened, his arrogance driven away by the realization that he was now both homeless and unemployed. Too late, he took off his hat and hung his head. He was still holding the filched book in his other hand. He offered it to Teddy, who refused to take it from him.

"Put it there," he said, nodding at the hall table, not allowing even that slight contact between them.

"What will I do?" Arturo asked, looking younger than ever.

"Come with me to New York," I said without thinking.

"Oh, really, Daisy," Teddy complained.

"And do what?" Arturo asked, some of his arrogance already returning.

"Not work in the garden, that's for certain," I said. "There will be odd jobs, perhaps some secretarial work since you are bookish."

Nostalgia is one of the strongest emotions. Arturo's dark good looks, his accent, his young man's arrogance, had reminded me so much of my long-ago beau, Giovanelli. He was certain to remind Gilbert, as well.

It had worked once. Perhaps it would work a second time. I had come to a decision, those last few days at the Mount. I had spent a week with Minnie, who had been divorced for a long time, with Edith, who was on the verge of divorce, it seemed, and with Beatrix, who had never married, and I longed for Gilbert, for my marriage, as flawed as it was.

That afternoon, our bags packed and loaded into Edith's automobile, Teddy behind the wheel looking dashing in his leather driving coat and goggles, Beatrix and I clambered into the crowded backseat and waved good-bye to Edith. Minnie sat next to Teddy.

"Don't forget that some of the peony roots still have to go in," Beatrix called to Edith, holding down her hat. "Make sure Reynolds waters them thoroughly."

"Yes, dear," Edith said. "Your instructions will be followed." She was obviously distracted, her thoughts still following the progress of poor Lily Bart's downfall.

As Teddy roared down the gravel drive, Beatrix and I looked over our shoulders at Edith and her home, both of them so lovely and regal, both haunted in their own distinctive way. Edith had already turned away and was partly through the door, her guests forgotten.

I never returned to the Mount again.

"I've never been back," I said aloud, interrupting the creaking of Walter's chair next to mine.

"It is so hard to leave lovely places," sighed Mrs. Avery. "My daughter has a home on Commonwealth Avenue. Not as grand as the Mount, I'm sure, but quite beautiful. Ceilings so high I can't touch them even with a stepladder, and lace at every window. She has a piano in her parlor and china from England. I go there at Christmas for the week."

It was our last night at the inn. The next day I would return to New York, and Mrs. Avery to Boston. Walter hadn't said his destination. He seemed out of sorts, undecided about something.

Because it was a Sunday evening and many of the other guests had already left, the inn was quiet and somehow desolate. No piano music wafted to us from the parlor, and the usual background sounds of conversation from the taproom were muffled. I was reminded of the day Henry and Edith's other friends had left the Mount, the day that opened the door into gray winter, my last day there. Mrs. Avery was right. It was hard to leave a lovely place.

"Shall we try the Ouija board again?" Mrs. Avery suggested.

"No, I think not," I said, remembering the *M* it had given us the other night. I didn't want to communicate with the dead. Not that way. "I have a better idea. Do you have gasoline in your car, Walter? Let's go for a drive. Mrs. Avery, get your wrap in case it grows chilly, and put on comfortable shoes."

It was a night of a bright moon and countless stars, a beautiful evening. I felt a sense of excitement, sitting next to Walter, the wind blowing on my face through the open window of his Frontmobile sedan. The automobile was different—Edith's vehicle had been an open black box set atop four wheels, and this sedan was faster, closed, secure—and the company was different. Yet as the trees flew past us, and the hills, and the new homes that had been built in the hills—as I instructed Walter, turn here, slow a bit there—I felt as if I were going to visit not just a house but myself as I had once been.

"It's been sold," I told them, holding on to my hat just as Beatrix had held on to hers the day we left the Mount. "Before the war, when Edith realized she couldn't continue with Teddy, she let it go. Her beautiful, beloved Mount. It was sold to a banker from New Orleans."

"My daughter married a banker," said Mrs. Avery from the dark depths of the backseat. "They are very well off."

"Is that where we are going, Daisy, to the Mount?" Walter asked.

"Turn here. Stop. Now we must walk a bit." For days I had

been just a few miles from the Mount, but it felt like a universe away, a lifetime away. I was going to see it again. It was time, and perhaps it would be part of my healing, part of that hard walk back from grief.

Walter pulled to the side of the road and turned off the motor. The night was still, the air thick with expectation and the occasional chirps and whirring of frogs and insects. We got out by the white picket gate at the entrance to Edith's former home. It was darker there than it had been at the inn. The house was at the far end of the drive, and if lights shone forth from those windows, we couldn't see them.

"This is trespassing," whispered Mrs. Avery.

"Shh. Look, all the windows in the gatekeeper's house are dark. He's asleep, if there is still a gatekeeper. If anyone stops us, we will say we are lost. Come on." I took her hand and pulled her out of the backseat. She laughed softly and gave in, following Walter, who was following me through the darkness.

There is something exciting about being in the dark night when you are supposed to be asleep, being where you are not supposed to be, when you are not supposed to be. It reminded me of the night in the Colosseum with Giovanelli, that sense of adventure and rule breaking.

We stumbled about till our eyes grew accustomed and we could make out treetops against dark sky, green grass reflecting patches of moonlight. When I felt the comforting crunch of gravel beneath my feet, I stepped firmly onto it, Walter and Mrs. Avery on either side of me.

"This," I said, "is the drive that Beatrix designed for Edith's house. It is one of the most beautiful paths in the world, a journey you make with your soul as well as with your body. Can you see?"

"Barely," whispered Walter, though I could sense he was excited, too.

We walked for almost half a mile through a tidy double avenue of sugar maples, that distinctly New World tree. Their leaves whispered overhead. Once the maple avenue ended, the drive curved into a dense wood where different varieties of trees huddled together in thick groups on either side of the path. "Do you feel the difference," I whispered, "moving from that formal avenue of trees into a dark woods? Beatrix meant this as a journey through time as well as space. You can move backward and forward. You go through the tame and the wild before you arrive. Appropriate for a writer's home, don't you think?"

"It's a little frightening," Mrs. Avery whispered back.

"But look. See what happens when you come out of the woods." We arrived in a clearing, and before us, on a hill, was Edith's beautiful Mount, white and regal, almost glowing in the darkness, surrounded by green shapes and gray paths illuminated by moonlight.

Mrs. Avery sighed. Walter took my hand and cleared his throat.

"Quite a house," he said. "They don't build 'em like this anymore."

"No," I agreed. "They don't. Edith planned every detail herself. I think she loved this house as much as she ever loved a person. Maybe more."

"Look," whispered Mrs. Avery. "There are lights in the windows upstairs. We had better leave, in case they set out dogs."

I didn't want to go. I wanted to sneak up to the window that had once been Henry James' room and look in and see if some shadow of him still slept there or wrote at the little desk. I wanted to sit in the Italian garden where Beatrix and I had sat after that evening, wondering what it meant to hear voices in the darkness, where no one was. I wanted to erase entire years, all the loss and worry, and go back to my week at the Mount, so that I could also go back to that day when I returned home to New York, and Gilbert was there, waiting for me.

"Come on, Daisy." Walter pulled gently on my arm.

We were quiet during the long walk back to the automobile and the drive to the inn, lost in our own thoughts. A visit to the past does that, makes you feel ghostly, like a visitor from a different world. It wasn't really that long ago since I had left the Mount, a decade in real time, yet I was so different.

The world was different, too. It wasn't just a matter of unused calling cards and dated flounced skirts, Irving Berlin being played in the parlor rather than Strauss. Since 1915, when the *Lusitania* had been sunk by the Germans, when fear became the common mood, and then in 1917 when we had formally entered the war . . . since then the world had become a changed place.

Some were calling those previous decades the Gilded Age, but I think Edith had been closer to the real meaning of those prewar years. They had been an age of innocence. A kiss in the moonlight could change a girl's destiny forever; a marriage that ended in divorce was a moral catastrophe, not a mere incident of living arrangements.

Had they been better times? Not for most. They had merely

been different. I think that was why Beatrix wanted an American rather than Old World sensibility for her gardens. We move forward. We must celebrate who we are now, not who we used to be.

And yet . . . in a garden time doesn't really exist at all, except as a season that comes and goes and then comes again.

It was well past midnight when we arrived back at the inn. Walter left his automobile parked on the street rather than waking the parking attendant, and we crept up the steps of the slumbering inn like teenagers sneaking in after curfew.

To our surprise, Mrs. Ballinger was sitting on the porch, waiting for us.

"I think you'd want to know," she said sternly. "They voted for women's suffrage in Tennessee. It was on the radio."

"Hurrah!" I shouted, not caring whom I awoke.

"Well, I'll be," said Walter, scratching his chin.

Every state in the union had approved voting rights for women. Soon they would have to make it a national law. We had won.

"Where have you been?" Mrs. Ballinger asked suspiciously.

"For a drive," Walter said. "Only a drive."

She sniffed, looked down her nose, then went upstairs to her room.

"Well, I'm for bed. Good night, Daisy. Good night, Walter." Mrs. Avery gave us each a little kiss on the cheek and disappeared into the dark shadows of the downstairs hallway.

"I'm not tired yet, Daisy. Are you?" Walter asked when we were alone.

"Not at all. Shall we sit on the porch for a little longer?"

"I've a better idea." He went into the darkened taproom and

came out with a bottle of whiskey and two glasses. "I left a dollar on the bar," he said.

We sat on a bench in the rose garden, surrounded by their fragrance and an occasional hint of pink where the moonlight fell on petals.

"What happened?" Walter asked, when he poured our second drinks.

"When? So much has happened," I said.

"Something that was like a curtain falling, or a door shutting." Walter was perceptive. "After you left the Mount."

And I resumed my story for him.

When I arrived home after my week at the Mount, Mr. Winters was there, waiting, and he was none too pleased to learn I had hired a new servant, and an untrained one at that, and without speaking of the matter with him first.

What he meant by "speaking of the matter" meant asking permission, and I knew if I had, he would have said no.

I said that to him.

"And yet you went ahead and did it. He looks somehow familiar. Daisy, what has happened to us?" His eyes were red, his collar loosened.

"Aren't you glad to see me, Gilbert?" I asked. "I am very pleased that you are here tonight. You've been away so much lately."

We were in his study, that room that always smelled richly of leather and cigars and newsprint. Gilbert, in our travels, had collected Oriental pieces, and his study was outfitted with inlaid tables, a wall-sized carved dragon screen, and displays of two-sided embroideries. It was, I thought, too busy for Edith's taste, but I enjoyed the effect and had always envied him that study.

We sat in the early-evening darkness, and when a maid came to light the lamps, Gilbert sent her away. Through the heavy closed door I could hear Robert speaking with the new footman, Arturo. Robert was home from school for a few days, taking time from his law studies to recover from a cough, except the cough wasn't going away. My son was ill, and there were Mr. Winters and I, frozen anew in silent combat over . . . over what? A new servant in the house?

"You should be thankful," Mrs. Manstey had said to me the month before, at her dinner party. "It is only the horses, a card game now and then. So many husbands keep mistresses. Oh, this new age. Where will it all lead?"

"I'm tired," I said to Gilbert. "I will go to bed now."

"Not yet. I have to tell you something."

"Tomorrow," I said. "Please." I feared what he had to say, and I wanted one more night of my old life, just one more. But it wasn't to be.

"Daisy, I've lost it all." He ran his hands through his hair.

I sat down in the chair opposite him. He reached for my hands, but I folded them into my lap.

"Surely not all," I said quietly. "We can sell the house in Newport."

He laughed unpleasantly. "I mortgaged that years ago."

I felt cold and wished we could light the fire in the hearth, but no wood had been left there. There was dust on the mantelpiece; the carpet was unswept; the twin vases on the mahogany bookcase were empty. They were antique Japanese bronze, and they had been an anniversary present from me to him; I couldn't remember when ever before they had been without flowers.

All this in a single week, I thought. What will it be like a year from now? Ten years from now?

"I've let two of the maids go," he said. "And the sous-chef. There will have to be more cuts."

"What about India?" She was to have a coming-out ball that winter. "And Athena's tutors?"

"Athena can continue her studies on her own," he said, running his hands through his hair, then flattening his hands against the top of the desk, the way people do when they are trying to get ahold of something to stop a fall. He looked like he was going to weep.

Everything was lost except the brownstone on Fifth Avenue, which was in my name. We would keep our home. But we would do what others had been forced to do: sell my remaining jewelry, some of the art we had acquired, make do with less, become invisible, people who lived in large houses behind closed doors and thick drapes, rarely seen in public, certainly no longer invited to the balls and opera opening nights, because we couldn't afford the box, return the supper invitations, purchase the necessary wardrobes.

I laughed, and Gilbert looked up in amazement. "Don't you see?" I asked. "This is how it began. Beatrix and I in Europe, hounded by Mrs. Haskell, who was buying everything she fancied, except the one thing that would have meant Beatrix's happiness. Amerigo's heirloom, *The Wolf of Gubbio*. Now we will be the sellers."

"I'll get you some brandy," Gilbert said. "Sit down, Daisy. Calm yourself."

"Have you told my brother?" I asked when he came back with the decanter and two glasses. Raymond had never liked Gilbert, even as a child, when he had found Gilbert in the garden in Vevey and Gilbert had refused to give him any candy. Oh, how Raymond must have gloated over this news.

"Yes. We will still have a small income from your trust, enough to live on."

"In reduced circumstances, of course."

"Of course."

I think it devastated Gilbert and the girls more than me. They had been born to wealth, but I could remember a time when my own mother cooked Sunday dinner, a time before the full household staff was hired, before the house itself changed from a two-story farmhouse to a three-story brick town house.

"I'm sorry, Daisy," Gilbert said that evening. When he wept, he put his head in my lap, like a little boy.

What a dreary autumn that was. The house staff shrank and shrank, one position after another gone, with tears and slammed doors, till there was a cook and a maid and not much else. Arturo stayed, having nowhere else to go, and worked for bed and board. I sent the seamstress away when she came with samples for new winter coats and gowns. I canceled our weekly order with the florist, and the French lessons and drawing tutor. India sulked when I explained her coming-out party must be held at home instead of in a ballroom, but she recovered herself soon. Athena promised she could learn as well on her own.

The four eldest children were already living on their own and doing well, but they felt shame for what their father had done. It was months before Gil Jr. would visit us, months before Robbie would look him in the eye and speak with him.

Life went on, just as gardens do. Winds and floods and frost may destroy them, but each spring some little green shoot appears, announcing that life does indeed go on. Some days, I felt like Lily Bart, who crept down and down the ladder instead of up, but I put that feeling away and determined there would be no self-pity, no long faces. My grandmother had milked a cow. I could darn my own stockings.

I did not leave Gilbert, as more than a few friends advised. He had come back to me in his troubles, he had wept with me, and there was more to hold us together than there was to drive us apart. I had loved him once with all the passion and ambition and dreams of a young girl, and to deny him would be to deny a large part of myself.

Eventually, I did forgive him. I realized his gambling was a weakness, stronger than himself, but not stronger than the promises I had made on our wedding day. Our love changed, became less about passion, about what intimacies happen between a man and a woman, and more about two friends trying to help each other through difficult times. He was much diminished and began to stoop and stayed at home rather than going to a club, but he was still Gilbert. I still belonged at his side.

Our lives grew smaller, yet some friends stood by. Minnie invited us over for her Sunday afternoon salons, and we met some of the more interesting minds of the time there, either in person or through discussion of their works, the writers and politicians who were slowly reshaping the world, Theodore and Edith Roosevelt, Upton Sinclair, Jane Addams, Theodore Dreiser; even that very strange woman who wrote in the rhythms of a stalling and starting automobile, Gertrude Stein.

One of the most argumentative salons was about *The Ladies' Home Journal* article by Grover Cleveland, who had written, "Sensible and responsible women do not want to vote. The relative positions to be assumed by man and woman in the working out of our civilization were assigned long ago by a higher intelligence."

"I don't know about that," Gilbert said. "It seems to me that society is doing the assigning of positions, and perhaps not all that well. Daisy has more common sense in her little finger than many men I know, and I don't see that women could make any more problems in the world than we men already have."

"Hear, hear," said Beatrix. Gilbert and I had sold most of my jewelry that week, and we would go home to bread and cheese for dinner, yet it was one of the happiest moments of my life.

TWENTY-ONE

It was snowing heavily the day Beatrix went to meet with Amerigo, almost two months after our week at the Mount. The sidewalks were icy and Fifth Avenue was a contrast of new white snow and brown ruts where traffic passed over.

Beatrix was working on garden plans for several commissions that autumn, and though she didn't speak of Amerigo, I knew she had been thinking about him. I could see it in the garden plans she showed me, the slight Italian influences that crept into her designs. We had made a point to meet once a week, and more and more it seemed those meetings with Beatrix were the lightest moments of my week. I could laugh, say anything that came into my mind, and know she would judge neither me nor Gilbert.

Minnie had found me a small job at the hospital dispensary, which was very kind and thoughtful, since I could permit people to think that, like Minnie, I was a volunteer rather than a paid laborer. Such things mattered, for the sake of my two youngest daughters, who still had to be settled in life; it was necessary to spin a few illusions about our circumstances. There is poverty and there is genteel poverty; we aimed for the latter.

So, that day when I met Beatrix, just before she was to have her reunion with Amerigo, I was coming from the dispensary, she from her office. We were two workingwomen meeting for an hour at the museum. I still had the smell of ether in my nostrils; she had ink on her fingers. That was the day when I looked hard at the question that had been swirling through my thoughts for months, perhaps years. Why should women be mere appendages to other people's lives?

Beatrix and I often spoke of the suffrage movement, but that day she had other things on her mind.

"What is the point of it?" she asked that afternoon at the museum. "I have agreed to meet with him. But to what purpose?"

They had just installed a new collection of Chinese porcelains, and we sat in front of them, admiring the whiteness of the glaze, the intense azure of the blue decorations, how a single brushstroke suggested a bird in flight, three strokes created a bridge over a river, eight strokes created a pair of lovers on that bridge. There was such a serenity to the ancient objects, a simplicity based on two colors, craft, a scene that the mind must register for exactly what it was: a lovers' tryst.

"Miss Jones?" A woman's voice interrupted our thoughts. "Beatrix!"

The wolfish Mrs. Haskett stood before us, cutting off our view of the Chinese porcelains.

After marrying off her youngest daughter to an English lord,

Mrs. Haskett had become, under Minnie's influence, a "woman who read" and, having read, enjoyed having the authors come to visit her and provide interesting talk for her teas and dinner parties. She had purchased one of the brownstones on Fifth Avenue, not far from my own house, though hers was newer, larger, and grander in every way.

"Mrs. Haskett," said Beatrix, standing.

Mrs. Haskett looked better as a woman of fifty than she had at forty. Her hair was white, but still very thick and full of waves, and the whiteness of her hair offset her olive complexion. The skin had shrunk back a little around her eyes, making them larger. She was well dressed, in sedate colors and soft lines—no more bustles and frills, but a sensible, if expensive, walking skirt and little jacket trimmed with fox.

"How is Minnie? I saw dear Mr. James last week," she said. "He came to visit and was full of tales about his adventures in the wilds of Lenox. Imagine. How clever of Mrs. Wharton to avoid Newport and instead build in Massachusetts."

"Are you here to see the new porcelains?" I asked, changing the conversation.

"No. I am here to meet with the acquisitions committee. I have offered to sell them one of my paintings. You know it, Beatrix. That sweet little painting that Amerigo Massimo was offering. *The Wolf of Gubbio*? I purchased it some years ago."

Yes, I thought. You made up your mind, finally, after you led him that merry chase, refusing to purchase the painting till Amerigo had married and performed his family duty. After he and Beatrix had parted.

Beatrix had gone ashen. She understood the timing as well as I. She lifted her chin higher. "That is wise of you," she said. "I've heard that painting does not bring good luck to its owner. Wasn't there a story about a murdered monk who follows the painting from place to place?"

Mrs. Haskett frowned. "I have heard that story," she said. "Old wives' tale." As if she herself wasn't fully convinced, she added, "Superstitious nonsense."

"Well, we must be on our way," Beatrix said, beginning a somewhat hurried step in the direction of the archway leading to the central stairs and the exit to Fifth Avenue.

"Wait." Mrs. Haskett reached out and put her hand on Beatrix's arm. Beatrix looked at it as if a spider or mouse had landed on her coat sleeve. "Will you come to my salon, Beatrix? This Sunday?" She pointedly did not invite me as well, but I was already getting used to that. Gossip spread quickly on Fifth Avenue.

"I wish I could say yes," said Beatrix, choosing each word with care. "But I am afraid I will be busy."

"Amerigo Massimo will be there. At four. And you, too, of course," she added as an afterthought to me.

She turned on her heel and left, her little maid scurrying behind her, trying to keep up with Mrs. Haskett's long, quick stride.

"Well?" I asked, after Mrs. Haskett had disappeared.

"No," Beatrix said. "It would be difficult enough to see him again, alone. But at her salon? No."

We spent a few more minutes pretending to study the porcelains, but Beatrix's thoughts were miles away, perhaps in Rome, in the Borghese gardens.

"That was a sign," she decided. "This must be ended." An hour later, she went to the park. Gardeners do not like unfinished stories; they are like bare ground that has been cultivated but not seeded. So much ruined potential, when there is a beginning without an ending.

Central Park was humming with activity that day. Children pulled one another on wooden sleighs, mothers and fathers playfully pummeled one another with snowballs, young girls and boys walked up and down the paths, whispering and laughing as their governesses flirted with their own beaus. It was a winter wonderland, and Beatrix took her time as she walked to the skating pond where she had agreed to meet with Amerigo.

Beatrix was filled with that sense of renewal that comes when a new year is on the horizon. She'd had a very busy year, many very busy years, in fact, since she had first met Amerigo, and she wondered what it would be like to go to him as a woman, a successful woman, rather than as the young girl she had been in Rome. She wondered what he would be like as a man with a wife and children and the fully accepted burden of responsibility, someone to whom she could no longer say, "Run away with me!" and mean it. Well, some people with responsibilities could say that—certainly many have—but she knew with all her being that Amerigo was not that kind of man.

She thought of Amerigo as she walked through Olmsted's

marvelous park, the gardens and forest, ponds and paths in the midst of what was becoming one of the grandest cities of the world, where everyone, rich and poor, tycoons and shoeshine boys, could enjoy nature.

She was glad the park was so busy that day, because gardens, she had come to believe, never feel complete until there are people in them, enjoying them.

Beatrix walked through Olmsted's miracle of green, not rehearsing in her thoughts what she would say to Amerigo, because she knew the words would come when they were needed. Perhaps they wouldn't even need to talk. They could just look at each other, hold hands for a moment, and know that all was well since all was as it should be. They had each done the right thing: he to marry and she not to marry.

Was she nervous? Who would not have been? She was not made of stone, and while she was pleased with how she had cultivated her life and made it bloom, she remembered, too, long nights of solitude. When you are as busy as Beatrix, it is difficult to be lonely. Loneliness requires a certain amount of free time. But solitude requires no such thing. Solitude can descend on you in a crowd, in your office, even in your favorite garden when it is filled with people.

Loneliness can be chased away as easily as a skittish alley cat. Solitude is a wolf that stalks you wherever you go.

There was an organ grinder in the park, with a little monkey all dressed up in a blue wool suit and hat. Beatrix paused and listened to the squeaky, sentimental music and put a nickel in the monkey's cup. He tipped his hat at her and the organ grinder began to play a different song. A *stornello* from the Spanish Steps of Rome. Had Amerigo arranged that in advance? Perhaps. Perhaps not. Such coincidences happen.

He was there, waiting by the skating pond, leaning on the railing, hugging his arms to his sides, a Roman man unaccustomed to the harsher winters of New York. A group of children, poorly dressed and too thin but laughing anyway, swarmed between her and Amerigo, reminding her again of that first meeting, when she had been swarmed by children in the Borghese gardens.

The air, she told me later, felt thick, as it had that frosty autumn night at the Mount, when we had heard conversation and music and wandered through the house, looking for their sources. As she walked toward him, another man, a stranger, stood next to Amerigo and shouted something to the skaters on the pond.

Amerigo laughed and began a conversation with the other man, who continued to nod and wave at the skaters. She was close enough now that she could hear the murmur of Amerigo's voice, but not the words. She stopped, listening to the music of his voice, a melody in a minor key that had both sadness and joy.

The stranger laughed again, louder this time, and moved away, leaving Amerigo alone.

She did not call out to him but he turned to her anyway, sensing her arrival in the way that lovers do, even years later.

He had changed from boy to man. His lean face had widened and acquired lines; his full beard had threads of silver. His eyes were the same, and his smile.

Beatrix would not tell me what they talked about, only that

they talked and walked for a good hour and it felt exactly as she had hoped it would, as a meeting of two old friends who once meant much to each other, lost touch, but then found each other again.

There are so many kinds of love. Some grow in deep soil and cannot ever be uprooted; some grow in thinner soil and their flowers bloom for a day. Yet even that is a kind of love.

As they talked, a burden fell from her. She, who had lived with the uncertainty of her hesitation, now knew that it had happened in the only way it could have happened, and she had nothing with which to recriminate herself. If they had eloped, they would have lost their families, their blameless friendship, their positions, and their plans for the lives they intended to live. Eventually, they would have lost each other, just as Minnie and her husband, Edith and Teddy, had lost each other, down long avenues of disagreement, disparity, resentment.

They had avoided that.

When Amerigo said he had to go, back to his hotel, to his wife and children, Beatrix felt sad, but not devastated.

I loved you, he said.

I loved you, too, she said. A long time ago.

They had met in one garden, and parted in a different one, and the parting, to her, felt complete. She was tempted, for a second, to turn back and wave one more time, but she didn't.

TWENTY-TWO

I went to Mrs. Haskett's salon without Beatrix. Curiosity would not let me stay away. Mr. Winters refused to come with me, but that was perhaps just as well. Aside from afternoons at Minnie's, he no longer cared for society and avoided the people who had once sat with him at card tables or at the racetracks in Saratoga and Longchamps. "Why fuel the gossip by appearing in public?" he would say, newly and painfully sensitive to the looks he sometimes received, the whispered condemnation he imagined he heard. He had failed in the worst way a man could fail in that world, financially. That was the standard, you see. Men could do as they wished as long as they obtained and retained wealth. Money was the great leveler, and once you no longer had it, you no longer counted for anything, with certain people.

Mrs. Haskett's Fifth Avenue home was luxuriously garish. To describe it would be to describe what has already been noted in her accommodations, even the temporary ones: the excess of gilt and glitter and plush, the expensive foods on the buffet, enough food to feed all of Little Italy for a week, had she been so inclined. The musicians were of the best, though they did not play well for her, knowing that she was no expert at pacing or expression. The servants were unobtrusive and well trained, but if you looked closely at them, you could see the narrowed eyes of employees unhappy with their posts.

"Beatrix did not come?" Mrs. Haskett accosted me rather than greeted me, as soon as I was announced.

"Miss Jones has an excess of work and is engaged with it."

"Even on Sunday," said Mrs. Haskett with great disapproval. "It is too bad, really too bad, that Miss Jones must work."

"She rather enjoys it," I said.

Mrs. Haskett moved on to the next guest. I took a glass of champagne from a passing maid and looked around, greeting those people I knew, though eyebrows lifted when women spoke with me. Some friends were kind and unchanged toward me. Some moved quickly away, as if misfortune were contagious.

Head up, my mother would have said. I kept my head high, shoulders back.

I found Amerigo in the music room, a gaudy overstuffed affair of spindly-legged chairs, grand piano, several harps, and gilded side tables. There was so much clutter in the room that the acoustics would have been terrible. Perhaps the hired musicians had refused to play there because of that. I couldn't help but think how Edith, with her gracious taste and fondness for simplicity and comfort in furnishings, would hate this room.

I made my way through the maze of furnishings to where he

stood beside a window looking out onto the street. When he turned and saw me without Beatrix, there was unmasked relief on his face.

"Ah. She didn't come. Good," was the first thing he said. I understood his meaning immediately.

"She has no particular fondness for Mrs. Haskett." I gave Amerigo my hand.

"It would be unspeakable," he said. "To meet her here, like this, with people like Mrs. Haskett." Amerigo flushed. "To have to make polite small talk with her. Unbearable. Will you sit with me for a minute?"

We sat near the window, a difficult silence winding around us. So much had happened, so long ago, and I could not reduce it to inane questions about his voyage, his activities in New York.

"She has made a name for herself," he said, breaking the silence. "She was modest about her accomplishments when we met, but I have heard other people talking. She said she would be a gardener." He smiled.

A couple, laughing at some secret joke, brushed past us and then fled into an adjoining room for more privacy. Her crimson dress was cut too low for the afternoon; his striped suit did not fit well. One could tell they were not husband and wife. Amerigo waited until we were alone again before speaking.

"I remember her, sitting in my garden with Magda. Magda remembered her, too. The American lady, she called her. I was sad when Magda passed away. She was the only person I could speak with about Beatrix, the only one who had known her."

"I am sorry."

He shrugged. "Magda was very old. It comes for us all."

The musicians began to play, and strangely enough, they played a song I remembered from Rome, something the street musicians had favored. Amerigo listened to them for a moment and smiled, the lines around his eyes creasing even more deeply.

"It is strange, hearing that old song played as a piece for chamber musicians. It needs the sound of crying babies and street sellers, doesn't it?" He tapped his fingers to the music.

"What is its name?" I asked.

"It is something they play at the Spanish Steps. 'The Poison Flower.' A young man falls in love with a girl who cannot love him back, who can never leave her father's garden. They say that your author, Hawthorne, heard this song and wrote a story about it."

"It is a sad story."

"Most love stories are, I have found." He realized that this sounded bitter and quickly amended his comment. "I have two sons now. And a daughter. They are the joy of my existence. They make everything worthwhile. I wonder that Beatrix has not married."

Was that hope in his voice? Pride that, after him, she would allow no other lovers in her life?

"She chose a different path," I said. "She wanted to do something that had not been done before. Marriage is, alas, all too common."

The musicians in the other room stopped playing, and I could hear how much laughter there was in the rooms, too much, and too many couples, not wedded to each other, stood whispering together. Their secrets melded with the gilt and excess of Mrs. Haskett's house, and I was glad that my husband had chosen not to come with me. I still valued his opinion, and I knew what his opinion would be of this house, these people. He had lost money, but he still had a sense of honor and loyalty, unlike some of the people at the salon. Some of Mrs. Haskett's guests had lost much more.

"This place is terrible," Amerigo said, a little too loudly. "I come only because I am trying to buy back from Mrs. Haskett a painting I sold her."

"*The Wolf of Gubbio*," I said.

"She has told you of it. Yes. My father is very old. He wishes to have the painting back, where it belongs. I sold it without his approval, and not for a very good price, I think, though that is not relevant. I sold it for a reason that no longer mattered. The painting belongs with my family, and now it is possible for me to purchase it back. My wife brought money with her to the marriage. I know you Americans speak freely of such things."

"Will Mrs. Haskett sell it back, do you think? She mentioned to me that she planned to sell it to the museum."

"So she threatens, but I think I will give her better value for her money. She will make me dance on her strings, I think. A puppet. That is how she sees those of us with less wealth than she has. She knows nothing, and when all is said and done, she is a very stupid woman. Without her husband's money, she would be nothing."

He turned away from the window. "And now, I will go to

Mrs. Haskett and try to amuse her. That is her price, you see. Good-bye, Mrs. Winters. I doubt we will meet again."

I left soon after and walked the long way home, up Fifth Avenue to the park, and then down again, the other side. It was snowing and very beautiful, but the roads were icy. Several vehicles had slid into half turns, tying up traffic and creating little groupings of angry men and frightened women and children who shouted and pointed at their automobiles or carriages.

The air had been so close in Mrs. Haskett's salon, so heavy with perfume and the smell of liqueurs. The cold air and the long walk revived me, and I thought of the world we had created, the world of Lily Bart and Henry James' poor unnamed governess, where women believed they must marry, and if they did not, they were mere weeds in other people's gardens, things to be plucked and discarded.

I thought Beatrix had found a better way.

My walk took me past the new Waldorf Astoria Hotel, with its long line of waiting carriages outside the sheltered portico of the front. Police in their blue uniforms stood by, trying unsuccessfully to look unobtrusive. The very wealthy do not like to be reminded of their vulnerability, of the crime and the criminals waiting to lighten them of their purses and jewels. Mr. Astor and his hotel managers usually stationed plainclothes detectives in the lobby and entrance of the hotel for that very reason. Yet today there were police in full uniform, swinging their billy clubs.

The reason was just opposite them, on the other side of the avenue, a group of men and women dressed in the drab and coarse garments of the working class. They stood quietly and fiercely holding placards on sticks, large-lettered signs asking for better wages, for reduced hours for their children, for decent housing. Some of the women carried signs demanding the right to vote.

This, too, was part of the world we had created, the haves and have-nots and that dangerous gulf between them.

Before I turned away I saw Arturo marching with them.

When I arrived home, Gilbert was in the study with the door closed. India was at an afternoon dance party—oh, how thankful I had been for that invitation, for India's sake— and Robert was in bed, trying to sleep away the cough that plagued him.

Rather than dine alone at that huge table, I had a tray sent into the library, where I could sit before a fire, my feet up on an ottoman. I kept the door opened and listened. When I heard footsteps in the hall, I called to him, and Arturo, still wearing his hat and coat, came in.

"That was dangerous," I said. "If Mr. Winters or anyone from this house had seen you marching, you would have been sent away."

"You saw me," he said. He spoke to me as if I were an equal, prepared to quarrel and stand his ground with me rather than wait for orders, instruction, or reprimand.

"That is different."

"How?"

"Because," I said. Because he reminded me of Giovanelli? It was more. We will be friends, he had said to me at the Mount. I thought we should be. "Was there trouble with the police?" I asked.

"No. There was an accident, though, at the corner of Fifty-first Street. Serious, I think. The police went away to that." He turned to leave, to warm himself in the kitchen with the other servants. He gave me a quick "Thank you" over his shoulder, and a grin of complicity.

A week later, Beatrix took an hour from her work to visit the museum again. I couldn't be there that day, so she went alone. She still studied the old masters, as Sargent and Olmsted had recommended, and was sitting in front of one of the Poussins in the collection, sketching the background trees and trying to identify the herbs in the foreground of the painting. She thought perhaps the painter had worked more for effect than accuracy, because she couldn't place the herbs in her well-informed taxonomy, but only knew they seemed familiar.

Had they been in Magda's garden, in Rome? A thrill went through her and she shivered a little at the memory of the old, wild garden in the courtyard of Amerigo's palazzo. She was certain that, indeed, these were herbs that had been growing there in a crumbling stone trough. She sketched them carefully, determined to go through her shelf of herbals for a definite identification.

JEANNE MACKIN

When she had finished her sketch she stood and, smoothing her skirts, turned to leave. On an impulse, she went to the balcony that overlooked the grand marble staircase of the museum. People milled about below, women in their heavy winter woolen dresses and fur wraps, men in their tall hats and black jackets, children in red and white with rabbit-fur mittens and muffs.

A face in the crowd turned and looked up at hers. Amerigo. He smiled, a warm, brilliant smile, and waved. He blew her a kiss, and that surprised her. He had never before, not in Rome or Berlin, not in Central Park when they had met days before, made such a familiar gesture in public. It moved her in unexpected ways, that kiss in her direction, and she decided to go downstairs and speak with him one more time. He would be leaving soon. They wouldn't meet again in this lifetime, she thought. She put her pencil and sketchbook in her bag and hurried down the marble stairs. That journey seemed to take a hundred years, and she realized she was very eager to see him once more, to say good-bye. It was a strange compulsion, different from when she had first seen him in the Borghese gardens, or at the ball in Berlin, or even in Central Park. She remembered, she wanted to tell him about the seeds that Magda had given her. She seemed no longer in control of her own feet, so inexorably did they carry her downstairs to him.

But he was already gone when she made her way to where he had been standing.

Why hadn't he waited for her? Well, it didn't really matter. She pulled on her gloves and adjusted her hat to prove to herself her own indifference. They had said everything that needed to be said, hadn't they? It would have been good, though, to tell him how unexpectedly well the seeds had grown in her Bar Harbor garden. Her face felt warm, as if that kiss blown through the air had actually reached her. She touched her cheek with her gloved hand and felt a twin kiss, there on her palm, where his lips had once rested.

TWENTY-THREE

"Oh, how lovely!" said Mrs. Avery. "Sad and happy, all at the same time." She dabbed at her eyes with her handkerchief.

"Control yourself, Mrs. Avery," Mrs. Ballinger reprimanded, tugging at her too-tight jacket, but her bright pink dress kept peeking through the gap. It was another warm August day, but one of the beeches outside the inn had already started to turn. It was the kind of day when gardeners hurry to give the phloxes and black-eyed Susans a last weeding and feeding before the blooming season is past. Beatrix would be sorting through iris and peony roots, already planning for next year.

The green, gentle hills around Lenox were as beautiful as a girl in first bloom, but I was looking forward to the colors and the coolness of autumn.

We were having a cup of coffee in the train station, Mrs. Avery, Walter, Mrs. Ballinger, and myself. Walter had driven us from the inn and decided to wait with us for the train. Our luggage was piled around the table in awkward mountains of plaid and leather cases. I had finally learned to travel with a minimum of wardrobe, toiletries, and books, but at such moments I missed the days when there were maids and footmen to ease the labor and discomforts of travel.

I hadn't traveled with a maid in tow for years and had learned the hard way to count my cases and make sure all were accounted for before getting on or off the train. My mother's mourning brooch, several unfinished novels, a knitted blanket, lambskin gloves, a silver cigarette case . . . all had disappeared with several of my lost travel cases. When I remembered how Mr. Winters and I had once traveled, with carts and carts of trunks and cases, all looked after by servants, it seemed inconceivable.

"You've come down in the world," Walter had said the evening before, when I had told him about Gilbert's gambling. Perhaps. Or maybe I had arrived early where many of us were heading—into a more equalitarian age, away from a world of preordained classes and positions. How I wished my mother were still alive, so that I could discuss some of these things with her. She would have laughed to see her little Daisy marching with a placard for women's rights, her daughter who once cared mostly that her gowns were flattering, that she caught all eyes when she entered a room.

Walter was quieter than usual that morning as we drank our coffee and waited for the train in the little Lenox station. He was still thinking about the vote in Tennessee, how women's suffrage would soon be the law of the land. My finishing a love story in which the woman goes her independent way had not lightened his mood.

"What next?" he grumbled. "I suppose women will want to fly airplanes or become doctors."

They already had, but I did not point this out to him. In my years of campaigning for women's rights, I had encountered so many of his type, decent sorts who worked hard, endured the good and the bad that life puts in their path, but despite their inherent goodness resist change with all their stubborn strength. He would come round eventually, perhaps by the time his granddaughters were old enough to vote. Change does not require unanimity, only that enough people agree that change is needed.

"Your story doesn't have an ending," Mrs. Ballinger complained, reaching for the last tea biscuit. She had given up trying to close the gap in her jacket. "What, for instance, happened to Mrs. Wharton?"

"She and Teddy were divorced just before the war. It was inevitable. An earlier generation of wives gritted their teeth and endured, but Edith, for all her love of classical styles, was a modern woman. After she sold the Mount, her beloved home, she moved to France. She was there during the war, working with refugees. She's still there and, from what Beatrix says, intends to stay there."

"All very well," said Mrs. Ballinger, taking a little folding fan from her purse and fanning herself vigorously. "But you promised us a ghost story. Where is the ghost?"

"There were those strange events at the Mount," offered Mrs. Avery.

"I think there was more to it," said Walter. "You haven't finished, Daisy." He winked at me.

I t's easy to remember the early years, when you are young and full of hope; even the middle years, when life is all busyness, raising children, housekeeping, travel, the constant social rounds. It's more difficult to revisit what comes after: the children who have moved away and are busy with their own lives, the husband who grows into early old age, the disappointments and worries and fears. Illness. Death.

"Think of spring," Beatrix would tell me when I felt weighted down. "Think of yellow tulips and red peonies. Remember the old yellow barn and the field of daisies, your namesake."

In the years after that last meeting with Amerigo, Beatrix was too busy to succumb to the darker moods that began to occasionally visit me. She helped design the grounds for Bishop Satterlee's cathedral in Washington; a walled garden with raised walks and a sunken center garden for Crosswicks, the Newbolds' estate in Pennsylvania; a country garden for Mrs. Gordon Bell in Connecticut; floral gardens for the estate of Emily Vanderbilt Sloane in Lenox; a magnificent drift of delphiniums and roses for Theodate Pope's estate at Hill-Stead. (This had been a challenge, because Theodate hated reds and the garden had to be exclusively blue, pink, and white.) For Edward Whitney's home in Oyster Bay, she built a trellis for roses and vines, and thirty-eight different flower beds, and a dell full of iris.

Beatrix proved, if there were still any doubt, that it was possible to be a lady and to be employed, to work as hard as a man works. She was born into an age when women were decorative and legally no more than children, and she helped bring women into a new era.

When she saw a weed in her path, she plucked it, never mind how regal the company or numerous the laborers available to do the work. The young woman who had hesitated in the Borghese gardens over that weed in the path had grown into a superbly confident woman, and one not afraid of either hard work or dirty hands.

Nor was any task too small for her. My Gilbert died of the Spanish flu. We had survived early passion, a house full of children, the quarrels and hurts of domesticity, and that longer-lasting, deeper pain of his gambling. We had survived all that, and the war, too, but when the soldiers brought home the Spanish flu, Gilbert did not survive that. Beatrix designed his monument, a simple tombstone engraved with a weeping willow—no angels or carved wreaths, just a few elegant lines of Gilbert's favorite kind of tree.

"He was weak, but he loved you, Daisy, and he was as true to you as he could be. A wife can't ask much more, can she?" she said. "A willow is for faithfulness."

But I get ahead of myself. Nine years after Beatrix's last meeting with Amerigo in New York, Princeton University was building its graduate college, and they asked her to work with them on the designs for the grounds. She agreed, after presenting her salary demands, and began her sketches.

At dinner one night with Mr. John Grier Hibben, who was

the college president, she was arguing in favor of a campus based on linkage rather than separation. "No false boundaries," she said. "Movement should flow freely through an unbounded landscape."

Mr. Hibben's eyebrows shot up. Would that mean moving the golf clubhouse?

It was a formal dinner, that evening in the spring of 1913, and conversation had wandered from Euclid to Freud. The dinner was long and the meal a little too heavy for Beatrix, who was a light eater. The windows were open and the spring evening wafted in, teasing her with the scent of blue and yellow hyacinths.

They had sat her next to an art historian who was writing a book on the Elgin Marbles, and Beatrix listened patiently. She became aware of a man seated on the other side of the table, another historian. He was talking with great animation to the woman next to him, his fingers dancing over the tablecloth in the eagerness of his storytelling. Beatrix began to wonder what they were talking about.

She looked at the professor more closely. He was not young. He was already balding, but he had the broad shoulders of a laborer, not an academic. There was something in his face that intrigued her. She decided he looked like Caravaggio's self-portrait as he painted it in *David and Goliath*, shaggy and shocked and intense.

Max Farrand wasn't as shaggy or as old as Goliath-Caravaggio, but his expression mimicked the painting strangely. It was, she realized, the look of passion in his eyes. Whatever were they talking about?

Mr. Hibben poured more wine and asked another question about borders and boundaries, obviously anxious over the proposed moving of the golf clubhouse.

"Lines of desire," Beatrix insisted.

This time, the historian on the other side of the table began to study her.

"Paths should be established only where people will actually want to walk," she explained. "Path follows desire, not vice versa. If it means cutting through a lawn rather than around it, that is what should be done. People don't always follow a route designated for them by others. Nor should they."

When dinner was finally over and they were allowed to stand, help themselves to brandy, and wander about freely, Beatrix went up to the historian and introduced herself. She gave him her hand.

He took it and kissed it, demonstrating how effectively he had studied the manners of the eighteenth century. This gallantry pleased her. People often think that once a woman has chosen a profession, she has renounced flirtation and any offer of courtliness from the opposite sex. Not true.

Max Farrand was a specialist on Benjamin Franklin and was, at that time, writing his great work, *The Framing of the Constitution*. He was forty-four years old, a bachelor in tweeds, and a man with an astounding memory.

"We met once before," he said, refusing to let go of her hand. "At the world's fair."

"Are you the young man who gave me his umbrella?"

"I am. Or was."

"Such a long time ago."

"Time has been kind to you, Miss Jones." Still he would not let go of her hand. It takes a certain stubbornness to be a bachelor for so long, and across that dinner table Max Farrand had already decided his bachelor years were over. Now he would be stubborn about his unwillingness to let her go.

"I am so curious," she said. "What were you talking about at dinner, with your friend? May I ask?" The staff had come in to begin clearing the table, so they moved away from the clatter to the French doors of the terrace.

Max grinned. "The first time Benjamin Franklin visited old Madame du Barry, she was in her bath. He offered to come back later, but the servant instead showed him into the chamber where Madame was in the tub. He never quite got over it."

"Do you speak often of Benjamin Franklin's flirtations?" Beatrix asked, amused.

"Whenever possible. He is my academic specialty."

"Then I should tell you, my great-great-grandfather was a friend of Benjamin Franklin, when his family lived in Philadelphia."

"What a strange coincidence. You must see if you can remember any family stories about him. I will take notes."

"Very strange," she agreed. "Yes. I will."

"Will you walk with me in the garden, Miss Jones?"

The garden was a formal one to match the Italianate house, and as they walked, Beatrix commented on the severity with which the hedge had been trimmed. She favored a technique of "plucking" rather than shearing, to produce feathery, soft edges.

"Lines of desire," Max Farrand said. "What an interesting

phrase." He was taller even than Beatrix, and when she looked up at him she knew her life had changed. The woman who argued the merits of New World gardens over Old had met a man of similar sensibility, a man who had devoted his life's work to Benjamin Franklin, that New World statesman who had been a friend to her great-great-grandfather.

The walk turned into several walks over the days, and then came letters and phone calls and visits. Max began to court her, and she let him. His conversation charmed her, and he made it quite clear that if he should marry, it would not interfere with his studies and he would expect any wife of his to be similarly concerned with a life of the mind, not just simple domesticity.

It grew into love. Why would Beatrix resist such a man? To be absolutely honest with him, though, she decided to tell him about her first trip to Rome, about Amerigo Massimo and what he had once meant to her. Not to confess anything, but to warn him, perhaps, that once she gave herself over to a declared passion, this time there would be no hesitation.

Max listened calmly and with a show of interest, though he was much more interested in Beatrix's future than her past. "I have heard of the Massimo family," Max said at one point. "They were in possession of a small sketch Franklin had made, or at least it had been attributed to Franklin, though it turned out to be a forgery."

In a garden, paths converge. There are vortexes around which everything revolves, plants, time, history. Beatrix felt the different paths of her life begin to swirl, like a waltz, into this growing intimacy with Max Farrand. She already knew they would be married; they had simply to pick the date.

But when Beatrix spoke of the last time she had seen Amerigo, in the museum, Max frowned.

"Impossible," he said quietly. "You must be remembering dates and events incorrectly."

"No, I am not," she insisted. "He was at the museum on Sunday, December fourteenth. I remember the date clearly. He waved up at me."

"No," Max insisted. "Amerigo Massimo died the week before, hit by an automobile on Madison Avenue. I remember it specifically because it was the day I learned that the drawing his family owned was not a Franklin sketch. And then that evening there was the little paragraph in the paper about the elder Massimo's son being struck down by a vehicle in New York."

"It was in the paper? But I read the papers. How did I miss it? And I saw Amerigo at the museum. I know I did. We waved to each other. He looked up and smiled at me."

Max led her to a bench, just as Amerigo had years before led her to a bench in the Borghese gardens.

Beatrix sat. "Dead?" she said. "All these years, when I have thought of him, I thought of him in his palazzo, with his wife and children. I have imagined him growing older. Portly and gentle. And he has been dead, all these years?" She took a handkerchief from her pocket and pressed it to her mouth. She didn't cry. The pain, the surprise, were such that tears would have seemed common, useless.

"I have made you sad," Max said. "I'm sorry." He took her other hand and held it.

"But how?" she said after a moment. "I saw him. I know I saw him."

"Sometimes," Max said, "we should accept an occasional miracle."

"I was going to tell him about the seeds," she said. "I had forgotten, you see, when we were in the park; I hadn't told him. He gave me some seeds when I was in Rome, for a vine. I planted them in my garden at Reef Point. I still haven't been able to identify the plant, but there it is, a Roman vine growing in Maine."

"Beatrix, my dear. Don't look so stricken. I think I am growing jealous. It is not an emotion Franklin approved of."

She smiled, as he had intended.

She didn't sleep well that night. She thought of the night at the Mount, the whispered conversation, sitting in the Italianate garden in the moonlight and thinking of Amerigo. "You will see wonders," the monk had told her years ago, at the catacombs in Rome. She thought, then, that he hadn't been talking about the ruins they were about to visit, but events later in her life. Sometimes, you see a wonder and don't even realize it till years later.

The next day, Max took her to the station, to get the train back to New York. "What do you say about a winter wedding?" he asked her. "I don't think I want to wait till next spring."

And that's what they had, a lovely winter wedding, so that Beatrix would be free to travel and work when gardening season began again in the spring. Minnie didn't cry, as mothers so often do at weddings. She put Beatrix's hand into Max's, and blessed them both, and with all her heart wished them a long and happy life together. Beatrix's first "heart history" had been a sad one, but Minnie liked the directness of Max Farrand's gaze, liked the way his eyes followed Beatrix, how their steps matched when they walked together. She knew, with all the special senses that mothers develop, that her daughter would have what she herself had not had: a marriage that strengthened her rather than weakened her, that made her larger, not smaller, that allowed her to be all she wished, all she was capable of.

TWENTY-FOUR

The train we had been waiting for arrived in a cloud of steam and grating of iron on iron.

"There's the ghost story," said Walter. "Massimo hadn't really been there. At the museum."

"Who is to say what is real and what is not?" I argued. "I think perhaps he was there, though not quite in the usual way."

"It is hard to be alone. I'm sorry your husband died," Walter said, following my train of thought.

When we love someone, are they ever really completely gone from us?

"It's been two years. I'm beginning to recover. I stayed busy." Too busy, even Beatrix had argued, as I marched with the suffragists almost every week, traveling, campaigning. And now it was over, Tennessee had voted yes, my week at the inn was finished, and there was nothing to do but go home, to the smaller apartment that had replaced the sold brownstone, where on Sunday children and grandchildren might visit but the rest of the week the apartment, small as it was, echoed with emptiness.

Gilbert's middle name was Maxwell. When the Ouija board had landed on *M*, I had almost jumped out of my chair. It was a coincidence, of course. *M* for Mary, for the master, or for the poodle, Mariah. *M* for Massimo. It was, as Walter said, a convenient letter.

I hastily swallowed the last of my coffee and grabbed my cardboard hatbox and leather travel case. Mrs. Ballinger was taking the same train and she had already cornered the single porter at the little station and was hoisting her bags into his arms until I thought he would topple over.

"I liked your stories," Walter said. "Maybe we'll meet again."

"Maybe." He took my two cases and carried them into the train compartment for me, ducking his head through the low doorways. When it was time to say good-bye, he took my hand. He didn't shake it. He kissed it.

"Good-bye, Daisy." He took a little notepad from his pocket and hastily wrote in it, then tore the page off to give me. "My address. And phone number." He blushed a little. "Maybe you'll call me sometime?"

When, a few months later, Beatrix asked me to join her at a new garden she was designing, she suggested I travel with someone rather than come alone.

"You are alone too much, I think," she said. She was fifty years old that year, and she and Max had become the kind of husband

and wife that other people wished they had become, wished they were. Whatever bad luck had hounded her mother and aunt into bad marriages and divorce, Beatrix had outwitted it.

"Is there someone you can bring?" she asked. "You might enjoy the trip more."

I dug into the bag I had used during my week at Lenox and found the scrap of paper with Walter's phone number.

He picked up on the second ring.

"Walter? This is Daisy."

"I know it's Daisy," he said. "I listened to you talking long enough to know your voice. I'm so glad you called." He chuckled into the phone.

We drove down to Washington, D.C., together in his sedan, windows open, talking sometimes, sitting quietly lost in our own thoughts other times. He was easy to be with. Some people wear silence like an uncomfortably tight suit, eager to be out of it. Walter was not like that. His silence was like the silence of dawn, a restful pause before the bustle of day begins.

Mildred Bliss and her diplomat husband, Robert, had just purchased the Oaks, the hundred-year-old brick Italianate house in Georgetown, with its rocky, sloping grounds. They wanted their friend Beatrix to design the gardens.

"The grounds are a dream," Beatrix said, rushing to the automobile and opening the door when we arrived. She was in her work suit, with boots, knee-length skirt, loose blouse, wide-brimmed linen hat, heavy woolen jacket, stained and frayed garden gloves. "Mrs. Bliss and I are in agreement on design, and she will give me free rein."

She took off her glove before holding out her hand to Walter, who shook it with enthusiasm.

"Have you known Mrs. Winters long?" Beatrix asked, leading us toward the old brick house.

"Not as long as I would like," he said.

"We will go into town for a tea later," Beatrix said. "Mildred and Robert are in Buenos Aires and the house is closed up, so we are, at this point, planning the garden by correspondence. Walk with me, and I will show you what we have in mind."

The grounds were, to my eyes, mostly uncared for lawn, unpruned hedges, huge oaks, and little else. But gardeners see differently. They see beneath the sod to the nourishing soil and ancient rock; they see the journey the sun will take in the southeast and the winter blasts of wind in the northwest corner; the colors of forsythia, not yet planted, seen from a distance; the curve of green bushes around a doorway.

"This," Beatrix said, taking long, eager steps, "will be a brick ribbon path to the library. I will add some carved stone arabesques off the path. There will be a terrace of beeches, a rose garden with a wrought-iron gate, an urn terrace—and the urn will be a copy of a French terra-cotta urn. The cutting garden will be edged with a double row of plum trees. In the northeast there will be a circular garden of lilacs. Imagine the color in the spring!"

Even Walter with his long legs found it hard to keep up with Beatrix as she walked us over the grounds, inviting us to see not what was there, but what would be there.

"And this," she said, coming to a complete stop and taking a deep breath, "this will be an Italian-style garden. Close your eyes, Daisy. Listen to the fountain playing, the birds singing in the bushes."

"It reminds me of Rome," I said, closing my eyes, imagining.

"Yes." Did one single word ever mean so much? "There's the delivery van. I have to go for a moment. They are bringing the bricks for the walk. We start next week."

Beatrix strode off, humming.

"Imagine this garden in the evening," I told Walter when we were alone. "Shadows, moonlight on white flowers, and the sound of water."

Walter closed his eyes, imagining.

"I think I can see it, Daisy," he said.

The late-winter sun was dazzling and sent red fireworks across my closed eyelids.

"Kiss me, Walter. Here, in the moonlight."

A Garden in Which No One Can Weep

Such a garden must be walled. There is no other way, and for those who are recalcitrant on this matter I would remind them that our word "paradise" comes from an ancient Middle Eastern word meaning, simply, a walled garden. Only in a paradise garden are tears impossible, and only a walled garden can be a paradise garden. Think of a medieval cloister, if you will, the sanctuary from the storm.

The trees should be fruit bearing: cherries, apricots, apples, and within this small grove of fruit there should be a bench large enough for two people to sit upon. The bench should be placed not on gravel but on Vinca minor, also called myrtle and "glory of the ground" because its pale blue flowers are the color of an April sky.

The walled garden should contain a large bed of woodland ferns growing on the north side of the fruit trees, and in front of the ferns, Galium odoratum, sweet woodruff, whose white flowers can be used to flavor May wine.

Roses of any variety may be planted, as long as they are in front of the south wall and receive plenty of sunshine. Highly recommended is an arbor over which grows a Réveil Dijonnais, the old French rose with its pink petals and white center, a rose of sturdy and serene character.

Other flowers should include the English daisy, sometimes also called "day's eye," and the daylily, both of which remind us that even in a garden in which no one can weep, joy may be fleeting.

This garden should have a fountain at its heart, and two paths at right angles meeting at the fountain. These paths divide the garden, and the world, into quarters: north, south, east, and west; past, present, future, and eternity, which encompasses all time.

All senses are activated in this garden: flowers for perfume and color, water for sound, fruit for taste and texture. The last element should be a wind chime that sounds in the key of C minor when stirred by the breeze, the key preferred by the writers of the old stornelli.

Sit in this garden. Listen to the water and the wind chime, taste the fruit, smell the fragrance. Tears will be impossible.

AUTHOR'S NOTE

Henry James called the factual reality upon which a novel was built his donnée. The donnée that prompted this novel was the European trip of Beatrix Jones Farrand (1872–1959), the famed landscape gardener and niece of Edith Wharton.

Beatrix Jones Farrand, like many ladies of good family of that age, valued privacy in a way we modern Facebook followers and Twitterers may not understand or appreciate. When her mother died in 1935, Beatrix burned many of her letters and many letters of her mother and aunt Edith as well, to preserve their privacy. Was there an Amerigo in her life when she visited Rome in 1895? There could have been, and that was my beginning point, as a novelist. I do know that she ceased keeping her journal of her European travels when she and Minnie arrived in Berlin. It could have been the fatigue of her travels that made her put down her pen. Or it could have been something else.

For the character of Daisy, I wanted to make amends for the

ghost of that poor character killed off by Roman fever (malaria) in the Henry James novel *Daisy Miller* ("I'll never forgive Henry James for what he did to Daisy!" some wonderfully passionate reader once posted on Facebook). I thought it would be interesting to take Daisy as her original creator presented her, innocent, playful, flirtatious, and see what she became after a typical marriage of the times. I don't think Mr. James would have minded. He himself rewrote *Daisy Miller* when he re-created it as a stage play, giving it a happy ending. He thought playgoers would prefer a more cheerful resolution.

The ghosts: Edith Wharton had a true fear of ghosts and wrote a collection of the finest ghost stories I've read, though she herself would not sleep in a room that had a book of ghost stories in it. After the Mount was sold, and then resold, it acquired a reputation for ghostly events.

ACKNOWLEDGMENTS

Thanks to Anna, Charlotte, Diane and Peggy, and Joyce, the reading group friends who a few years ago pointed me back in the direction of two of my favorites, Henry James and Edith Wharton; thanks also to Nancy Holzner and to Tom and M.K., and as always, special thanks to my husband, Steve Poleskie.

My editor at NAL, Ellen Edwards, has been a spectacular colleague, and I am grateful for her advice, encouragement, and perception; I owe a happy debt of thanks to my agent, Kevan Lyon.

The lovely and haunting epigraph that begins this story is from the professional writings of Beatrix Jones Farrand, contained in the Beatrix Jones Farrand Collection, Environmental Design Archives, University of California, Berkeley.

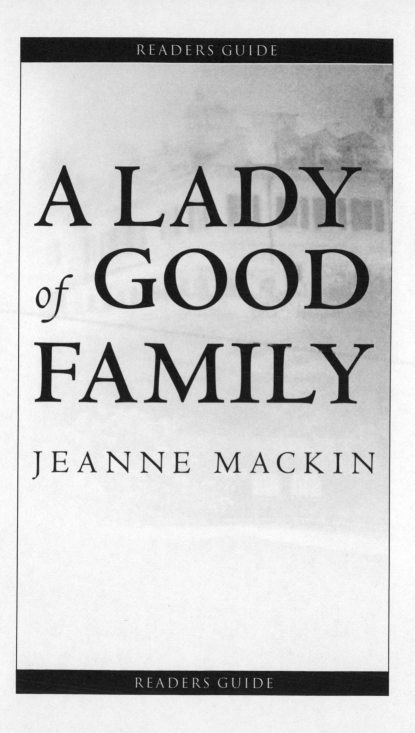

A LADY *of* GOOD FAMILY

JEANNE MACKIN

A CONVERSATION
WITH JEANNE MACKIN

Spoiler alert: A Conversation with Jeanne Mackin and the Questions for Discussion that follow tell more about what happens in the book than you might want to know until you read it.

Q. Which interested you more about Beatrix Farrand—her passion for gardens or her connection to writer Edith Wharton?

A. The two worked together for me. The bond between Beatrix and Edith, aside from family kinship, was that they both loved gardens. In fact, Edith used to call her writing time her "secret garden," and when she decided to build her home at the Mount, the garden was one of her primary concerns and delights. It made such a strong impression on me that Edith Wharton's niece became one of our country's most famous garden designers.

Edith and Beatrix didn't always agree on gardens and their designs: Edith favored a more classical, European approach. Beatrix had a strong sense of place, and she thought gardens in America should reflect that sense of place. Perhaps the two women helped balance each other's proclivities and provide a sounding board for their ideas.

I am myself a passionate gardener, have been since I moved to the house I now live in, more than thirty years ago, so I understand that twitching in the thumbs that gardeners feel when they see a weed and want to pull it, even in someone else's garden. It's as automatic a response as brushing lint off your darling's jacket before he goes out, and it's a response I believe Beatrix would have had. And, as a writer, I am a great admirer of Edith Wharton's work; in fact, I am more in awe of her than I am of Henry James' novels, so I very much appreciated the time I spent rereading some of her work in order to also understand Beatrix. They were both groundbreakers but also very much women of their time.

If Beatrix hadn't been related to Edith, I'd still want to write about her and her passion and her gardens. She was a fascinating person and she made gorgeous gardens.

Q. In A Lady of Good Family, *you focus on a small part of Beatrix's life rather than covering a major portion of it. Can you tell us more about the genesis of the novel?*

A. When I finished college, I packed a knapsack and spent a year traveling in Europe and some of the Middle East. It wasn't the grand tour that earlier generations made; it was hitchhiking and hostels. In some ways that wanderyear was more important to my education than what I received in formal classrooms. The impressions were so strong and memorable: the taste of autumn beer in Germany, spicy with herbs; the heat of the Sahara; the colored light streaming through rose windows in French cathedrals. When we travel, our senses are more alert, and our memories more ready to hold impressions. At least that is so for me.

So when I knew I wanted to write a novel about Beatrix, I decided to begin it with her travels and some of her impressions: the information she took back with her to New York and Maine as she began her professional life. I wanted to choose a particular moment and place—that accidental meeting with Amerigo in the Borghese gardens—and make that the beginning of an arc that wasn't a full life story, but a story about how she became a professional gardener.

Q. The epigraph—"One felt more and more that some moonlight nights in May . . . the ghosts of the people who once lived there must come back"—suggests why you wrote the novel as not just a love story but also a ghost story. Care to elaborate?

A. Gardens are such haunted places! Some of my earliest memories are of my grandmother's garden behind her house on Elisha Street, in Waterloo, New York. I still dream about that garden, and when I began planting mine I realized, one day, that I was more or less trying to re-create her garden, to get back to that place and to those people, many long dead. Sit in a garden, any garden, and you can't help but feel the presence of the other people, dead and alive, who may have sat in the garden.

Gardens are mystical places, part natural and wild, full of green and growth, and part manufactured and artificial, in the true meaning of the word, with laid paths, wooden benches, and terra-cotta pots. The old Celts believed that whenever there was an important transition and overlap—when day meets night, or when one season gives way to another—that's when magic happens and doors open into other worlds. In a garden, wild meets cultivated, nature meets human made, so a garden, for me, has always been one of those transitional places, where magic comes alive and mystery abides.

And isn't lost love always a kind of ghost story? The lover may be nowhere around, and yet he's always with you in some sense. Ghost stories are about loss and regret and failure; hauntings are about unfinished business.

I love ghost stories, and so did many people of Edith's generation. She herself wrote several and they are my favorites, especially one called "Afterward," which was another touchstone for this novel. And of course there's Henry James' *The Turn of the Screw*, one of the greatest haunting stories ever. It made sense, when I was writing about gardens and those characters, that a ghost would also emerge.

When I found Beatrix's quote that opens the novel, I was ecstatic.

Q. *The novel contains obvious references to two Henry James novels*—Daisy Miller *and* The Turn of the Screw—*and to Edith Wharton's* The House of Mirth. *Why was it important to you to explore and echo these writers' work?*

A. I was never satisfied with the way Henry James ended Daisy Miller, by simply killing her off.

Daisy, as James created her, is a great character, all innocence and feistiness. She is full of potential, as we say now, and I wanted to explore her potential, to take her places James did not. When he wrote his play version of *Daisy Miller*, Daisy and Winterbourne (I changed his name to Winters) actually have a happy ending, but James ends the play quickly, with the embrace of the two lovers. I wanted to pursue the story, test Daisy with problems and difficulties, and see what kind of woman she would grow into.

Daisy Miller and Lily Bart from *The House of Mirth* have much in common: they are both social outsiders, both on the lookout for advancement, both aware of the limitations their culture places on them, but hopeful that they can avoid those limitations. When I reread *The House of Mirth*, I found some two dozen places in the text where marriage is referred to as a financial transaction, and a woman, the potential bride, is a "good" or "product" to be sold or at least exchanged. John Galsworthy's novel *The Man of Property* is my third touchstone for this concept: the property referred to in the title is not just the Forsyte wealth, but the Forsyte wife. She is her husband's property.

As for *The Turn of the Screw*, it is one of my favorite novels. When Henry James wrote or talked about this novel, he said that the evil was in the reader's mind, not in the story itself, so we all become coconspirators with the governess when we read this story. Do the ghosts really exist or are they the result of a fevered imagination? It is the question that every good ghost story needs to ask.

Q. It's tempting to be drawn to the wealth and glamour of New York's "aristocracy" during what came to be known as the Gilded Age, until we're reminded of the social restrictions they lived under. Especially shocking is the male attitude that he could do what he wanted—even drive his family into financial ruin—and his wife had no right to question his actions. What was life really like for these families?

A. Divorce, for any reason, was a terrible scandal and almost always seen as a failure on the wife's part. Wives, happily married or not, were expected to endure, to simply look the other way, to cope. A man's home was his castle, and he ruled that empire. If a woman married unwisely, that is, to a man with bad habits such as gambling, visiting prostitutes, keeping a mistress, or conducting blatantly illegal business deals, the wife suffered the consequences along with the husband, although she had no say in the activities.

The law made wives subordinate to husbands, making women legally little more than children themselves. Once women married, they had no say over their own bodies (rape within marriage wasn't legally recognized until recently) and no say over their children: the father was the authority, and if a couple did divorce, the father, not the mother, had the right to keep the children.

Do you see why mothers made such a to-do over whom their daughters married, and why?

It was a little different, perhaps a little easier, for the wealthy. Money is a form of power, and if a woman had money of her own, as Edith Wharton did from her writing and a family inheritance, she had more say over her own life. Being divorced and penniless could mean starving on the streets; being divorced and well-off with your own income meant having to survive gossip and harsh judgment from others—it wasn't life threatening.

Q. The novel continually compares the Old World of Europe with the New World of America, and specifically of New York City. Can you expand upon the differences between the two in the years preceding the First World War? How did the war change that?

A. Europe, the Old World, had—still has in most places—the aura of long history and culture. In Rome, for instance, some of the buildings have foundations that date back to the Roman Empire; new apartment buildings lean up against Roman amphitheaters and medieval churches. When you walk in cities like Rome and Paris, you walk through centuries and centuries of history and art.

New York in the eighteenth century was still a village of wooden houses and Native American footpaths turned into mud roads; by the nineteenth century the city had grown tremendously, and by Beatrix's childhood there were the wide avenues, the stone mansions, the new hotels and department stores that came to define New York, as well as the downside of quick growth and unequal wealth: the tenements, the homeless. By 1913, New York Harbor was the world's busiest port, even more important than London's. The New World represented energy and speed and optimism for the future.

Still, when people wanted "culture," they looked to the Old World, to the art and the museums, and they traveled there. That was the point of the grand tour, to acquire that sense of history and art and culture still based in the Old World. Remember, the Metropolitan Museum of Art in New York didn't open its doors until 1870!

Artists like Henry James had a perplexing relationship with their native country, admiring America for its energy and novelty and opportunities, yet choosing to live in what they perceived as the more cultured Old World. James settled in England, Edith Wharton in France. It's revealing that when Henry James wrote the happy ending for the play version of *Daisy Miller*, the last thing that Daisy and Winterbourne say is that they are going home to America to be married. "Oh, yes; you ought to go home!" Daisy says. Yet James did not.

After the First World War, New York and the other American cities became even more important. We won the war without suffering damage to our own infrastructure; we moved forward even faster than before. There were important societal changes: women who had done war work outside the home, replacing male labor, were not always happy about being sent back to the nursery and kitchen. And many servants who had gone to offices and factories were even less eager to return to stables and sculleries to work. There was a large shift in labor from servants to employees. While the rich will always have their maids and assistants and private chefs, the middle class had to become much more resilient and self-sufficient. Daisy learns to pack lightly and carry her own bags.

Q. Can you expand upon the many changes in attitude and opportunity that women increasingly enjoyed in the twentieth century? When did laws regarding marriage begin to alter, and when did women really get the vote?

A. Marriage and attitudes about divorce changed drastically in the 1960s, with no-fault divorce. Before that, when couples wanted to divorce, either the husband or wife had to prove that the other spouse had committed adultery, deserted the family, or been violently cruel. That's why divorce was such a scandal: it meant either that the wife had been a sinful, deceitful person or that she had been a victim of some terrible action.

A hundred years before no-fault divorce, in the mid-nineteenth century, laws and attitudes about marriage and divorce began a slow, important change. Property rights and other rights of married women were decided by the states rather than by the federal government, and varied greatly. In New York State in 1845, the legislature established that working married women could keep their salaries—before that, any income they earned became the property of their husbands.

The Married Women's Property Act of 1848 further altered the law regarding the property rights of married women, saying that a wife's property kept in her own name couldn't be sold without her approval or used without her permission to pay her husband's debts. That's why Daisy wants to put the New York house in her own name, once she realizes how dangerous her husband's gambling impulse has become.

The decision to allow women to vote was made on a state-by-state basis. The Fourteenth Amendment, of 1868, said that the right to vote "shall not be denied or abridged . . . on account of sex," yet not all states immediately agreed, so the

Nineteenth Amendment was introduced in 1878 . . . and debated for the next forty years! During those years, the women's rights movement grew ever stronger and more politically savvy, thanks to leaders like Alice Paul, who, with other members of the National Woman's Party, picketed the White House for the first time in history. During the First World War, women marched with posters reading, "How long must women wait for liberty?" They burned effigies of President Wilson; they went to prison; they went on hunger strikes.

The last state legislature needed to ratify the Nineteenth Amendment was Tennessee, and the deciding vote in favor was cast on August 18, 1920, by Harry Burn. Supposedly, his mother told him to be a good boy and vote "aye." His mother should be canonized. What is discouraging is that Alice Paul and the other members of the NWP believed that once all states allowed women to vote, an Equal Rights Amendment would soon follow. We're still waiting for that one!

Q. Women have always struggled with the age-old question of how to find fulfillment in both their personal and professional lives. Some readers might conclude from Beatrix's example that achieving such a balance requires great wealth and a lack of children. Do you agree?

A. No, I don't agree, or at least I don't think that is how it should be. Let's be honest, though. Enough money and freedom from duty to do as you please to build a career can't hurt! Women and girls today might find it difficult to understand what married life was often like before birth control was readily available. Some women experienced one pregnancy after another, in fact, spent their entire premenopausal life in some stage of pregnancy and child rearing. It was their work, and it consumed their time and quite often killed them. The wealthy had nannies, nurses, and governesses to take care of child rearing, and I suspect they knew a little more about birth control than we give them credit for.

Today, women have more freedom and more choices. But achieving a balance, as you say, is a struggle. Fulfillment comes from doing what you love and being surrounded by people who respect your choices. It's a day-to-day struggle, doing your work and also being available to family and friends. My one rule is this: never, never, ever call me in the morning when I'm working. I'll hang up on you, if I answer the phone at all. I can't write in bed like Edith did, though. I envy her that.

Q. Mrs. Haskett is a truly disagreeable woman, cruel and acquisitive. She seems to embody the negative aspects of the nouveau riche. Did you have a particular model in mind when you created her?

A. Thankfully no, if you're referring to living people I know. I thought of Mrs. Haskett almost as a metaphor for the greed of the times, that "I have the money and I can buy whatever I want, whether you want to sell or not" attitude.

I love art museums second only to good libraries, and it pains me that so many collections were built on war, looting, and the rich buying from the newly poor. There is no way around this problem, however. How else can art be moved from private collections to public viewings? Henry James covered some of this territory in his novels, the rich Americans buying art off the impoverished Europeans.

As to Mrs. Haskett's social ambitions for herself and her daughters, firm placement in the respectable upper classes, in her generation, was as important as money in the bank, as poor Lily Bart discovers. If you were rich enough, you could buy a title, an ancestral home, and all the toys and benefits that came with them. There's a reason why it is called the Gilded Age and not the golden age. Gilding is a superficial layer that wears off in time. And it's why, in the title, I refer to Beatrix as a lady. Breeding and a generosity of spirit, empathy, are deeper than gilding: they don't wear off.

Q. Beatrix's mother, Minnie, seems open-minded in her love for her daughter and willing to defy strict social convention to find meaningful work for herself. Can you tell us more about her? Was she warm and accessible with people outside her class? Were she and Beatrix able to remain close even as Beatrix's career flourished, and following her marriage to Max Farrand?

A. Minnie (Mary) Jones was known for her warmth, wit, and intelligence. Henry James was a great admirer of her and a lifelong friend, so she must have been a wonderful conversationalist and a perceptive reader. She's one of the people I'd love to invite to dinner and ask what she thinks of my own favorite books, and which of Edith's books she most admires.

Aside from her intelligence and energy, Minnie was also a woman of great social conscience. She didn't just give loose change to charity; she worked for the poor and for the working class. I suspect that her dedication to helping the less fortunate might have been one of the things that damaged her marriage: Freddie Jones was a son much loved and spoiled by his mother, and he expected a wife to be dedicated to his comfort, not to the well-being of others.

Beatrix and Minnie's close and loving relationship wasn't changed by Beatrix's marriage, though the time they spent together was necessarily reduced. When the Great Depression arrived, Minnie was short of cash, and Beatrix did all she could to help her; Minnie often spent summers with Beatrix and Max in Bar Harbor.

One of the great sorrows of Beatrix's life was that she wasn't with Minnie when she died, at age eighty-four. Minnie had traveled again to Europe to see Edith, but caught a cold, and the cold turned into pneumonia. She died before Beatrix could get there.

At the memorial for her mother in New York, Beatrix

chose this beautiful passage from Proverbs to read: "A good name is rather to be chosen than great riches, and loving favor rather than silver and gold."

Q. Can you tell us more about the projects Beatrix worked on after 1920, when the novel ends?

A. Dumbarton Oaks is the jewel in Beatrix's crown, and visitors can still admire her work there, especially how she designed the gardens to suit the rocky, sloping grounds, letting the original shapes of the land guide her choices.

Beatrix was already fifty years old when she began her work at Dumbarton Oaks, a good age for remembering earlier days, and these gardens do reflect Beatrix's earlier trips in Italy. There are references to Renaissance gardens and also to the American Arts and Crafts movement. The terraces function as outdoor rooms and courts leading into other outdoor rooms; there are fountains, pools, rose beds, sculptures, walks lined with flowering trees. There are places to be meditatively alone, places for talking with friends. The Dumbarton Oaks Gardens are absolutely magnificent.

Before, during, and after her years of work and maintenance at Dumbarton Oaks, Beatrix worked on some two hundred different projects: college campuses, private gardens, town gardens, village greens, memorials and memorial stones, including one for President Theodore Roosevelt in the Oyster

Bay cemetery of Long Island, a rose garden for the New York Botanical Garden . . . the list is extensive and varied, showing Beatrix's determination to bring green and growing beauty to as many settings and people as she could.

Beatrix's other famous garden didn't share as happy a fate as Dumbarton Oaks, however. After Beatrix and Max married, the couple spent a large part of every year in Bar Harbor and together created Reef Point Gardens: home, horticultural library, and botanic garden all at once, a place where Beatrix could showcase native American plants and provide educational resources for horticulturalists and gardeners. But after Max died in 1945, funding for Reef Point fell short of what was needed to maintain the extensive garden and library. Rather than let the house and garden dwindle into mediocrity, Beatrix had her childhood home torn down and the gardens dismantled.

I think that grim and mournful action testifies to the depth of her feeling both for her husband and for her mother: without them, the house no longer made sense. A friend bought the property to rebuild on; another friend purchased many of the plants and created two new gardens with them: the Asticou Azalea Garden and the Thuya Garden. There is a kind of eternity to gardens: they are rarely completely destroyed; they continue either in individual plants moved elsewhere or in suggestions of paths and walls, outlines.

Beatrix transferred her library and papers to the University of California at Berkeley and moved to a smaller cottage in Bar Harbor. She died there in 1959.

The Beatrix Farrand Society (www.beatrixfarrandsociety.org) lists thirteen gardens where her work can still be admired, including the Abby Aldrich Rockefeller Garden in Maine; the Beatrix Farrand Garden at Bellefield in Hyde Park, New York; the Peggy Rockefeller Rose Garden in the New York Botanical Garden; and her most famous work, Dumbarton Oaks, Washington, D.C.

Q. Your novel The Beautiful American, *published in the spring of 2014, received glowing reviews from print publications and from readers who posted comments online. Does anything about your experience in publishing that novel stand out?*

A. Some wonderful comments: a male reader said it made him cry! Someone else said that when she finished it, she started it all over again. The response, in general, was really wonderful and very encouraging. The novel received the CNY Award in Fiction for 2014, and I was delighted about that. I'm a storyteller and I'm over the moon when people like the story and the way it is told. Some friends, though, thought that my portrayal of Picasso was much too kind. I had to explain that I was writing Picasso the way Nora, the narrator, would have perceived him, and Nora rather liked

Picasso. He was kind to her, which is not the same as saying he was kind to all women. He wasn't. He was, we all know, a bit of a rascal.

Q. Since you liked this question last time, I'll ask it again. Where do you keep the pile of books you're reading and what's in it these days?

A. Ah. I have a new system. I placed a bookcase on top of my desk, not beside it, so all I have to do is look up from my typing and there they are, all the titles I need for reference and inspiration. I just hope the legs of my desk are really, really strong.

I also have a nightstand with very strong legs and lots of books on it. The desktop books are mostly research for the novel, along with the novels of Edith and Henry, and several histories of gardening. The nightstand books are my distraction reading: I believe in the Zen theory that sometimes to hit the target you have to look away from it, so during my research and writing I also read lots of books that had nothing to do with Beatrix and gardens. A few that stand out: *Shakespeare's Pub*, by Pete Brown, a really fine history of the George Inn in London. Sounds starchy, but believe me, it isn't. *Wild*, by Cheryl Strayed, was a great read and thoroughly convinced me I'm not the extreme-hiker type. Marina Warner's *Once Upon a Time* is a fascinating new look at fairy tales, and my reading group devoured the *Old Filth* trilogy by Jane Gardam. I reread *The Pursuit of Love* by Jessica Mitford for perhaps the thirty-second time.

Q. Do you find new electronic devices changing the way you read? Do research?

A. Not the way I read. I still prefer the old-fashioned paper-between-boards kind of reading experience. I remember one day when my computer had gone all squirrelly and my husband's had as well. I was weeping and wailing and he picked up a book and said, "Look! This is perfect technology! Portable, no power source needed, and no software." That's how I still feel about books. I admit, though, that being able to carry around an entire library in your handbag is beginning to sound appealing.

Research is a trickier question. I will use online databases for quick facts and fact-checking, but I still prefer volumes, actual books, for deeper research. For instance, for an earlier novel, I read some twelve hundred pages of text (library books) to write a five-page scene about falconry. Mostly I still roam my various libraries, fingering actual books on actual shelves. If I ever come back as a ghost, I plan to haunt a particular library at Cornell, where I've done most of my research. It is a wonderful, fantastic place, as good as a garden, and I think I'll make a decent ghost for it.

Q. Do you have a book that you've always wanted to write and haven't written yet?

A. Yes. It's . . . I can't tell you. I'm superstitious about this. If I talk about a book before I begin it, the book doesn't get finished. So, stay tuned!

QUESTIONS FOR DISCUSSION

1. Did you enjoy the novel? What was your overall response to it?

2. Although the novel is primarily about historical figure Beatrix Farrand, fictional Daisy Winters tells the story. Did you find Daisy an effective narrator? What are the advantages and disadvantages of hearing the story from her point of view?

3. Discuss what life was like for Beatrix as an upper-class woman coming of age before 1900. What restrictions did she face early on that began to fall away as the new century progressed?

4. Beatrix and Amerigo first meet by chance several times, which seems to suggest that fate is conspiring to draw them together. Have you ever had a similar experience of a romance that seems "meant to be"?

5. Discuss the references to novels by Henry James and Edith Wharton. Are you familiar with *Daisy Miller*, *The Turn of the Screw*, and *The House of Mirth*? Are you inspired to seek them out and read them?

6. The author suggests that falling in love was an important part of Beatrix's growth both as a woman and as a professional landscape gardener. How does the experience enrich her? Do you agree that an experience of passionate, romantic love is essential for a woman's fulfillment?

7. Why does Beatrix hesitate when Amerigo suggests they elope? Have you ever had to make a split-second decision with far-reaching consequences for your life? What did you choose?

8. There are happy and unhappy marriages in the novel. Discuss the ingredients that go into making each marriage successful or disastrous. How much freedom to choose do the couples really have, and how much is driven by social convention? What role does luck play? And how do the marriages in the novel compare to marriages you know now?

9. Discuss the various ghosts in the novel. Why do you think the author includes them? Does the epigraph, taken from Beatrix Farrand's writing, provide a clue?

10. Discuss the many cruelties Mrs. Haskett inflicts and the

possessions she accumulates in an effort to gain entrée into New York society's highest echelons. Does she remind you of anyone from history, literature, or today's pop culture?

11. Why do you think the author includes the three descriptions of gardens—for first meetings, second chances, and "where no one can weep"?

12. Does the novel make you want to create a garden, visit a garden, or read about gardens?

13. Before reading the novel, had you ever heard of Beatrix Farrand? Consider making a list of accomplished women of the last one hundred and fifty years that most people have never heard of.

14. Did you find the end of the novel satisfying? Why or why not?

ABOUT THE AUTHOR

In addition to several other novels as well as short fiction and creative nonfiction, **Jeanne Mackin** is the author of the *Cornell Book of Herbs and Edible Flowers* and coeditor of *The Norton Book of Love*. She is the recipient of a creative writing fellowship from the American Antiquarian Society, and her journalism has won awards from the Council for the Advancement and Support of Education, in Washington, D.C. She lives with her husband, artist Steve Poleskie, in upstate New York.

CONNECT ONLINE

jeannemackin.com
facebook.com/jeannemackinauthor
twitter.com/jeannemackin1